ABANDON ALL HOPE

DEDICATION

~For Maggie, Mitchell, Ryan and Hannah~

Thank you for your patience and the encouragement you offered when I was writing ABANDON ALL HOPE. My wish is that watching me reach for and work for my dreams will fuel you as you strive for yours!

ACKNOWLEDGEMENTS

This book wouldn't have come together without the contribution of my editors: Dani Crabtree, who did the first round; Carmen Ferreiro, my big picture girl and a fellow author; RT Wolfe, fellow author and friend, who held my hand, offered a listening ear, and taught me a lot about point of view; and, finally, Brenda Rothert, fellow author and friend, who was able to pay attention to detail where I couldn't. I thank you.

I'd also like to thank the ladies & gentleman of Heart&Scroll, my local RWA chapter, who challenge me to become a better writer. My gratitude goes out to the members of Authors Helping Authors who retweet for me and help me to get the word out about my writing. And finally, to the Ladies in Red, who offer advice, encouragement, and support for their fellow writers.

"Love
is patient,
Love is kind.
It always protects,
Always trusts,
Always hopes,
Always perseveres.
Love never fails."

1Corinthians 13

CHAPTER ONE

C hase Hatton was bewitched by Hope from the start.

He was...ten...no, twelve. Definitely twelve, as he was playing American Junior League baseball that summer. There had been a break in the team's schedule, so his mom had asked the new neighbor lady over for dinner, along with her twelve-year-old kid. He was told he couldn't go over to Bobby McGraw's to play catch. He was needed at home to entertain, of all things, the new neighbor's daughter. A girl.

Chase sat on the back porch steps smacking a ball into his glove over and over. In his frustration, he dropped the ball. It hit the edge of the step, and ricocheted, rolling down the small slope of their backyard. He glanced up and saw them crossing the lawn.

Mrs. Creswell had on a dress; she had no doubt worn it to work and had just gotten home. Hope wore cutoff jean shorts and a blue, checkered, sleeveless blouse tied at her waist. She held a present, and as she walked, a long ponytail swished behind her in a somewhat mesmerizing rhythm. The sun was just beginning its descent behind the pair.

Chase held up a hand and squinted, wrinkling his freckled nose. The sun rays seemed to be shooting off the two, as if they, themselves, were the source of the bright light. Hope bent down and picked up his ball. He heard the familiar sound of the screen door opening behind him: his mom coming to greet their guests. She was probably wiping her hands on an apron as she descended the steps, blond hair swept up in a loose bun. The smell of her famous fried chicken wafted out the door and his stomach rumbled on cue.

Hope gestured as if to throw the ball back and he stood, holding out his glove. With amazing accuracy, and equally impressive velocity, especially considering she still held the present in her other hand, Hope zinged it into his glove. The adults greeted each other with that loud, grown-up hullabaloo, but their voices faded into the background as she approached.

She smiled at him. "Hi."

"H-hey," he stammered, his palms becoming sweaty. He was caught up by those stunning eyes, unusual in some way he had yet to figure out. Bangs curled over her forehead, and her face was clear and bright. Maybe entertaining the neighbor girl wouldn't be so bad after all.

"Oh, this is for you." She handed him the gift. He turned to set the glove and ball down on the step. The ball squeezed out of the mitt and rolled toward Hope again. She bent and scooped it up, tossing it back and forth as he tore open the wrapping paper.

"Oh, wow! Cool!" Chase gushed, unveiling a model airplane. An Albatros D.V. Diecast Model German Air Force Jasta 11, also known as "The Red Baron." It was the sweetest model he had ever seen.

"And its propeller really works!" She tucked the ball back into his glove on the steps.

"Thanks," he breathed.

"No problem." She stuck her hands behind her back and rocked from heel to toe, beaming with pride.

He interrupted the adults' conversation, eager to check out his new plane. "Mom, can we go put this together?"

"No, Chase." She put a hand on top of his head. "It's time for dinner. And after dinner, I want you to show Hope around."

"Yes, Ma'am." He and Hope exchanged a look of disappointment and shuffled into the house with the grown-ups. "You're a pretty good throw, for a girl," he stated flatly.

She seemed unsure of how to take his comment. "Tha-anks?"

When they entered the house, Chase's father greeted the Creswells warmly. He had been upstairs changing from work clothes into khaki shorts and a polo. Greg Hatton was tall, with jet black hair and a gleaming smile. Though in his mid-thirties, he still retained his boyish good looks and was a lover of puns and corny jokes. Chase alternately laughed at his dad and groaned, shaking his head and rolling his eyes at Hope whenever the grown-ups weren't looking. She seemed to take to his dad within minutes.

The dinner conversation was pleasant, the women having discovered a common love for card games and cozy mysteries. As they compared reading lists, Hope helped herself to generous portions of mashed potatoes and gravy, corn on the cob, and fried chicken.

"M-mmm. Your mom makes the best chicken."

"She sure does." He swiped another drumstick off the platter in front of him. "Does your mom cook?"

She leaned in conspiratorially. "If you can call it that," she whispered behind her hand. "Last night, she made 'Tater-tot Casserole'"—she wrinkled up her pretty little nose—"and it was de-e-e-sgusting!"

They both laughed.

"Hey, what are you two doing down there?" Chase's mom asked with mock suspicion.

"Oh, leave them alone," his dad answered. He gave her a light elbow to the ribs and subtly changed the subject. "Where's Jeff tonight?"

"He's having supper at Danny Calvin's."

"Ah. Our eldest son has quite the social calendar," he commented to Mrs. Creswell with a wink. His eyes slid down the table to where

Chase had polished off the chicken and pushed his empty plate away. He raised his eyebrows and chuckled. "Chase, would you like to be excused?"

"Yes, sir." He grabbed his plate and glass and motioned for Hope to do the same. She glanced at her mother, and getting a nod and a smile, followed suit. It was mere seconds before the screen door slammed behind them and their feet pounded down the wide steps in unison.

"Wanna see our corn maze?"

"Sure," Hope responded gamely. They headed for the wall of cornstalks edging the west side of the yard. In the fading light, she peered across the field connecting their two properties at her cracker box of a house. She turned to examine his. After a few minutes, she commented, "I like how your porch goes all the way around your house."

Chase glanced back, reflecting, having never really considered this aspect. "Yeah, I guess it is kind of cool."

Out of curiosity, his eyes followed hers between the two houses. Across the way, on a small, neat lawn, the Creswells' tiny, white bungalow perched. A shallow porch spanned a portion of the front of the house, sitting low to the ground. The previous owners had torn up much of the landscaping for some reason, giving it a barren look, the foundation exposed by the lack of shrubbery. Still, it was homey, he surmised, and just the right size for Hope and her mom.

Turning his head again to look at his house, Chase tried hard to imagine what it must look like through Hope's eyes. Physically, it was a white two-story with black shutters. The lawn rolled away from the house, sloping toward a wooded area. A huge oak tree shaded the whole right side of the house, its arms extending protectively over the roof. In short, it was the quintessential home every child drew as soon as he was able to hold a crayon in his chubby, little fist, usually pictured under a rainbow.

Chase stole a peek at Hope. She was still gazing at his house, the corners of her mouth turned up, eyes dreamy. He knew she was not seeing those material aspects of the house he had just taken in, but was, instead, imagining the life within its walls. Looking through her eyes, it was easy for him to do the same. He heard the hum of family life when his brother was home, the two of them chasing each other up and down the stairs as their father hollered at them from the TV room and their mom clanged plates together, her arms elbow-deep in suds. As he stood there, Chase felt for the first time the overwhelming need Hope would always stir within him, the need to give her everything she longed for, to fill the emptiness he sensed inside of her.

His heart beating rapidly, he prayed she hadn't noticed him staring at her. He stuck his sweaty palms deep into the pockets of his denim shorts as they turned back toward the cornfield. Hope fell into step beside him, mimicking his posture by sticking her hands in her pockets. As they ambled across the lawn, he watched her out of the corners of his eyes.

He didn't think he had ever met a prettier girl. Her face was perfectly proportioned, and seeing her in profile now, he admired the way her nose turned up just slightly at the end. But it was the eyes that drew him in. Warm and inviting, they had a way of looking at you with alarming frankness, offering up all the feeling within Hope's heart and seeming to see clearly into yours. The pair became submerged in an easy silence, like old friends rather than new acquaintances, both caught up in their own thoughts.

It was still warm, and in the distance they could hear the sound of a lawn mower's gentle humming. The smell of the fresh-cut grass that hung in the air, carried to them by a soft breeze, was comforting. The August evening held a sense of fleetingness. It whispered in seductive tones to savor the summer before it was too late; stuffy schoolrooms waited just beyond the horizon.

Despite his heavy sense of contentment, after a while, Chase felt it was necessary to breach the silence. He turned around to walk in front of Hope, backward, so they could converse face-to-face. "So, how did you know to get me a model plane?"

"Oh. Your mom told me. I have five of them. When I grow up," she said decisively, "I'm going to be a pilot. Or a photographer."

Chase considered this. He had never put any serious thought into what he would be someday. "A pilot...or a photographer," he said slowly. "They don't exactly go together, do they?" A teasing grin played over his face, but Hope didn't seem to notice.

"No, I guess not." She shrugged, not worried by the observation. They entered the green tunnel weaving through the corn, the stalks just tall enough so they could not see out. "This is cool!"

"Yeah," Chase returned in a self-congratulatory way. "My uncle owns all of this land, from here all the way down to the ridge. He lets me carve a maze every year."

With a proprietary air, he tore a part of a husk from a stalk as they sauntered by. He rubbed it thoughtfully as they ventured on, still walking backward. He made sure he didn't trip over the stubble covering the path in places, not wanting to look foolish in her eyes.

Hope reached out and grabbed the husk out of his hands, grinning at him. He smiled back, happy she felt comfortable enough to be playful and challenge him. He watched as she brought the green husk up to her nose and took a deep breath. He snatched another husk, and they both split and shred their finds into confetti-like pieces, their hands becoming sticky and sweet-smelling.

"So, where's your dad?" he asked finally.

"My mom...left him." Hope ripped carefully now, as if making straight edges had become imperative. "He was..." Her face contorted as she struggled to describe what she was thinking. "Not a nice man." Her nose wrinkled as if she had gotten a whiff of something rotten.

Chase thought he saw a slight tremor in her hands as she worked them along the leaf, finally dropping it to wipe her palms on her shorts. She glanced up, but he pretended to concentrate on his own husk. She looked off to the side. He was certain he saw tears mounting in her eyes. It was the first time she had avoided making eye contact with him. He turned around to stroll beside her, though there was barely room for two to pass in the tall corn. He searched around for a change in subject.

"What was your old school like?"

"We weren't there long." Her voice was again subdued.

She stooped to pick up a piece of dry cornstalk. He wondered if she did it in order to have something to look at, so she could hide her telltale eyes. She rubbed it in her hands, and he listened to the crinkling sound the dead, crisp layers made. She deliberately shook her head, as if to physically cast off bad memories.

"But we'll be here for a while," she declared with what sounded like forced brightness. She paused, whispering under her breath, "Hopefully." She stopped abruptly where another branch of the path opened up on her left. "What's this?"

"Why don't you find out?" Chase answered, an eyebrow raised in challenge. She took a few steps forward, and then turned back. "Aren't you coming?"

He smiled mischievously. "Nope. I'll just wait for you here."

"O-okay." She drug the word out, as if unsure of what he was up to, but certain he was up to something. She turned and continued down the path, which veered at a right angle after several yards, blocking out her view of the original path. Chase ducked into an adjacent trail. He heard her steps quicken. He had been right about her being curious about what lay ahead. He knew the path twisted and turned a number of times before she would end up in a wide, circular dead end.

"Chase?" she called out. "It just ended." He made no reply. "Chase?"

As he peered between the stalks he hid behind, he saw her smile. She seemed to understand she had been suckered.

"Chase!" she shouted, but the corners of her lips turned up. Hope began to run back in the direction from which she had come.

With a loud cry, he jumped out in front of her.

Hope's scream of terror hurt his ears. She stumbled backward, landing on her rump in some mud. She stared up from where she lay, resting on both elbows for a second. "You are so-o-o-o dead!"

"Oh, come on," he responded amiably, ready to make peace. "I'll help you up." He reached his hand out to her. She stretched out to clasp it, but not before she had clutched a handful of mud.

"Ugg!" Chase, mud dripping from his palm, was unable to hide his delight at her deception. "Now *you're* dead!"

She laughed but scrambled to her feet, pushing him off balance. She ran with wild abandon down the path. He waited, good-naturedly, until the count of ten, giving her a head start, and then took off. Although dusk was playing tricks on his eyes, it was easy to find her by listening to the laughter as she ducked into several of the side paths.

But abruptly her laughter ended, replaced by a loud *thud* and Hope calling out his name in fear and pain. Chase picked the path he thought she was on, and ran as fast as he could through the green walls hemming the trail. He turned a corner, and saw her up ahead. She was rocking back and forth, clutching her leg and moaning. As he got closer, he saw her white sneaker, despite the gathering darkness, wedged underneath a tree root. It snaked across the path where it had wound close to the edge of the field.

He raced up and crouched down beside her. Her face was contorted as if she were trying not to cry. "What happened?"

"O-o-o-h! It's my ankle." She spoke through gritted teeth, although unable to keep the tears in check now.

Chase looked from the ankle of her extended leg, which still had a sneaker on it, to the ankle of the leg she was hanging on to, whose foot was bare. It was clear, even to him, the latter was swollen considerably. Her foot also seemed to jut out at a strange angle.

"I'll go get help."

He was already halfway down the path when she called out, nearly hysterical, "Chase! Please, wait! Come back. Come back. Don't leave me here!"

He returned to her side, where she was crying in earnest now, and squatted down, rubbing her back. She kept repeating over and over again, "Please don't leave me. I don't want to stay here by myself. Please don't leave."

"It's okay, Hope," he responded quietly, sitting down next to her. "I'm not leaving." He put an arm around her and she leaned in, her tears dampening his shirt.

"It hurts! It hurts," she whimpered.

"I know it does."

He looked down the path, longing to return to the house for his dad. But the dark was falling quickly now, and he knew Hope would be afraid out in the cornfield alone.

He was torn, wondering what was the right thing to do, when, to his immense relief, he thought he heard his older brother calling out. Hope raised her head, too, as if she had heard it.

"We're in here," he called. "This way. Hope's hurt!" He heard the sound of his big, football-playing brother tromping through the corn. With as much trouble as his brother gave him on a regular basis, Chase was surprised by how good Jeff's voice sounded as he continued to call his name. "This way."

Within just a few minutes, his brother appeared around the bend and hurried the last several yards toward them. A sophomore in high school, his build was different from Chase's. Tall and muscular, with wavy blond hair and a brilliant smile, Jeff was the object of all the girls' affection, and the envy of all his male peers. He wore a gray t-shirt that read, "Property of Lincoln High School," the fabric taut across his expansive chest, and a pair of navy gym shorts.

He bent down, peering into Hope's tearstained face. "Hi," he said in a friendly manner. "My name's Jeff."

Hope lowered her eyes, voice soft. "I'm Hope. Hope C-creswell."

"Hi, Hope. Wow!" He whistled with compassion. "Looks pretty painful. I'm going to carry you back to the house, all right?"

She nodded with a small smile, blinking back tears. Chase moved so Jeff could slip his hands under her knees and around her back. He made sure to keep the hurt ankle away from his body so it wouldn't be squeezed. Hope put her hands around his neck and he rose, untroubled by his burden.

Chase was looking up at his brother's broad back with a mixture of pride and jealousy when Jeff called over his shoulder, "What were you thinking, bringing her here in the dark? It's a wonder she didn't break her neck."

Chase's mouth hung open, until Hope explained, "It wasn't his fault. I just wasn't watching where I was going."

It felt unbelievably good to hear her defend him. He bent down and tugged on the sneaker stuck under the root for several minutes until it came loose and he fell backward into the dirt. He stood up and hurried after Jeff and Hope. When he caught up to the pair, all he could do was stare resentfully at her arms clasped around his older brother's neck. *He* should be the one carrying Hope, not Jeff. He knew it was illogical to think this way, since Jeff was twice his size. Yet his frustration burned within him all the same.

When they arrived at the house, Jeff laid Hope down on the couch within the soft light of the living room lamps. It was evident to all concerned that her ankle was broken. Chase was shocked by the deep purple-black color of her injury. He peeked up into her pale face and she gave him a weak smile.

It was decided Mr. Hatton would drive the Creswells to the hospital. Chase watched from the porch as his father carried Hope out to the car and snuggled her into the backseat with a blanket his mother had provided. The phone rang and Jeff hurried inside to answer it. Chase and his mom stood on the porch and waved to the car's taillights as it zoomed off toward town.

Chase felt lost after she was gone.

A few weeks later, Hope showed up on the first day of school using crutches. Chase was bending down by his locker, putting his new school supplies away, when she hobbled in the door with her mother. He stood, with a huge smile on his face, but Hope was swarmed by others who were asking all sorts of questions about her injury. She was leaning on her crutches just inside the doorway, pausing before maneuvering down the few steps to the hallway. Her hair was down and glowed, even in the low-wattage lighting of the hallway, and she had that beautiful smile on her face. He took a step toward her, but she started off down an adjacent corridor, not having seen him. Several kids followed, one boy even relieving Hope's mom of her backpack.

Chase froze, a huge wave of disappointment nearly knocking him backward. He had waited through the final days of summer until he could see Hope again at school, and things hadn't turned out quite the way he had imagined they would. The noise and general confusion in the hallway seemed to be twinned with the commotion inside of his head. He turned around and slammed his locker shut, trudging down the hall in the opposite direction.

The rest of his elementary days were much the same; he, gazing on from afar, as a group of admirers flocked around Hope. It wasn't until his senior year of high school that he finally had the nerve to ask her out. He remembered her responding, teasingly, in a way that melted his heart, "It's about time."

CHAPTER TWO

A wooden magnet on her refrigerator read, "The rat race is over. The rat won!" and Hope had never found it to be truer.

Today, she had wanted to look good for her Monday morning assignment meeting so she could land a big story, but the day started out as any typical bad day does, with the alarm clock set to p.m., not a.m. When Hope finally peeled her eyes open and saw the numbers 7:04 glaring at her, knowing she had a 7:35 train to catch, she flew out of bed in a panic. She fought through a head rush and scrambled to find something to wear that didn't need to be ironed. On the way out the door, she grabbed a diet soda from the fridge, and an oatmeal cookie from a package on the kitchen counter. *Oatmeal IS a breakfast food*, she reasoned. Twenty short minutes after her alarm clock didn't ring, she rushed out the door and hustled up the street, filled with a multitude of people who had apparently set their alarm clocks incorrectly as well.

Despite this bad start, at exactly 8 a.m., Hope entered the conference room clutching her portfolio determinedly—determined to make the best of her rotten day; determined not to be stuck with another story about the wallaby's birthday at the zoo, or some elderly lady winning her ninth consecutive quilting bee; determined to win a hard-hitting news story she could make memorable. Though she had been a photographer for the paper for years, it had only been about six months since she first requested a writing assignment. Since then, she had been stuck with the crap stories no one else wanted to take. But that would not be the case today.

Hope took her seat as others claimed their own, all of them wearing stiffly starched shirts and pressed trousers, or tight-fitting skirts and silk blouses. One by one, her colleagues pulled up to the table, sliding out their cell phones and tablets. Hope glanced down at her pad of yellow legal paper and wrinkled blouse. On top of that, in her haste to leave her apartment, she had shattered a glass in her bathroom sink. Trying to clean it up, she managed to imbed the tiniest, and most painful, shard into her finger. Now she noticed a spot of blood on her blouse, presumably from her bad-morning-massacred fingertip. With a sigh of resignation, Hope debated a possible career switch.

A honey-toned voice whispered in her ear. "Good morning, Gorgeous."

Hope's boyfriend, Phillip, lifted his head and continued to orbit around the table until he was sitting opposite her, ostensibly in the best position to gaze on her face. Handsome blue eyes darted in her direction as he lowered his ex-college-football player frame into a seat. An electric-blue shirt set off those eyes, making him look like he belonged behind an anchor desk, not a byline. His blond hair contained more styling products than Hope's did, something she liked to tease him about, though she liked the results. Usually, Hope was not drawn to men with Phillip's cookie-cutter good looks. She preferred men with a lopsided smile or a crooked nose or a scar, something slightly off-kilter, but Phillip's down-home, South Carolina charm had won her from the get-go.

Just as Phillip took his seat, Jack Delaney, chief editor of *The Chicago Globe News*, entered the room. He strode purposefully to the head of the table and turned his back to the windows overlooking Michigan Avenue. He chose not to take a seat. Instead, his shoulders hunched slightly, he stood behind his chair, grasping the top of it with his hands. A big man, Delaney's stature had seemed to inflate as his importance to the company did, growing taller with each rise in the ranks. He was barrel-chested, a thick shock of dark gray hair slicked back on the sides, giving it an oddly aerodynamic look in Hope's eyes. In his usual brusque manner, he began the meeting as if he were one of those announcers at the end of car commercials, verbalizing the fine print.

"Good morning. I'd like to, first of all, offer my congratulations to a pair of staff members who recently won awards for their fine work in the field of journalism. Liz McPherson was honored last week with the coveted Robert F. Downy Award for her series on the insurrection in Kosovo."

Liz McPherson, a tall blonde with perfectly coiffed hair and a catty smile, sat to Phillip's right. She was given a resounding round of applause and thumps on the back by those sitting around her. She nodded her thanks.

"And I would also like to recognize Hope Creswell who was recently given the Ladies' Garden Club Award for her work describing the ongoing renovations in Grant Park. Congratulations, Hope."

There was a smattering of polite applause before the chief editor resumed the business of the day. Hope studied her hands, embarrassed. Phillip coughed quietly and she raised her eyes a little to catch his proud smile. It made her feel better, if only by the slimmest fraction.

"Now," Jack Delaney said, clearing his throat, "I'd like to get through these assignments quickly, as I've got a plane to catch. I will list each project first, and then we will discuss who would be best suited for them. First off, I need a couple of seasoned veterans for a series on Afghani politics. This will be an in-depth report, running four consecutive Sundays, and will require these reporters to be out of the country for at least a month, so let's keep that in mind before you volunteer for this one..."

This is it! Hope thought wildly. *This is the piece that will make everyone take me seriously.* She tried to talk herself into a reasoned calm. *Okay, so this may be a little out of my league, but if I could convince Delaney I could learn from being paired up with a pro on a project like this...* Hope was so engrossed in her thoughts she almost missed his next words.

"Mr. Hatton will be in town for a day or two doing a couple of shows and, I believe, shooting a video. I'd also like this to be a lengthy article, or couple of articles, for our entertainment section, and the reporter would need to shadow Mr. Hatton for the duration of his stay, which I'm sure, for many of you female reporters, would not be too much of a hardship." He gave a low chuckle.

"Hope, aren't you from Nebraska, like Chase Hatton?" Liz piped up.

Hope was speechless. Chase Hatton was not a name she had expected to hear, not this morning, not now.

"Yeah. Didn't you tell me once you grew up in Lincoln with Chase Hatton and went to school with him?" Phillip added.

"I...well...I..." Hope wondered if she looked as panicked as she felt.

"Is that true, Hope?" Jack Delaney asked in his bass voice. She nodded faintly. "Well, good. Good. You already have an in. You'll be perfect for it. And Liz and Phillip? I'd like to put you on the Afghani story, if you're up for it."

"I'd be thrilled," Phillip was saying.

"Yes. Of course," Liz interjected.

"Good. Then that is decided." The big man continued to hand out assignments, but Hope's head was buzzing. *What had just happened?* She felt like a quarterback lying on the turf after he'd been waylaid by a blindside tackle. *She* was to interview Chase? The discombobulated feeling she had started off the day with returned in spades.

Jack Delaney cleared his throat one final time. "I will leave the remainder of the assignments in the hands of the senior editors, who will pass them on to the rest of you. Thank you for your time this morning. Let's get out there and write some more award-winning stuff." With that, the whirlwind of a man was gone and the door was shutting behind him.

It wasn't until Hope heard the general shuffling of a meeting coming to an end that she came out of her stupor. People gathered their belongings and pushed back chairs noisily, though she still sat, dazed. She glanced up and thought she saw Liz McPherson winking at Phillip. Then, Liz seemed to realize Hope was watching her.

"Congratulations, Hope," she said patronizingly. "I'm sure you'll enjoy hanging out with a rock star for a couple of days, huh?" She gave Phillip's hand a squeeze, and followed the others out of the conference room, leaving them alone.

"Hope," Phillip began, "you're not mad I took this assignment and will be gone for a while, are you? 'Cause I could tell Delaney I don't want it. It's just...it's a great assignment."

She found her voice. "No, I'm not upset about that. You should go. I understand."

Phillip strolled around the table and leaned on its edge next to her chair. "Then what are you upset about?"

"Nothing. Nothing. It's just been one of those mornings, you know?"

"Well, maybe," he murmured, bending down to nuzzle her ear, "it's because you didn't let me stay all night."

She didn't even hear him. "Phillip, I wanted to be ready for this meeting. I wanted to get a good assignment. Ugh! Liz McPherson. I swear she did that on purpose."

"What? You mean the Chase Hatton story? Oh no. I'm sure she didn't—"

"I'm sorry, Phillip, but I think that woman has it in for me."

"Liz? Oh no, honey. I don't think so."

"And I'm not thrilled about you traveling with her either," Hope added peevishly.

Phillip laughed. "Well, just think about me, leaving you here with Mr. Hunky Rock Star."

"Oh, believe me, Phillip, you have nothing to worry about with Chase Hatton. That's for sure."

"That bad, huh?" When she didn't elaborate, he changed the subject. Leaning in, he whispered mischievously, "Why don't you and I go back to your apartment to 'do a little research' for our stories before I have to start packing?" He toyed with the lapel of her blazer, and then gave it a playful tug.

Hope smiled up at him. How was it, even at her lowest, he could still pull a smile from her? "I'm up for 'a little research.'" She, in turn, fingered his tie, pulling him to her with it until she felt the warmth of his mouth on hers. Hope's fingers glided up Phillip's chest and explored the familiar skin of his face. His hand traveled to the back of Hope's neck, caressing her bare skin there. Before they could get carried away any further, they heard someone's hand on the doorknob. Jumping apart guiltily, they turned to see Liz McPherson in the doorway.

Liz frowned, appearing annoyed at having obviously interrupted something. "Phil, our flight leaves in four hours, so you may want to get packing," she snapped. She turned to go, purposefully leaving the door open in her wake.

Their faces fell as they looked at one another. Phillip hung his head, mumbling. "Damn Delaney! Why does he have to be so gosh darn..." He scrambled for the word he needed.

"Efficient?"

"I was going for something more like hyperactive." He gazed at her with a sigh. "Walk me to my car?"

"Sure."

Phillip slung his hand over her shoulder, and they left the conference room.

On the way to the parking garage, Hope was quiet. She knew Phillip would attribute it to his leaving, but she had more on her mind. *Chase Hatton.* The name stirred up so many emotions she had trouble sorting through them all. He had been the first man she loved. *Boy,* she corrected. *He was barely eighteen.* In truth, he was the only person she had ever given her heart to, not foreseeing Chase would simply throw it aside.

Phillip nudged her from her reverie as they headed down to the ground floor in an elevator. "You gonna be okay?"

"Sure. I'll be fine. I'll just miss you is all."

"I'll miss you, too, babe."

The door of the elevator dinged open, and they exited, their footsteps ringing in the empty parking garage. Minutes later they stood beside Phillip's sporty convertible. Hope leaned against the door. Goodbyes like this were always difficult. And it was true, she would miss him. Okay, so theirs wasn't the heart-stopping love affair she had dreamed of once. But she had grown up. Those relationships happened only in romance novels. Passion in real life was little more than a momentary physical urge, quickly satisfied, though still leaving you empty.

As if to emphasize the point she was making in her head, Phillip pulled her close, sticking his hands in her back pockets and, as she raised her head, kissing her hard on the mouth. He moved his right hand to her throat, letting it rest there briefly, and then slid it downward, under the fabric of her blouse.

She giggled and squirmed. "Phillip! There have to be security cameras in here."

"So let them watch," he muttered, not fully taking his lips from hers. "Maybe they'll learn something." She felt her passion rising to meet his. He suddenly grabbed her hips and spun Hope so her front was pressed against the car. His mouth was on her neck, and his hands sought her breasts again, though covered with the blouse this time. She thrilled to the sound of his voice near her ear. "We could be quick, you know? It'll only take me an hour to get my stuff ready."

She chuckled, making a small gurgling sound in her throat, and checking the elevator, praying no one would get off. "It'll take you that long to decide what to wear on the plane."

Phillip's hands stilled; he must have realized she was right. He was a terrible packer, always second-guessing himself or feeling as if he were leaving something behind.

"Phillip." Hope pushed her tush into him, giving herself enough room to turn around. She straightened his tie, which was comically askew. "You *have* to go."

"All right," he sighed. "You win." He tugged Hope in once more, growling in her ear. "You drive me crazy, you know?"

"Yeah," she whispered back. "But it's a very short drive."

"Hey," he said, pretending to be hurt. Phillip disengaged himself and slapped her rear before opening the car door. Sliding into his seat, the reporter started the engine smoothly. He rolled down the window and reached up to pull her in for a last kiss. "You know, the boys in the security booth are very disappointed right now."

"Oh, I'll make it up to them," she teased as she stepped away from the car.

"You better not!" Phillip called as he pulled out. And, with a flashy squeal of his tires, he was gone.

CHAPTER THREE

C hase strolled out of his hotel bathroom wearing only a pair of jeans. He rubbed a towel over his damp hair. His muscular chest still held a few sparkling drops of water, glistening, in fact, all the way down his toned abs to the waistline of his jeans, darkening their top. He had arrived in Chicago just this morning, and already completed a charity concert in Grant Park. Since the facility had no dressing room, the singer had come back to his penthouse for a shower after the live performance.

His manager, Hal Westwood, sat at a table with papers spread out in front of him, his ever-present cell phone amidst them, at-the-ready. Hal was tall, sober-looking, with thick, brown hair, which was always professionally styled. He was more often than not dressed in a suit and tie, even when attending casual affairs. Hal was good at what he did, and well-respected in a field where flash was more the call for the day, and professionalism was sometimes seen as "being uptight."

Chase picked up a piece of pineapple from a heaping tray on a side table as he asked, "Okay, Hal, what's next on the agenda?" He popped the pineapple into his mouth and listened to his manager's reply.

"As a matter of fact," he cleared his throat, referencing notes, "I just set up an interview with you for tomorrow morning with a...Hope Creswell, of *The Chicago Globe News*. I agreed to let her shadow you for a week or so. It will be good publicity because of the paper's wide readership. Later in the afternoon, we have to get started on the video shoot..."

But Chase had tuned him out.

Hope. He had abandoned all illusions of hearing from her years ago, and now this. She had requested "an interview" with him. He was dumbfounded. After all these years, why had she contacted him? Just for a newspaper article? Or could there be something more behind it? He stood and stared blindly out of the windows of his penthouse, awash in memories. Some tugged at the corners of his lips, making him want to smile; others twisted his stomach in knots.

Hope was coming here, to his penthouse? Hal glanced up from his schedule when Chase didn't answer. "Chase? Did I overwhelm you? Does it sound like too much?"

Chase turned to face him. "No, no, Hal. It sounds fine. I guess I'm just tired is all."

"Okay," Hal gazed at him thoughtfully, then gathered up his things. "I'll just head back to my room for now then. I'll come by at 8:45 or so for the interview—"

"No, it's okay. I actually know Hope. I'll be fine on my own."

He frowned. "Are you sure?"

"Yeah. I'd prefer to see her alone, at least at first."

"All right, then." He sounded doubtful and seemed to weigh the matter for a minute before his face relaxed into a smile. "See you in the morning then."

HOPE STUMBLED IN HER front door, much the same way she had stumbled out of it earlier, with a sense of confusion and anxiety. She closed the door behind her and leaned against it, as if trying to keep the rest of the world from getting in. Exhaling loudly, she dropped her purse, keys, and notebook, which all seemed to weigh about fifty pounds apiece, at her feet, one at a time. Three satisfying *thumps.* She reached up and yanked the clip from her hair, shaking it loose and letting it fall all around her, so that, for a minute, it blocked her view of the room.

Meow.

Hope stuck a lip out and blew air up her face in an exasperated way, clearing a few strands of silky brown hair from her eyes. Reaching up, she pushed the rest back. Despite her bad day, the cat's greeting cheered her. "Hello, Mr. Mewford. How's my kitty?"

A black ball of fur uncurled from a plush, off-white couch, which she had come to regret purchasing. It was constantly covered in Mewford hair. The cat trotted across the room, mewing his hello and wrapping around her feet. As he circled, he began to purr loudly. She reached down and picked the cat up, cooing, "And how was your day today, sir? Mine sucked!"

She ran a hand over her companion's back in long strokes meant to comfort them both as she crossed the apartment. She strolled past the fur-laden couch to the windows on the far side of the room. Her place was tiny, but she figured that left less to clean. The surroundings bordered on sparse, as she liked nice clean lines without a lot of clutter. A set of four arched windows, running nearly floor to ceiling, was one of her favorite features, as they flooded the small space with light. Hope set Mewford down on his velvet paws with a soft *thud,* and the cat continued his trek around her legs as she stared out the windows. Stretching one hand out, she touched the cool pane before her.

Traffic bustled far below her, silenced by distance and glass. She watched the tiny cars, which somehow looked fake from this height. They reminded her of the lost pieces from her childhood board game, minus the blue and pink plastic drivers. The cars blurred in and out. She switched her hand to steady herself against the edge of the brick that ran between the windows, her stomach pitching. The simplicity surrounding her was a foil for the turmoil she now felt inside.

Tomorrow she'd be face-to-face with Chase.

Hope closed her eyes for a second or two, and then deliberately turned away from the windows. She surveyed the mess left at the door, and considered picking it up. Instead, she headed for the bedroom. She needed a bath.

The bedroom was also small and cozy. It was dominated by a white, wrought iron bed, covered with a downy comforter, also with its fair share of cat fur. In the far left corner, another window let in abundant light, which fell across the floor, climbing the bed and reaching halfway across it. It spread along the sheets, still jumbled from her crazy morning. In the right-hand corner of the room, on the wall between the living room and bedroom, a large, white armoire sat diagonal to the corner, a necessary piece of furniture, since the designer had forgotten to add a closet to the room. Most women would have found this an impossible situation, but Hope generally dressed as simply as she decorated, so it was not a problem. She frowned at the delinquent alarm clock before turning to head to the bathroom.

Mr. Mewford followed. He stretched up Hope's leg, emphasizing his need for attention and gazing at her with his aren't-I-good-do-I-get-a-treat eyes. "Did you keep all the bad guys out? Huh?" Hope entered the bathroom, bending to retrieve his kitty treats from underneath the sink just as he jumped up on it. He stuck his paw out and tapped her on the head in a friendly way. She laughed at his transparent attempts to butter her up. "You know you're getting your treats, don't ya, fellow?"

As her feline friend munched on the treats she had placed in front of him on the counter, Hope turned the water on in the tub. This was another one of the things she loved about her place. In fact, it was the main reason for her renting from "The Claw-foot Condominiums" in the first place—that, and its nearness to the L. Each apartment in the building held a big, claw-foot, porcelain tub.

When the owners renovated the old building, instead of removing the heavy, old-fashioned tubs, they had, quite successfully, turned them into a theme for the entire building. Hope loved everything about the tub, from its hardware, which felt sturdy and solid in her hands, to its depth, in which she could completely submerge herself.

She went to the kitchen and poured a glass of wine, grabbing a butane-lighter from the drawer on her way out. After returning to the bathroom, she lit the four thick candles, which sat at different levels on individual stands surrounding the tub. She enjoyed the commingled smell of melting wax and shampoo. She turned the dimmer switch, and smiled to herself as she pulled out thick towels and stripped her clothes off to step into the steamy water. Her day may have started out bad, but she'd be damned if it would finish that way. She lowered her weary body into the hot water with a sigh, entering her own personal oasis. Closing her eyes, she laid her head back against the smooth, cool, porcelain lip of the tub, letting her hair spill over the edge. Her arms melted along the sides.

Phillip would be halfway around the world by now, but strangely, she hadn't thought about him since his taillights had vanished in the parking garage. Her mind was filled to overflowing with her apprehension over meeting Chase Hatton once again.

When they first met, he had been a welcome playmate. His warm, brown hair and ready smile were complimented by his gray-green eyes, which would alternately appear thoughtful or full of mischief. He had the cutest set of freckles, sprinkled like fairy dust, just at the edge of his cheekbones. But what drew her to him like the pull of gravity was his relaxed air. Like he never let anything ruffle him. Like he was simply content with his life. She longed to dip her foot in the tranquil waters of his world, to let it offset her life, which had often been visited by chaos. She was attracted to Chase's perpetually unperturbed spirit, by the ease in which he moved and breathed. When they were together, she wished only to immerse herself in his pleasant calm, just as she now submerged herself in the soothing bathwater.

Hope let herself slip under the surface, allowing the water to fill her ears and block out the noise of her day. The sound of Phillip's goodbye, the memory of Liz's condescension, the abrupt importance of Jack Delaney, all blocked out and replaced with the singular sound of "Chase." She would only think of the good times they had together, not permitting her thoughts to slip back to the night of prom, when her heart had been wrenched away for good.

In the beginning, she thought of Chase merely as a neat kid, a good friend, fun to be with. But somewhere along the line, her vision of him began to morph. She tried to figure out just when her feelings for Chase had changed...maybe during her freshman year.

She remembered seeing him sometime during that first week on campus. Sidelined all summer with a broken ankle, the same one she had injured at Chase's house the night they first met, she had seen neither hide nor hair of her young neighbor the entire time. But she recalled running into him that day.

She stepped into the shade of a tree, getting out of the traffic along the intersecting sidewalks that crisscrossed the main quadrangle, to again retrieve her schedule. She had missed orientation the day she got her cast removed, and the layout of the buildings turned out to be more complicated than she had initially believed. When she looked up again to get her bearings, she saw Chase approaching with a group of his friends. When their eyes met, he stopped abruptly, causing one of his buddies to run into him.

"Sorry, Chip," she heard him say.

The other boy followed his gaze.

"No problem, buddy. Hey, who's that?"

"Nobody you need to know," Chase responded vaguely. "Hey, take my books, would ya?" He handed them over without even looking in his friend's direction. "I'll catch up to you in Mrs. Kelly's class."

"All right," his friend replied, clearly disappointed.

Hope watched Chase as he strode toward her across the grass. He had put on weight over the summer, and his broad chest was beginning to look a lot like his brother, Jeff's. His hair was longer, and his eyes more startling than she remembered, but he still had a killer white smile.

"Hey, Hope. How's it going?"

She allowed herself to bask in the richness of his voice for a second as a gentle breeze fingered through his hair. His voice had what could only be described as a seductive smoothness. A bit flustered, she tried to form a coherent answer to his oh-so-ordinary question. "Oh, um...not so good, I guess. I can't seem to find the music building."

"That's because it's kind of off the beaten path. Come on, I'll show you. Let me carry your books." Without waiting for a response, Chase lifted the load from her hands and they fell into step together. "Do you have a lot of classes in the music building? I'm taking guitar from Mr. Stalwart after school, but that's the only time I'm in there."

"I just have mixed chorus with Mrs. Flasher."

"Ah. I heard she plays favorites, so try to get on her good side." He grinned and it reminded her of how much she had missed seeing him.

"What other advice do you have for me?" she queried, handing him the printout of her schedule.

"Mrs. V. is cool. Jeff had her and even *he* liked her class."

"A high recommendation, indeed."

He chuckled. "Yes. Mr. Johnson's supposed to be really cool, too, but A.P. history is tough. You'll have to work your butt off."

"Mmm." She frowned, somewhat concerned.

"Are you going out for volleyball? I heard they're having tryouts already at the end of the week."

"I hadn't really thought about it."

"You should. I remember you had a wicked serve in Mrs. Nal-away's gym class."

"I did?" Hope responded, surprised but pleased. She grinned, sliding in a quick peek in his direction.

He nodded, grinning in return.

All too soon they found themselves in front of Hope's classroom. They stood awkwardly for a few seconds.

"Well," he said, clearing his throat. "This is it."

She tucked her hair behind her ear, suddenly nervous. "Thank you for—" The bell sounded loudly, cutting off her sentence.

"Better go," Chase suggested, urging her toward the door.

"Oh no! Won't you be late?"

"I don't care," he said with the same wonderful grin he had shot her earlier. He turned and started to walk away. "See ya around," he called over his shoulder.

She watched him saunter away, admiring the way he looked in his jeans. Hot was not a strong enough word for it. Sizzling, searing, blazing...

That was the first time she remembered her heart skipping a beat in Chase Hatton's presence. Since then, she couldn't remember a time when it hadn't.

CHAPTER FOUR

Later that evening, after Hal left, Chase found himself in a nostalgic mood and threw on a "Property of Lincoln High School" t-shirt he frequently wore without even thinking of its connection to home and Hope. Now, he found he could think of nothing else as he stood with arms crossed over his chest, gazing out the windows of his penthouse at the twinkling lights of the big city. They reminded him of the scads of fireflies he and Hope collected in jars over the summers back in Lincoln.

Chase caught his reflection in the glass, and wondered if he had changed much since then. Whatever his reflection told him, Chase felt the same on the inside as he had eight years ago as a high school senior. Had Hope changed? Was she still the same ponytail-wearing beauty with the wicked jump serve? His mind drifted back to a game near the end of her volleyball season their junior year.

At the time, Chase was dating number seventeen, Susie McNamara. As he sauntered in with his friends, Susie looked up and saw him. She waved just as the opposition served. Hope, who was playing behind Susie, dove to save the ball as it was about to drop at Susie's feet. She made an incredible play, popping the ball up in a position to be spiked over the net by another teammate to score a point.

The crowd went wild, but Chase had eyes only for Hope. She lay writhing in pain on the floor; blood was everywhere. She held her elbow and rolled from side to side. Whistles blew and coaches and officials rushed out onto the floor, blocking his view. He was reminded of the first time they had met, when Hope sat clutching her ankle in the middle of a cornfield. His friends had already climbed into the stands, and Chase hastened up behind them, hoping to obtain a better view of the court. As he took a seat, he heard someone address Chip Carter, who was presently dating Hope, and sitting right behind him.

"Hey, Chip, it looks like Hope is hurt."

Chip, who was stuffing his face full of popcorn, glanced up, mumbling, "Serves the little Ice Princess right."

Chase felt his jaw tighten at the sound of Chip's callous response.

"What? She's not that good a kisser, or something?" his companion teased.

"Oh no! She's a good kisser. A *fantastic* kisser, in fact. That's the problem. She gets you all worked up and then can't finish the job. I had to practically take her hand and show her what to do." He snorted derisively.

Chase could feel his face, ears, and the back of his neck get hot in anger, but he concentrated on making his voice sound casual as he turned around to say, "Ever think maybe she's just not that into you, Chippy?"

Chip's face turned a bright shade of red, a hue deep enough to coordinate with the cheerleaders' uniforms. Other boys around them hooted and slapped Chase on the back, and he felt good about having embarrassed Chip...until the next week.

The following week the same scene played out again, Chase at the volleyball game, finding the only seat open to be right in front of Chip. Hope was in the middle of serving for about a ten-point run, an Ace bandage covering the elbow she had broken open in her previous game. She drew her arm back like an archer extending the bow string. With a loud *smack* her hand met the ball as she twisted her wrist to one side, putting such a spin on the ball, it made it nearly impossible to return. When an opposing player would try to pass a ball she had served to their front row, no matter how squarely they hit it, the ball would careen off their hands in an unexpected direction, generally out of play.

"Geez, did you see that serve, Chip? Your little Ice Princess is kickin' butt tonight."

"Yeah," Chip said proudly. "Only, she's not really an Ice Princess," he added, loud enough for Chase to hear. "Last night when we went out, well, let me just say she did things to me with her mouth I ain't never had a girl do to me." His friends "oohed" and "ahed" in appreciation. Chip leaned forward and whispered in Chase's ear. "Maybe you were right, Hatton. Last week, Hope was off her game. But this week, she couldn't keep her hands off me."

Chase contemplated planting a fist in Chip Carter's overly large mouth, but the principal walked by right in front of them just at that moment, and he had to resist. A second later, thunderous applause filled his ears, and students began rushing out onto the court. They had beaten their longtime rivals, Southeast Lincoln, 25-11, to take the conference championship.

Chase followed the mob as it oozed out of the stands. He searched the floor for Hope. He saw her near the net, being congratulated by someone. Her face was flushed with excitement, but when she glanced up and caught his eye she stilled, her smile broadening. He grinned, gliding toward her, but Susie cut across his line of vision and came running to him. She jumped up and Chase caught her, surprised.

"Hey," he offered, "great game!"

"Yeah! Wasn't it awesome!" she screamed over the crowd.

He hugged Susie, but was hunting over her shoulder for Hope. He saw her familiar ponytail as she threaded through the crowd in the opposite direction. "Hey, Suz," Chase said hurriedly, "I'm gonna go congratulate Hope before she leaves, okay?"

But Susie was already in mid-squeal as one of her girlfriends approached. She nodded to Chase even as she was engulfed in an embrace.

Chase maneuvered through the mass of people on the gym floor, keeping Hope's bouncing ponytail in sight. He saw her entering a doorway at the far side of the gym. He picked up his pace, banging his hand on the metal bar to open the door. He found himself in the long corridor that led to the locker rooms, his nose assaulted by the smell of stale air and sweat. Hope was halfway down the hall, pulling the rubber band from her long hair and shaking it loose as she walked.

"Hope!" His voice echoed weirdly off the cinder block walls. As she turned, he caught a sad expression in her eyes a split-second before she recognized him, then a smile eased across her face to replace it.

Chase ran the several feet between them and spontaneously threw his arms around her. He pressed Hope to him tightly, and they stood together for a second, her cheek resting on his shoulder, his eyes squeezed shut. Strangely, he felt a sigh of relief escape him, and realized he had been anxious over the thought of somehow missing her before she left. They drew apart and stood awkwardly for a beat.

Hope tucked a strand of hair behind an ear, and dropped her eyes. Her cheeks were still glowing from excitement and exertion, and small tendrils were stuck to her face with sweat, but she was still drop-dead gorgeous. He felt that lurch in his stomach being close to her always gave him, like the feeling he got when he went over a dip in the road at too high a speed and became briefly airborne.

"Great game!" Chase blurted out.

"Thanks," she said, seeming both proud and slightly ill-at-ease with the praise.

"Boy! That's some serve you have."

"Thanks," she said again, glancing up, her smile becoming a little wider. She seemed uncomfortable, as if she were searching for something else to say, but she remained silent.

"How's your arm?" Chase offered.

"Oh, it's better. I got eight stitches," she added, unwinding the bandage to show him. "I just put this on to cushion it in case I fell again." The cut was long and jagged.

"Oooh!" he said sympathetically. He touched her arm to turn it to get a better view. "Looks pretty bad." Without thinking, he rubbed her forearm a little before releasing it. Her skin was velvety soft, and he was filled with a need to touch more of it.

She let the arm drop to dangle at her waist, the other arm coming up to cross her chest and grip the bicep. She stood uneasily, shifting her weight from side to side and again appeared to be struggling for elusive words. She pressed her lips into a thoughtful expression. Chase reflected that even though mussed, her soft, brown hair framed her face appealingly.

"Susie had a good game," she said at last, looking up to search his face. Chase's heart skipped a beat as he stared into those unbelievable eyes of hers, feeling as if she could see right through him.

"Yeah," he replied, shrugging a little. "So," he added, digging for information of his own, "are you and Chip going out to celebrate?"

For the briefest of seconds, something flitted through her eyes, as if the mention of Chip's name was a slap in the face. She stiffened. "Chip and I are no longer going out. We broke up last week."

They both started as the door slammed open behind Chase, and Susie, with two of her friends, moved toward them, their talking and laughter sounding hollow in the stuffy hall. "Well, I guess I better grab a shower," Hope said in a rush, not taking her eyes from the approaching threesome.

"Yeah, okay," Chase responded lamely as she backed away. He watched her as she took a few steps in the opposite direction.

Before she had gotten far, Hope turned around and spoke quietly, "Thanks, Chase." Then, she pushed through the locker room door and disappeared.

Chase saw her again a few days later as he was searching for a book on the shelves of the school library's balcony. As he was running his finger along the spines of the books in the most remote part of the stacks, searching for the correct series of letters and numbers, he heard her voice.

"I don't care what Chip told you!"

Her voice sounded tight and irate. He squinted through the crack between the top of the books and the next shelf up. Practically swallowed up by a red letterman's jacket, he could barely see her form pressed against the wall. He heard the low growl of a male voice, and then Hope, even more loudly. "Get your hands off me!"

Abandoning his search, he raced down the aisle. As he rounded the bookcase, he heard the noise of several books hitting the floor. He saw Hope, arms extended, pushing against the chest of a football player. The guy's hands were bracing the wall on either side of her, effectually pinning her there.

"Is there a problem, Hope?" Chase inquired, jaw clenched.

The football player turned, releasing one hand from the wall, and he recognized him as one of the school's star linebackers, whose name he couldn't recall. The behemoth stood twice his size, but he didn't care.

Hope shoved the football player as hard as she could in the shoulder that he still had toward her, forcing him to remove his other arm, her eyes spitting fire. "No," she replied angrily.

There was a tense moment when the football player glowered at Chase, sizing him up, and then back at Hope, seeming to try to determine if there was any give there. Having gotten in trouble the week before for a fight he started in the cafeteria, the football player, perhaps, didn't want to push his luck with the coach. He glared at Hope one last time before shrugging his shoulders and marching past Chase without a word.

Chase eyed him as he left, then turned toward Hope. She was bent, picking books up off the floor. He stooped and began helping her. He could see her hand trembling as she reached for a book near him; whether it was in anger or fear, he didn't know. She slammed the books onto the shelf haphazardly, and then picked her backpack up from the floor, swinging it over a shoulder.

"Are you okay?" Chase began.

"I'm fine," she snapped, brushing past him, eyes flashing, hands clinging to her backpack strap, the knuckles white.

He followed her at a distance and watched her go into a ladies' room. He waited, trying to appear casual, for ten minutes, keeping an eye on the door. When she came out, her eyes and nose were red, and he was sure she had been crying. He followed her to class, listening as the teacher gave her an afterschool detention for being late.

At three o'clock Chase strode into the detention room, hauling his backpack off his shoulder and placing it onto a desk next to Hope with a *thump*. "What are you in for?" he asked her in his best gangster voice.

She beamed. "I was late to class fourth hour. How 'bout you?"

"The same."

She turned in her seat to touch his arm. "I don't even know why you're talking to me. I was so rude to you earlier. Chase, I'm sorry. It's just...some guys are real jerks." Her face darkened with the memory briefly, but then she hurriedly added, "But not you." She shut her mouth tightly, perhaps afraid she had revealed too much about the strange encounter in the book stacks.

"It's no biggie, Hope." He covered her hand with his, squeezing it.

Just then, the teacher on duty arrived with his stack of papers to grade. "Ahem," he cleared his throat pointedly, and the pair turned to face the front of the classroom. The rest of the detention time they were forced to spend silently, but Hope gave Chase a smile every now and again. She had this way of smiling when she was tentative about something or uncertain of herself. He found it to be the sexiest smile, her upper lip turning up a fraction and quivering in a way that made his stomach do flip-flops.

Chase rubbed his arms, turning from the window that had served as a type of TV screen for his memories. He switched off the lamps in the room one by one and meandered into the large bedroom on his left. He sat down on the edge of the bed for a minute, suddenly tired. The memories of her were so vivid. Even now it seemed he could smell the sweet fragrance of her skin, a scent that reminded him of ripe pears and apple blossoms. He imagined touching her arms, brushing the hair away from her face.

Chase shook his head angrily. Hope had *left* him. Without a word, she had left him. That pain, too, he could taste as if it were yesterday, the bitterness like rancid milk on his tongue. He pulled his t-shirt off over his head in one swift motion, balling it up to toss it at a chair across the room. He overshot and watched it land, in a heap, in the corner behind the chair. He leaned forward with his elbows on his knees, feet spread apart. Fingers raked through long blond hair furiously for a minute, as his broad chest expanded with each deep breath.

Chase laughed mirthlessly, surprised by the intensity of his emotions after so much time. With a practiced deliberateness, he pushed the thought of her from his mind. He slipped his jeans off, letting them lie in a puddle on the floor, and climbed into bed. Switching the last light off, he let darkness engulf him, as if being submerged in water. He slept restlessly, thoughts of the meeting with Hope in the morning running through his head painfully, like a long family slide show.

CHAPTER FIVE

A half-finished glass of Riesling sat on the tile floor of her bathroom. Hope stretched a foot out and expertly turned the hot water back on to warm up the now tepid tub. The candles burned low as Hope drew in a breath and let herself slip under again. The water closed over her face with a gentle kiss, and she could hear its deadened roar as it cascaded into the tub, hair floating lazily around her. That sensation of being light as air transported Hope back to a summer night just before her senior year of high school.

"Are you ready to go to the Hattons?" her mother called.

Hope peeked in the mirror one last time, applying a final layer of lip gloss, just in case Chase happened to be home. The teen turned sideways, pleased with the way the halter top she had chosen accented her newly curvy figure. Though athletic, she was no longer the tomboy she had been when they first moved next door to Chase Hatton, and for the hundredth time, she hoped he would notice the difference.

"Arggh!" She laughed at herself, grabbing a purse from her bedpost. "He'll probably be out on a date anyway." Chase had been seeing a number of girls since his basketball playing had led the way to Lincoln's victory at the state playoffs.

"Come on, Lady Jane!" her mother chided.

Hope hustled out the door and crossed the lawn with her mother, as they had when she was twelve all those summers ago. She held a chocolate cake in her hands, something she had spent the hot afternoon baking, necessitating a second shower before they left the house. She was disappointed when she did not spot Chase on the porch, and decided he was almost definitely out on a date. But when they entered the door, he came scurrying down the stairs. He had on a pair of khaki shorts and a black polo shirt with leather sandals on his feet. Dressed to go out, she decided, but at least she had gotten to see him, if only for a moment.

"Hi," she greeted him, feeling a little shy.

"Hey, Hope."

"Hope, honey, that looks delicious," Mrs. Hatton commented, taking the plate from her.

"I'm afraid it's melted a little on the way over here."

"I'll stick it in the fridge and it will be just fine."

"Can I help?" Hope's mom asked.

The adults moved off into the kitchen through the swinging door separating the two rooms. The door closed behind them with a *swish,* leaving Chase and Hope alone. After a moment of nervous silence, they both began talking at once.

"How's your summer—?"

"You look—"

They laughed. "You go ahead, Chase."

"I was just going to say, you look nice."

"Thanks," she said, feeling her face get hot. "So do you. Are you going out on a date?"

Chase seemed surprised by the question. "No. I'm eating here with you."

"Ah. Sentenced to entertain the neighbor girl again, eh?"

"Not hardly," he replied quietly, holding her gaze for a beat. The door swung open and the adults started filing in, laden with platters.

"Do you need any help, Mrs. Hatton?" Hope asked quickly.

Chase's mom seemed to sense she had interrupted something, but smiled at the pair. "I think we have it all," she replied lightly.

Hope couldn't remember what they had for dinner that night, only that it was delicious. At the end of the meal, she and Chase escaped to the garage for a game of table tennis. The garage was large, with a low, raftered ceiling holding bikes and boxes, and shelves built into all of the walls along the sides and back. It had a nice, damp, woody scent, albeit somewhat musty. There were center support poles running between the two garage doors, and on one side, a large table tennis table awaited.

The game started off friendly, but soon the pair's natural sense of competition heightened and it escalated into a battle of major proportions. Hope couldn't help but notice the muscles on Chase's arms tightening as he played, his skin tanned from hours at the pool. He shook hair out of his eyes with a smile, and she felt her insides melt like the cheese oozing out of a grilled cheese sandwich.

Chase found he had his hands full, as the same twist of the wrist that sent a volleyball spinning, also sent a table tennis ball spiraling out of control. Hope had a knack for hitting the ball just close enough to knick the table before it tumbled out of bounds. Add to this the fact that he seemed distracted at times. She served and his reaction was just a tad slow as the ball hit the paddle, sending it into the net.

"Ohhh!" he groaned.

She grinned. "15-16." The next serve he didn't have a chance at.

"Geez! What was that?" Chase exclaimed as the ball whizzed past him.

"16 all!" Hope began hopping around.

"What are you doing?"

"My sandal strap came undone." She set her paddle down and bent to fix it, and he went to retrieve the ball from where it had rolled behind a rake. After he scooped it up, his eyes swept across the floor under the table to where she curled her leg up to fiddle with the buckle. She caught his eye.

"Ouch!" he muttered under his breath with a half whistle.

"Huh?"

They both straightened up, gazing across the table into each other's eyes.

"Nothing."

He bounced the ball to her.

"Ready?"

"Damn straight!" he returned.

The battle raged back and forth until Chase stood ready to serve, the score 24-25, in Hope's favor. Game point. But he wasn't about to quit.

"You stick your tongue out when you're concentrating."

"I do not!" Hope replied, slightly embarrassed.

"*Yes*, you do. It's cute."

Hope felt her cheeks get hot. "You're just trying to distract me," she rejoined, shifting her feet from side to side like she did on the volleyball court, her paddle poised.

"Darned right I am! I can't let myself get beat by a girl."

Before he had even finished his sentence, Chase tried to zing the ball past her, but Hope's reactions were too quick. With a flourish, she returned the ball, hitting it off the side of the table for the final time as she scored the winning point. She hooted and hollered, enjoying an elaborate victory dance on her side of the garage. Chase laid both hands on the table, appearing exasperated. Catching his glare, Hope stopped her dancing.

"Oh. That wasn't very sportsmanlike of me was it?" She grinned. "Oh well!" And with that she started dancing triumphantly again.

"I'm going to kick your ass!" Chase taunted, coming around the table toward her.

"You and what army?" she threw back, skirting around to keep the table between them. Chase faked in one direction and moved in the other, but Hope wasn't taken in. She laughed and darted about so as not to lose her positioning.

He chuckled. "I give," he said, breathing hard. "Want to go for a walk?"

"Sure."

Chase turned toward the door.

"You're not going to leave my body out in the cornfield, are you?" Hope teased.

"Don't give me any ideas," he called over his shoulder dryly.

They strolled across the lawn at a diagonal to the wall of corn defining the edge of the Hattons' property, heading in the direction of the woods, which stretched to the east of the fields.

"Have you ever had Mr. Stout?" Chase asked out of the blue.

"Yeah. Freshman year, for algebra. He's great."

"Yeah. I love it when he's in the middle of an equation that takes up half the board and then he goes, 'Oh, who cares what x is anyway? Have I ever told you about my train collection?'" Chase mimicked his teacher's baritone voice.

Hope laughed at his imitation. That was what made Mr. Stout memorable; his students enjoyed his obvious enthusiasm for his hobby. "Yeah. He'd spend a whole hour talking about his models." She smiled, remembering the way the big man would sit on the edge of his desk and gaze out the window and talk about engines and track designs.

Chase eyed her, his head cocked sideways. "Did he have a nickname for you, by any chance?"

She glanced up quickly. He had lured her into a trap. She turned to look straight ahead, a faint smile playing on her lips. "Yes," she said slowly.

"And what was it, exactly?"

Her lips quivered as she smiled, but she remained silent.

"Was it...Harlequin?"

"Maybe."

"And why did Mr. Stout call you Harlequin?"

"You're really enjoying this, aren't you?"

"Maybe."

They were meandering, taking pleasure in the night air, which had brought a slight respite to the day's heat. After entering the shelter of the trees, they followed a dirt path, which was worn in the wooded lot over the years.

"Okay." She took a deep breath. "Even though I'm sure you *know,* Mr. Stout called me Harlequin because he saw me reading Harlequin romance novels in his classroom, a lot."

He sniggered and Hope hit him hard on the arm.

"Ouch!" he said, rubbing it. They walked a little farther, Chase still seeming to revel in his verbal victory, until Hope started chuckling.

"What?"

"Oh, nothing. I was just thinking about this one time in Mr. Stout's class."

"What happened?" Chase was curious now.

"Oh, well..." She debated the wisdom of telling this particular story, but having gone this far... "I was looking out in the hall instead of paying attention. My desk was by the door. And this cute guy passed by—"

"Who?" Chase interrupted.

"Robbie Lips," Hope said dreamily. "Do you remember Robbie Lips?"

"Senior class president, star quarterback, golden child," Chase spouted, sounding irritated. "Of course I remember Robbie Lips, who wouldn't?"

"Well, Mr. Stout caught me looking out into the hall, so he called Robbie Lips in. He said, 'Robbie, I'd like you to meet Harlequin. Harlequin, this is Robbie. Harlequin here was just wondering if you were free Friday night.' I was mortified. Robbie nodded, a little stunned I guess, and Mr. Stout said, 'Great. He'll pick you up at seven, Harlequin. *Now*, do you think you can concentrate on algebra?'" She shook her head with a smile, amusement finally able to overtake the humiliation of the past.

"So, did he?"

"Did he what?"

"Pick you up at seven?"

"No." She chuckled. They had broken out of the trees and now stood on the edge of a large pond. "Wow! I never knew this was here." There was a long dock sticking out into the water. "Is this your land?" They wandered out to the edge of the dock; the moonlight shimmered across the pond, inviting them.

Ignoring her question, Chase let the same mischievous grin play on his face that he had been wearing all evening. "Wanna go for a swim?" Without waiting for an answer, he pulled his shirt off over his head and laid it on a post. His hand went to his belt buckle.

"Chase!"

"What? You scared?"

As he dropped his shorts and stripped off his underwear, she turned away, her heart racing. Chase ran the rest of the way down the dock and jumped into the water with a wild whoop of freedom. Hope turned back at the last minute and got a glimpse of his naked form right before his feet parted the water, then devoured him like some huge aquatic dragon. The sound of his voice reverberated for a few seconds against the surrounding trees, and then there was a complete silence that seemed strangely out of place after his war cry. Hope heard only the crickets chirping, as if they were waiting with her, watching and waiting for the stillness to be disrupted. After what seemed like an impossibly long amount of time, Chase broke the surface, sputtering and laughing without restraint at his own daring.

"Man!" he screamed in delight. "This water feels great! Come on in, Hope."

"What? Are you kidding?"

"Come on. I'll turn around. I promise. You've got to try this."

She bit her lip. "Are you crazy?"

"Yes. The question is," he commented, treading water and raising an eyebrow in that sexy way he had, "are you?"

She smiled at him, feeling suddenly adventurous. His reckless-ness was contagious. "All right." She was shocked to hear her re-sponse as it cut through the night. Had she really just said that? Before her brain had any time to think, she kicked off her sandals. "Turn around," she demanded, staring at him.

He acquiesced without a word, seeming to hold his breath.

Hope untied her top and laid it on Chase's. The air kissed her warm skin, and she shivered despite the heat.

Chase heard a splash and turned around quickly. He could see the ripples where the water had swallowed her up, but everything was hushed. He searched the top of the pond for a clue as to her loca-tion, until, without warning, she popped up in front of him, laugh-ing and splashing. He grabbed her wrists instinctively. "Hey, cut it out," he snorted.

With his touch, she became motionless, suddenly realizing the only thing separating them now was an insubstantial liquid shield. He gazed at her, his eyes straying to her lips. Her eyes, too, were drawn to his lips with an equal desire to feel them pressed against her own.

He pulled her infinitesimally closer. "Hope..." His voice sounded raspy.

Hope remembered the lightning bolt of panic she'd felt then, quick, hot, unexpected. She was naked, with this boy she had loved for so long, alone in the woods. "I...I..." All she wanted to do was kiss him, be his, but she couldn't, not this way. She forced the words out. "This is wrong."

Hope couldn't look into his confused face. She broke free and swam to the dock, each stroke feeling as if it were ripping through her heart. Unaware of her nudity now, only thinking of the hurt she'd seen in Chase's eyes, she climbed up the ladder and out of the water. She hurriedly scooped up her clothes and ran off into the trees. Once inside the protection of the trees, she scrambled into her clothes, though sobbing.

It was that feeling Hope felt now. Confused, perhaps still wanting him in the way she had that night, but most of all, afraid. Hope slowly became aware she was lying in an empty bathtub, shivering. At one point she had kicked the drain plug off and let the warm water siphon away from her skin. She felt cold, alone, empty. It took all of her strength to pull herself up, grasping the sides of the tub, and get out.

Seconds later, she stared at a blurred reflection in the steamy mirror, a towel wrapped under her armpits, another turbaned on her head. She remembered, with a sad smile, how he had come after her that night. She ran her hands along her arms as Chase had when he had tried to offer comfort, feeling the magic of it all over again. If only things could have ended then, before she had truly lost herself to him. She picked a hand towel up off the bathroom sink, and rubbed a hole in the steam so she could see herself clearly. She flashed back to the girl who had assessed herself in the mirror that summer night, before leaving for the Hattons'. The two reflections stood side by side in her mind: one young and innocent, one older, and hopefully, wiser.

Tomorrow she would see Chase; that she could do nothing about. But, she promised herself, she would write her story about him, and then it would be over for good. Thoughtfully, she blew out the candles and went to bed.

CHAPTER SIX

Across town, Chase lay in bed, staring at the alarm clock's reflection in the dresser mirror, caught up in the same memory.

When his mom told Chase the Creswells were coming for dinner, he had been thrilled. He saw it as an opportunity to finally ask Hope out. He'd be on his own turf. He always felt more comfortable with her there, away from the high-pressure social setting of school. He got dressed up, and hoped neither of his parents would notice and mortify him by commenting on it in front of Hope.

Seeing her, his hormones simply seemed to go into overdrive that night; it was the only way he could explain it. The table tennis game was a struggle, not just because Hope was good at table tennis, but because he was so distracted by her presence. For instance, when he retrieved a stray ball and turned his head, catching sight of her, what could only be described as *fantastic,* legs, he all but drooled. Watching her toned arms and forever legs, he kept imagining them locking around him with surprising strength. It was not only that, but also the way she flicked her gorgeous hair over her shoulders, making him want to twine his fingers through its thickness and draw her close. It was that damned halter top, hinting at those sumptuous curves underneath, and the glowing skin, taunting him as the light danced off it. It was the cute, quivery thing her smile did when he teased her about the nickname Mr. Stout had given her. All of this compounded to drive him to his stupid, immature behavior at the pond.

When she surfaced like some Naiad—water dripping from her hair, lashes damp, face bright with the initial thrill of her actions—he froze. Her eyes were wide and even more intense in the moonlight, her breathing still uncontrolled after the excitement and exertion of a nocturnal plunge. His eyes strayed to her lips, which had been wide in laughter, and then trembled, as if they were momentarily unsure of how to act. He longed to feel their warmth, even as the heat was radiating out from her tiny wrists, caught in his hands. He could feel her heart beating furiously under his fingertips.

And then, just when it seemed they would kiss, Hope pulled back.

When she climbed out on the dock, Chase was too shocked to look away. It was only after she had disappeared that he moved, swimming as fast as he could to catch up with her. He pulled himself out of the water and threw on underwear and shorts. He grabbed his shirt, stepped into sandals, and zipped his shorts on the run, pulling the shirt on before he left the shelter of trees.

He retraced their steps, but saw no sign of Hope. She wasn't in the garage, which was still lighted. He cracked the door to the house open, and only heard the pleasant hum of the adults' voices. She was not there. Slowing down to think, he realized there would have been wet footprints on the concrete had she come that way. He plodded around to the back of the house.

That was when he saw her. Hope was silhouetted in the moonlight where she sat on one of the swings dangling from their old swing set. Hands clasped the chains, but her head was down and she barely moved. Chase approached her with caution, almost afraid she would run again. As he drew near, he was certain Hope could hear him, but she remained still, not even lifting her head. Chase moved slowly around the slide to stand in front of her. He knelt down, placing his hands just below her small ones, still gripping the chains.

"Hope—"

"I'm sorry, Chase. I—"

"*You* have nothing to be sorry for, Hope. I'm the one who should be sorry. I shouldn't—"

"I didn't want you to think I was..." she blurted out. She lifted her head and looked vaguely past his shoulder, seeming to search for the words to make him understand. Now that the moonlight was on her face, he could see she had tears running down her cheeks. "I was"—her voice shook—"like Chip told everybody I was. Ugh! I sound like such an idiot!" She flew out of the swing, nearly knocking Chase over, and turned her back to him.

He thought Hope was going to run off again, but she didn't. She leaned one hand against the deck of the slide, the other hand on a hip, shaking her head in frustration.

"Hope." Chase gently took the distraught girl by the shoulders and turned her. Peering into anxious eyes, he struggled to find the words to say to reassure her. He suddenly understood the difficult position girls were in. If they didn't give in to a boy's demands on a date, they were frigid. If they did, they were easy. It was a no-win situation. Chase wondered if he had made any girl feel as frightened and torn as he could now see Hope was. He reached up and touched her face, brushing a tear away with his thumb.

"I know you are not anything like what Chip has been saying. I know who you are, Hope. It's okay. You don't have to explain anything to me."

"But I shouldn't have—"

"*I* shouldn't have teased you, or made you feel uncomfortable by...jumping in like I did." Suddenly, blinding white light lit the yard. Chase stepped instinctively in front of Hope, hiding her from those in the house. They heard the porch door creak open.

"Chase!" his mom called. "Time to come in."

"Okay, Mom," he called hurriedly. He could see the figure of his mom turn away and hear the door bang shut behind her.

"Oh my gosh! What am I going to do?" Hope said in a panic, her hand reaching up to feel her damp hair. "My mom's going to know I went swimming."

Chase thought quickly. "I'll tell them you weren't feeling well...and I walked you home. You can act like you just hopped out of the shower when she gets there. She won't suspect a thing."

Slowly, Hope's face relaxed into a smile. "That's brilliant."

Happy to see her brighten at last, Chase said proudly, "Yeah, I'm good."

"Only, not so good at table tennis," she teased, seeming to have recovered her former cheer. "Chase." She looked down for a second, then returned her gaze to his. "Thanks. Thanks for everything. You're really a great guy," she added softly.

As he gazed down into her face, he knew he wanted to kiss her. But he knew just as surely the time was not right. Someday though, he promised himself, he would kiss her. He rubbed his hands along the soft skin of her arms. "You're pretty great yourself." He sighed, glancing back at the house. "You'd better go." He squeezed her arms, and then released her.

She nodded and turned toward home. "Good night," she called over her shoulder.

"Good night, Hope," he murmured softly. It was the most provocative night of his life, and he hadn't even kissed her.

That thought kept him up half the night.

AT EIGHT A.M. CHASE again stood transfixed before the windows of his penthouse. Soon, Hope would be knocking on his door. He had never felt this nervous before, not even his first time on stage. *She's just an old flame, is all,* he told himself. *That was all years ago. She dumped me the night of senior prom and went on with her life, just like I did.*

But, despite his best efforts, the words remained hollow. Hope wasn't just an old flame; she was the only one to have ever lit his fire at all. Sure, he had dated many women in the intervening years. Being a rock star had its benefits, after all. But no one had made him feel the way he had felt around Hope Creswell, and he doubted anyone could.

He stopped pacing in front of the windows and picked up his guitar, strumming it fretfully, hoping music would calm him down. And it did, a little. He closed his eyes and softly sang the familiar lyrics, feeling them as he had felt them many years ago when he had written them down on the back of a laundry claim ticket.

You took from me my Hope, leaving me empty and cold,
Now these arms ache, 'cause it's you they want to hold,
The woman I hold thinks I love her, she hasn't a clue
All I can think about when I hold her is you.
Empty and aching you sent me away
And all of these years, they have kept me at bay
And others have come, but there's no one to stay
And at night I keep searching for words I could say
To keep you from turning away
To keep Hope from draining away
To just get me through 'til the day

Agitated, Chase swept a hand angrily across the chords, creating a harsh, jarring noise suited to his temper. He jumped up, throwing his guitar on the couch and taking up pacing again in front of the windows. He sighed and threw his head back, running hands through his long hair, and laughed brokenly.

You're a fool, Chase. You're not the boy you once were. You've grown and changed, and so has she. Hope Creswell was nothing more than a childhood crush. Sure, she hurt you once, but she doesn't have that power anymore. I'll let her have her little interview, and that will be the end of it.

The doorbell rang and he jumped. *So why is it my heart is going a hundred miles an hour?*

He went to answer it.

WHEN CHASE OPENED THE door, Hope was looking down, her thick, black eyelashes contrasting with her fair skin as she examined her shuffling feet, waiting for someone to answer her ring. There was an innocence in her face that was captured in the first millisecond before realizing she was being observed. But hearing the noise of the door opening, she glanced up quickly. Their eyes locked, and they both froze for several seconds, unable to speak.

Although he had seen her brilliant eyes a hundred times in his dreams over the past eight years, seeing them here, now, even though he had mentally prepared himself for her visit, took his breath away. His heart, which had been beating wildly in anticipation of her visit, now seemed to stop, and then a second later, charge ahead, as if trying to beat its way out of his chest. His palms on the doorframe became sweaty, and he tried to gather his wits so as not to appear like the lovesick whelp he now felt himself to be.

Hope looked very much the same as she had eight years prior. She wore her long, golden-brown, straight hair in two braids dangling past her shoulders. He was barely able to suppress a desire to touch the feathery tips below the rubber bands holding them together. Her hands were stuck deep into the pockets of the slouchy tweed coat she wore over a tight-fitting, baby-blue, v-neck t-shirt, which fit snugly over her hips and dark blue jeans, hanging slightly lower than the bottom of her jacket. As in high school, she had a camera slung carelessly around her neck, like an Olympian's gold medal, and nearly as valuable to her.

Slowly, a smile spread across his face, and he forced himself to exhale, saying, "So, it *is* you."

She smiled in return, a little shyly, he thought, responding, "Hello, Chase."

She held out her hand and he was taken aback, the gesture seeming too stiff and formal considering their intimate past, but after a second, he took it and shook it warmly, covering it with his other hand as well. His touch and smile seemed to relax her a little. Maybe this wouldn't be so difficult after all. They both were adults now; they should be able to act maturely.

"Come in," he invited, standing aside to allow her to pass. He never took his eyes off her as she entered, soaking in the details they offered. Her short jacket, coming just to her waist, permitted him a clear view of her tight tush and shapely hips. She had filled out some since her tree-climbing days when they had first met. She still had the muscles of an athlete, and the tomboy she once was, but now, time had added the soft, tempting curves of womanhood. Though her t-shirt hugged her hips temptingly and covered the tops of her jeans' pockets, he still fantasized about sticking his hands in those pockets and feeling her warmth.

He watched her face as she gazed about, seeing the glow of excitement that was sweetly familiar to him. He had almost forgotten just how lovely her face was. She had a clear complexion, delicate features, and big, expressive eyes. Whatever she felt could be seen on her face; she had no gift for pretense. Her eyes were unique, a pale blue with thin rays of yellows and browns radiating out from the center, like a starburst, the outside of the iris a thin circle of black. The mix of colors was not a distracting feature. In fact, it was something that wouldn't be noticed at a distance, but up close, they were mesmerizing.

Hope had expected someone else to open the door—a manager, a groupie, a chauffeur, anyone—but not him. She had been in the initial phases of bracing herself for seeing him again, when suddenly he was there in front of her. She was unprepared.

She eyed him. He hadn't changed much, except for his hair. When they were younger, it had been about the same shade of brown hers was. Now, someone, a manager or promoter, perhaps, had convinced him to dye his hair blond, and he wore it longer than he had in high school, just to his collar, and long on top. The clothes he wore now were different, too. He seemed to have traded in his t-shirts and shorts for black jeans and an expensive-looking, scarlet-colored, button-down shirt. But when Hope peered into his eyes, she was flooded with memories of past times, and a warm feeling spread over her, both welcome and uncomfortable at the same time.

She took in her surroundings, resisting the urge to run across the wide, circular room and peer out the windows covering the far wall where the light streamed in across the lush carpeting. Directly in front of them was a sunk-in area with two large, semicircular couches with an ornate, round table between them. To the left was a wet bar with funky v-shaped stools, which looked somehow top-heavy, as if they would tip over at any moment. To the right was a big screen, plasma TV surrounded by comfortable seats, which had attached cup holders like in a movie theater.

"Wow, Chase! This is great!" She turned back to him. "You really have made something of yourself, haven't you?"

He grinned. "I've done all right, I guess."

"Done all right?" she exclaimed in surprise. "You've had six songs in the top ten in the past two years, and your first album went platinum in less than three months. I'd say you've done pretty damn good!" She laughed.

The sound of her voice was intoxicating, like a heady perfume, and he recalled now how she would occasionally insert a curse word into her speech just to catch him off guard and make him laugh.

"You haven't changed a bit."

"Oh yes, I have," she said quickly, unable to keep the edge out of her voice. Hope looked down, moving her foot back and forth across the carpeting, watching as the color of the nap changed with each sweep, her hands clasped behind her back. *I'm here for a story, that's it,* she reminded herself. She moved over to the window and gazed out over Chicago. Suddenly, she swayed forward and placed her hand on the glass to steady herself.

"Still afraid of heights, huh?"

Hope hadn't realized he had followed her. She nodded mutely, surprised he had remembered something about her she had forgotten herself. Unable to resist the temptation, she turned to gaze at him, the pain engulfing her with a suddenness that was frightening. She didn't want to remember or be reminded that he knew these things about her.

Chase stood beside her silently. When she had been looking out over the city, he had been peering at her, trying to read her. Now, as she turned toward him, he caught a glimpse of anguish in her eyes, but like a wave washing over the beach, she put her guard back up, something she must have learned how to do since he had known her last.

Thinking reaching for something concrete would help to stabilize her, she pulled a notebook out of an inner pocket of her jacket. The ordinariness of the gesture gave her a comfort she could hold on to. "Well," she said, in as businesslike a tone as she could muster, her voice starting out small but gaining strength, "should we get started?"

He continued to study her for a minute in a way that was unnerving, but then he stood back, waving an arm and dipping his head slightly so she could pass to the sofa. He removed his guitar, balancing it so it leaned against the arm of the couch. They sat down opposite each other, the table a solid, reassuring barrier between them. He leaned back, stretching his arms over the back of the couch in what appeared to be a rather relaxed, almost smug, position. Hope tapped her pen on the top of her notebook.

"Okay, I read your bio this morning. Please correct me if I have any of this information wrong." She opened her spiral, pretending she had notes written there. "You have a home in L.A., but you're on the road a lot. You're not married." She glanced up and he nodded impassively. "You...don't have any children," she added, a hint of sharpness seeping in. Again he nodded, and she popped off the couch like a jack-in-the-box and moved to the window.

Chase tried to gauge her strange reaction. What was going on inside that pretty head of hers? There was a time when he knew her every emotion, but ever since prom night, she had become a mystery to him. She stood for a minute—her legs spread apart, her hands crisscrossed behind her back—still holding the spiral and pen, her head bent. He stood and moved to stand next to her. He wanted to be angry with her, but the vulnerability he sensed in Hope made his own pain distant. He still felt the need to protect her from...what? She raised her head to stare out the window, the sunshine forcing her to squint a little, although he knew she was seeing nothing.

She sighed. "I'm sorry, Chase," she said softly. "This is just...strange." She lifted her face to peer into his eyes for a moment.

"I know." He touched her shoulder, and for a fleeting instant, he thought she might just slip into his arms. They stood unmoving for several seconds, like a pair of statues, until a knock at the door shattered the spell.

"That's probably my manager," Chase explained, crossing to open it. Hal bustled in with his briefcase.

"Hope, this is Hal Westbrook."

Hope stepped forward and reached out to shake his hand. "Nice to meet you, Mr. Westbrook, and thank you for allowing me to tag along with Chase."

"Ms. Creswell—"

"Please, call me Hope."

"Nice to meet you, Hope." He sat down on the couch and stretched out to take the same position Chase had taken earlier, with his arms extended along the back of the couch. "So, you two know each other from...?"

Chase and Hope exchanged a look. Chase answered for them both. "We went to school together in Lincoln."

"You did? Well you probably have more of a scoop on Chase than I do." Again the pair looked at each other. Little by little, smiles spread over their faces.

Oh, God, Chase thought, *that incredible, wavering little smile that makes me crazy.*

"So, did you know each other in grade school?"

"We met when we were twelve," Chase answered without hesitation.

Hope nodded, seeming pleased he had remembered.

"And you were together all the way through high school?"

Their smiles slowly faded. "Until Hope moved away." Chase's voice was uncharacteristically icy.

His eyes flew to Hope's face. There was a flash of something in her eyes...hurt? Anger? But just as quickly as it had come, it went away, as if she were closing the safe door on her emotions, spinning the combination to keep them locked up for good. It was apparent to him she was determined to be professional.

"I moved to Chicago with my mom after college."

Chase turned his back on them and strode over to the wet bar. While she was talking, he clinked ice noisily into a glass and filled it with water. He stayed behind the bar, drinking his water and staring at them. "I got a job at *The Chicago Globe News* in the mail room, hoping to eventually become a reporter. I've been reporting now for about three years."

"I see," Hal responded, nodding at the camera around her neck. "And you take your own photos?"

"Oh," she said, touching her camera, "yes, I do. It's like a second passion. Of course, I will get your approval, and Chase's, before I print any photos."

Hal nodded. "Well," he said, staring at Chase and rising from the couch, "are you ready to go down to the studio, Chase?" Hope stood as well.

Chase nodded, setting his glass down on the counter roughly. "I'll get my guitar case."

CHAPTER SEVEN

The trio left from the hotel in a limousine, Hope facing the back, both men sitting opposite her. Chase stared out the window, his arms crossed in front of him, not saying a word.

For her part, Hope seemed extremely pleasant, if maybe a little forced. Hal talked to her as she took notes. "Today we're going to shoot some video of Chase dancing with a young lady named Jennifer Bogar, a model. The video is for a song called, 'In Your Eyes.' Have you heard it?"

Hope nodded. She thought it was one of the most beautiful rock ballads she had ever heard, and wondered who Chase had written it for.

"We usually take a whole lot of video, then come back to the studio and piece it together with the music." Hal went into great detail, explaining the process to Hope, who listened attentively, jotting down notes from time to time and asking an occasional question. As buildings flew by outside his window, Chase tuned out their voices, recalling some voices from the past.

It was their first date. Hope was laughing. "Okay, how do I do this?"

"I still can't believe you've never played miniature golf before," he said, feigning exasperation. He came around behind her to demonstrate. "You grip the club like this. Good." Her hair smelled sexy. They both knew he didn't need to get this close, but it was all part of the dance. "Use that notch on the club's head to line up your shot, and hit it gently." Chase spoke into Hope's ear, his lips inches away, longing to kiss her there. "Now you try," he murmured, releasing her arms.

Chase stood off to the side as she practiced the way he had shown her, concentrating with great effort. Hope pulled the club back and brought it swiftly down, rocketing the ball into the side boards with a bang. It ricocheted wildly off the course.

"Holy shit!" Chase hot-stepped out of the way. "You could have killed me!"

She laughed, becoming nearly hysterical. "I'm s-sorry, Chase." She put a hand to her mouth to suppress giggles.

As Chase passed her, he muttered loud enough to hear, "Maybe you should just stick to table tennis." She raised the club to threaten him with it, but Chase grabbed it out of her hands. "Ah-ah-ah, it says right there on the rule board"—he gestured with the stolen club—"'no striking other players with your club.'"

"It does not," Hope said, reading it despite herself.

He chuckled, eyeing the angle of his lie. "You're so gullible." He handed back her club and lined up his putter. Just as he began to move his hands forward, Hope elbowed him, sending his shot off target. "Hey, you!" he shouted as she took off running. He chased Hope, catching up and grabbing her around the waist, both of them laughing.

Hope improved with each shot, and by the time they got to the eighth hole, she was giving him a run for his money. On a difficult seventeenth hole, Hope made a hole in one. She jumped up and down with glee.

Chase dropped his putter on the ground, grabbing her. "You did it! You did it!" He kissed her cheek happily, proud of his little protégé.

They ate pizza in the clubhouse, reenacting the miraculous hole-in-one. When they were finished, Chase asked her, "Why don't we go back to my house? We can walk down to the pond and dip our feet in the water."

"No swimming?" she asked tentatively.

"No swimming," he promised, crossing his heart.

"Sounds good."

The night had fallen by the time they got to the dock. They slipped shoes off and sat down on the edge, swirling their feet in little circles as they talked about every subject under the sun. During a pause, Chase said, "Hope, I had a lot of fun tonight."

She beamed. "So did I."

Their feet stilled in the water. "I've been wanting...to kiss you all night," he whispered, staring unflinchingly into her eyes. He leaned closer, bringing his lips slowly to hers. As he kissed her, something sweetly stirred within him, a tingling need for more of her. They parted unhurriedly, and she smiled at him. Hope reached up, placing her hand behind his neck. Her full lips searched for his this time with growing desire. She pulled her feet out of the water and swung her legs up over his lap, dripping water on him, speckling his shorts with dark spots, but he was oblivious. Every movement she made filled him with wonder. He pulled her closer, his hands skimming over shoulder blades as another wave of passion thrilled him.

Hope explored the muscles of his back, discovering bare skin at the waistline and moving her hands underneath his shirt. Chase sought and touched her soft flesh at last, along her side, feeling the indention of her waist. He continued downward, over her shorts to feel the curve of her hips, finally ending at her smooth legs. He let out a moan. "Hope," he said between kisses, "we need to stop."

She groaned her displeasure, but pulled away, laying her head on his chest, their heartbeats slowly returning to near-normal. They sat for several minutes without saying a word, until Chase checked his watch. "I should walk you home." She slid her feet around, and they put their shoes back on silently and stood up. He reached for her hands, and they stood in the moonlight at the end of the dock, wishing for time to stand still.

Chase had plenty of attractive girls crank up his temperature, but with Hope he felt like he was always on the edge of losing control all together, and it wasn't entirely out of lust. Something inside told him this was so much more than that. Yes, the body responded, but so did the heart. He desired Hope because of her open nature; she reminded him of a flower unfurling its beautiful and delicate petals. She could playfully meet him head on, but at the same time there was a vulnerability about her. It made him want to scoop her up and ride off to some castle where he could simply love her for the rest of his life. He knew the honesty and candidness he adored made her easy prey for those less scrupulous than he, and Chase wanted to protect that, to keep it pure before the world destroyed it.

Chase bent down again to kiss her, and eventually they turned to stroll hand in hand through the woods.

When they got to the edge of the tree line, Chase stopped abruptly and turned to Hope. She slid her hands around his waist, seeming perfectly at ease, stepping close enough for him to feel their bodies pressed together. He brought a hand up and smoothed the hair away from Hope's face, kissing her again, unable to get his fill of tasting her. A burning heat surged inside Chase and he spun Hope around, backing her up against a tree, his hands moving over neck and shoulders where her sleeveless blouse allowed him to again touch skin. He brought his mouth to her neck.

Hope clutched at his arms, a sigh escaping from her. "Oh, Chase...." He moved his head to gaze at her. Hope slowly opened her eyes. They burned like the sparks drifting lazily up from a fire, filling him with the same kind of light and warmth. Chase knew then he had touched a sacred part of her, the part that needed him to make her happy.

He laughed in his throat. "You are *amazing*!" He squeezed her tightly to himself, whispering in her ear, "I know it's foolish to say this right now, but...I love you. I really do. I think I always have."

She tightened her hands around his neck and they stood there, just holding each other for a minute. Then, Hope leaned back, taking his face in her hands so she could look deep into his eyes. "I love you, too, Chase Hatton."

Even all these years later, Chase could remember exactly how those words had sounded, how each syllable was pronounced. His eyes shifted from the window to consider her. She was right here with him, after so much time, their knees practically touching, yet a world separated them. She glanced at him, making eye contact and not looking away. *Why, Hope? Why did you leave me?* he shouted in his head. Her eyes mirrored his own, appearing for an instant empty and lost, trying to express something to him, but what, he could not fathom. Seemingly unable to bear it any longer, she dropped her eyes, staring at the toes of her shoes. Swallowing his heartache, he turned to peer moodily out the window again.

CHAPTER EIGHT

Hope tried to pay attention to what Hal Westbrook was saying while at the same time sneaking peeks at Chase in the back of the limo. Chase was leaning back, his elbow resting on the window ledge, hand curled into a fist, which rested against his lips. She wondered what he was thinking about. Various emotions seemed to swirl through his eyes, and then, without warning, he turned and looked directly at her. Hope's heart caught in her throat. *My God! How is it he can still move me so*? She found it hard to breathe and had to examine her feet to steady herself.

Hope knew it wasn't just Chase's good looks that had her heart aflutter. Somehow, even after what he had done, she couldn't shake the original image she had of him. It was like when you learn someone's name wrong. When you find out later it's not their name, your tongue still goes to the first name, no matter how many times you try to relearn it. She thought she knew Chase, but she had been mistaken. Yet, here she was, still unable to rid herself of the feeling she got whenever they were together.

When they had first started dating, Chase had been the one boy she had felt at ease with. He didn't pressure her to be anyone she wasn't; he simply appreciated her for who she was. She felt safe with him, protected, cared for...until prom night, when everything she knew about Chase turned out to be false.

She had cried for months afterward, especially when she heard their song, "My Girl" by The Temptations. It had been on the soundtrack of the movie *The Big Chill*, the first movie they had seen together. She had come to loathe the song. After finishing college and moving to Chicago to work for the newspaper, Hope had found herself driving home from work, thinking of picking up the phone to call Chase and tell him about her day. Or, she would get tickled about something and think, *Chase would think this is hysterical,* and not be able to think of anybody else who would understand the humor in it. There were times, too, she would simply feel sad about something, and be in need of the warm feeling he always provided just by walking into the room. And then there were the times when Hope wondered how she was ever going to make it through another day without him.

She had promised herself not to ever let anyone have that power over her again; yet, here she was, letting those same feelings resurface.

I can't believe I'm letting my emotions run away with me like this. It's like I'm eighteen all over again. Haven't I learned anything?

To her relief, the limo pulled up to a big building and came to a stop. Chase got out and held the door for her, but remained distant. *Which is fine with me,* she told herself.

When they got inside the atrium of the Zulu Records building, several men approached their party, greeting them warmly. Hope faded into the background while they conducted their initial business. She wandered off and started shooting pictures of the impressive interior of the building. It was all light and glass and brass, the lobby open up to the top of the building.

Chase watched her as she ambled around, snapping shots. She may as well have still been taking pictures for the Lincoln High School *Lincs News.* He could see her focusing on architectural details, like a bee hovering over a flower. He knew most of these pictures were for her personal collection, the newspaper wouldn't be interested in these more artsy photos she was taking. But he also knew she just had to capture the things she saw that pleased her, gold filigree around the elevator, an antique mail chute, which was for display only, a shadow on the atrium floor.

Hal and the producer started down a hallway, and Chase followed, keeping half an eye on Hope. Hope noticed their movement out of the corner of an eye, and left her study of a unique light fixture to trot after them. When they entered the large set that had been put together for the shoot, her spellbinding eyes lit up like a child's. Chase had gotten used to the glamour and glitz, having done five videos before this one, but now he enjoyed seeing it all anew through her eyes.

The room within the room, which all the big lights and cameras were focused on, was set up as a ballroom. Lush red carpeting with gold vines forming a diamond pattern outlined the room. Tables were draped with starched tablecloths, and behind these lay a polished wood dance floor. A few men in white tuxedoes with black ties were already tuning up instruments on the stage at the far side of the room. Actors and actresses milled about dressed in ballroom gowns and tuxes, killing time before the shoot.

Chase could tell Hope had forgotten all about anything else. She roamed around, snapping pictures of ladies in black dresses, and men in animated discussions, standing with their feet up on chairs as they leaned in to make a point. She had a gift for these types of candid shots, shots which captured the mood of a subject without them even knowing they had been photographed.

Hope snapped a shot of a woman wearing a long, sapphire dress. The gown pooled around the slender woman's feet as she stood pulling back the heavy, velvet drapes from a window. She had dark hair, pulled up and plaited elaborately on top of her head. Light streamed in the window, making her glow. With bright red lipstick on, the woman stood, her large, dark eyes searching pensively out the window for what Hope imagined to be her lover, arriving late for the party.

Swinging her camera around, Hope refocused it on the next image, only to find the lens had captured Chase. He had changed into a black tuxedo with a white shirt and a short tab collar over a wide silver tie. She pulled her eye away from the viewfinder as if it had burned her, and then lowered her camera to gawk at him for a minute. Chase was unaware she was observing him. He spoke to a man in blue jeans and a blue jean shirt. Probably the producer, Hope guessed. Slowly, she brought the camera back up to her eye. She began to take picture after picture of Chase, pictures of him laughing, pictures of him wearing a serious expression. She was so caught up in this, she almost missed the girl who came barreling in from out of nowhere.

The woman threw her arms around what looked like a surprised Chase and planted a passionate kiss on him. Hope's camera came down, along with her jaw, as she stared at this newcomer. She was tall, almost as tall as Chase, with a striking jade-colored satin dress on. Before Chase even had time to react to her exuberant greeting, Hal rushed over.

"Jennifer. How are you?"

"Great, Hal. How the hell are you?" The woman spoke in an overly loud voice and seemed to sway a little on her feet. Chase put a hand on the small of her back to steady her, where the crisscross lattice work of the top part of the dress ended and a deep oval cutout left skin bare.

"Jen—" Chase began, but she grabbed his face.

"You are just as hot as ever." She locked her lips over his again.

Chase stepped back, taking her hands gently from the sides of his face and holding them. His cheeks turned red, and he glanced around the room nervously, catching Hope's eyes for a second.

Hope felt cold, her stomach sinking as if she had swallowed a boulder whole. She took a few unsteady steps backward, and then turned away, marching across the room. She stopped suddenly, unsure of where she was even going. Hope heard Chase's calm voice speaking quietly, "Jen, what's wrong? You seem upset?"

Hearing the sound of weeping, Hope turned to see Chase's arms folded protectively around the young woman, whose shoulders were shaking. "I'm sorry, Chase."

Chase glanced at the producer. "Is there someplace private we could go to talk?"

"Sure." The man started to lead them off. Chase glanced in Hope's direction, but she could not read his expression.

Hal was visibly upset. Hope could hear bits and pieces of his conversation with another man who appeared to be on the crew. "She's obviously drunk. What are we going to do? We have twenty people here, plus the crew. How are we going to find somebody at this late date?" After a minute, he stormed off in the direction Chase had taken.

Hope sat down on the edge of the stage, feeling tired. She fiddled with her camera, trying not to dwell on the image she'd just seen and on the fact that it mirrored her prom night, but she couldn't help herself.

It was prom night. She and Chase had been dating for several months and had become pretty much inseparable. They studied together, went to games together, sometimes just sat and watched TV together. Tonight would be bittersweet as, at the end of the summer, Hope would be going to journalism school at the University of Missouri, and Chase would be staying home to develop his music career. They planned to visit each other frequently, but the kind of daily togetherness they had been enjoying would be coming to an end.

Chase came to pick her up in his yellow Camaro, which he had paid for with money from several gigs his band had played. They had been playing everybody else's proms, but when asked to play for their own high school, Chase had opted out, wanting to spend the entire evening of their last dance with Hope. But that wasn't how things were to work out.

When he came in the door of her house to pick her up, Hope was just coming down the stairs. Her hair was swept up, with a rhinestone headband running through it. Her dress was made of a crinkly material with a bright purple, orange, and pink floral pattern. A twisted scarf made out of the same material traversed the front, high above her waist, and tied in the back, leaving long tails swishing elegantly behind her. Hope was fidgeting with the wrist corsage Chase had brought over earlier in the day as she descended. Hearing her mom's voice, she lifted her head.

Chase stood just inside the doorway wearing a white suit with an orange shirt that matched her dress, open at the collar. When he caught her movement on the stairs and looked up at her, a huge grin slowly spread over his face. Slipping past her mom, he met Hope at the bottom of the stairs, taking both of her hands in his and kissing her on the cheek. "You look *fantastic*!" he whispered. She dropped her eyes, a little embarrassed, but she could feel a familiar warmth spread through her, a warmth only he could give her.

The magical beginning of the evening continued at the school, where they danced and laughed with friends most of the night. At one point, though, Chase came back to their table with a couple of sodas looking troubled.

"Hope, I just ran into Susie and she was very upset about something. I'm sorry to have to ask this, but would you mind if I went and talked to her for a few minutes?"

"No, no. Of course not." Hope shooed him away. "Just let me know if there is anything I can do to help, okay?"

"I may take you up on that, if it's some kind of 'girl thing.'" He smiled, kissing her on top of the head before leaving. After taking a couple of steps, he turned around. "Don't go dancin' with some other guy now."

"Not even if it's my brother?" she teased.

"You don't have a brother," he growled, suppressing a grin. "Am I gonna have to stay here?"

"No. Go. I'll be good. I promise."

He came back and kissed her one last time, and then disappeared into the crowd. And that was the last happy memory she had of Chase Hatton.

After about twenty minutes, Hope decided to go see if Chase needed any help. Leaving the gym behind, she was about to cross the hall and go into the cafeteria when she found Chip Carter blocking the door.

"Hope, you don't want to go in there."

"Why?" she said suspiciously, still angry at Chip for spreading rumors about her the year before.

"'Cause, Hope, I never wanted to tell you this...but..."

"Chip." She sighed. "If you have something to say, just spit it out."

"Okay," he said, sounding a little angry now. "Chase has been cheating on you."

Hope's mouth dropped open in shock.

"I probably should have told you, but Chase and I used to be friends, and he made me promise. Chase drops you off at your house after a date, and then goes to pick up Susie McNamara, 'cause, as we all know, Susie, well, puts out. I'm sorry, Hope, but you just weren't giving him what he needed, and Susie was more than willing to step up and take care of Chase's needs—"

"You liar!" Hope spat, trying to push past him.

"Wait, Hope. There's more." Chip put his hands on her shoulders. "Chase's foolin' around has finally caught up with him. Susie has a bun in the oven and that's why she's so upset. They're having a baby." Hope stood there with tears in her eyes, trying to figure out why Chip would say something so cruel. "You don't believe me, do you? Well, just see for yourself."

Chip pushed the door open a crack, and Hope shifted so she could see into the room. Chase and Susie were sitting together at a table, Chase's arm around her, Susie's head on his shoulder. "I'm sorry, Chase," Susie was saying.

"Don't be silly, Susie. Hope will understand. You and the baby come first right now. I'll help you through this."

"Chase, you've always been so good to me." She lifted her head, and kissed him tenderly on the lips. Hope pulled her head back, feeling sick. She took off running, unseeing, down the hall, accidentally heading in the opposite direction of the parking lot.

Now, seeing Chase being kissed in the studio today by someone in a formal gown was just more than she could take. Job or no job, there was only so much she could put up with. She headed down a hallway in search of Hal Westbrook.

She found Hal and the producer outside a door talking with Chase.

"She's been trying to get pregnant and found out today the in vitro didn't work. So, since she hasn't been able to drink while she was trying, she...had a few."

"A few bottles, maybe!" Hal fumed. "I'm sorry, Chase. I really am. But that doesn't change the fact that we have the studio rented out for the day, and a slew of people here are expecting to be paid for a day's work."

"Can't the agency just send someone else over?"

"Yeah, I guess. But we're losing valuable time."

Taking in their grim faces, Hope found herself feeling sorry for Chase. Obviously, this wasn't his fault. This time, anyway. As she approached the group, she heard herself say, "Is there anything I can do to help?"

Hal peered at her and then at Chase. He smiled.

As if reading his mind, Chase started protesting, "Hal—"

A young woman poked her head out of the door. "She's asking for you, Mr. Hatton."

"Thanks," Chase responded with a sigh, following her back through the door and insisting, "Please just call me Chase." He turned back to Hal. "*Not* a good idea!" He gave him a warning look before the door closed behind him.

Hal hesitated only a beat.

"Hope, I know this is totally not in your job description, but..." He raised his eyebrows at the producer.

"Yes! Yes! She would be perfect!"

Hope glanced from one to the other. "Perfect for what?"

The next thing she knew, Hope was standing in front of a full-length mirror, her hair done up, wearing the green gown. The dress was a little tight, as Hope was curvier than Jennifer, and far too long, but the producer promised to keep all of the shots above her pinned hemline. She was hustled into the ballroom by a hairdresser, a make-up artist, and a clothes designer, all reassuring her that she was, indeed, "fabulous."

On the set, Chase sat alone, looking thoughtful and drumming on the table, his feet propped up on a chair. When he saw her enter, his fingers became motionless on the linen tablecloth. Slowly, he swung his feet down and stood up, his face unreadable. She crossed to him nervously.

When he saw her, Chase felt as if the wind had been knocked out of him briefly. *That dress.* It seemed to stretch down a mile before it slid tantalizingly over the curve of her hips. For a second all he could think about was grabbing those hips and pressing his body to hers, hip bone to hip bone.

Chase cleared his head and then cleared his throat. "I'm sorry, Hope. I know you didn't sign up for this—"

"No, it's okay. I wanted to help."

"Thanks," he said sincerely.

"Places, everyone!" someone yelled. While Hope's little entourage had been working to doll her up, everyone else had been practicing, and they quickly scurried to their assigned places. Hope glanced around, unnerved by the commotion. The band started up, and Hope's attention was diverted to the stage.

Chase cleared his throat again uneasily. "We're...supposed to dance." He held his hand out to her.

"Chase," she whispered, peeking at the others who had already begun to dance, "I haven't danced since..." Her heart beat rapidly. "Since..."

"Hope," Chase said calmly. "It will be all right. Just follow me."

Slowly, she placed her hand in his outstretched one. Chase pulled her to him, placing a firm hand on the small of her back, where the fabric dipped away, just where her body began to curve outward. He led her to the dance floor, and they began to sway to the music. After a few steps, Chase accidentally stepped on her gown, which nearly toppled them as they fought to keep from crashing to the floor. He grabbed at Hope clumsily, and she began to laugh. "Good Lord, Chase! We're going to make one hell of a video." He laughed, too. Their nerves fed their laughter until they were both nearly hysterical. He pulled her close and kissed her lightly on the cheek, and they both seemed to relax a little.

"Just keep going," the director called out, "we can edit that out if we need to."

As they began their dance again, the mood became more serious. Chase's hand was on Hope's bare skin, where, had they been alone, he could have easily swept it to other areas of her body. That thought was driving her wild. *Hope Alexis Creswell, get a grip!* her brain screamed. Despite this, she dared to peek up at his face. He appeared impassive, yet she could not turn away. The strong cheekbones, the arch of his eyebrows, all so tantalizingly familiar...she had not forgotten him. She could never forget the way it felt to be in his arms. Even now—although she knew in her mind they were in a room full of strangers, paid to dance this strange dance with them, and although she knew she was only with him for the sake of a music video—he had the power to move her just by his proximity and touch.

Chase felt her eyes on him, and while he tried to resist their pull, his eyes were drawn to Hope's face nonetheless. She looked stunning. The color of the dress set off her eyes all the more, and the way her light, chestnut-brown hair was pulled up accentuated high cheekbones, perfectly arched brows, and the elegant sweep of her neck. The vision was quite a contrast from the braid-wearing girl who had graced his doorstep just that morning, but both were equally fetching in their own way. Her lips were parted slightly, and she seemed to be concentrating, perhaps on the dancing. He longed to kiss her, or at least to touch her full, moist lips with his finger, and he had to shake his head slightly to banish the idea from mind.

When he gazed at her, Hope became lightheaded. She concentrated on breathing. *In, out. That's a girl, Hope.* She twirled around the dance floor, melting into him to synchronize their movements. She felt like a figure inside a jewelry box, flowing with Chase as if she had been doing it all her life. The sound of the violins pulled on her heart, the music so exquisite it seemed as if it were coming from inside them. As the music slowed, so did her partner's movements.

Chase was gazing at her with an absolutely riveting intensity and before he even made a move, she anticipated the deep dip he would give her as the last note hung in the air. They stood frozen a minute: he poised, holding her in midair; she breathlessly surrendering to him. The dip, she thought fleetingly, was so seductive because it took the vertical dancing one step closer to the horizontal dance. She straightened, breathing hard. Chase's face was inches from hers.

Whether from the switch in blood flow from vertical to horizontal and back again, or the general lack of oxygen to her brain she experienced around Chase, Hope felt a whoosh starting at the base of the skull and washing over it, blurring her vision. She knew there were only seconds before she passed out.

"I have to get air," she managed to say, breaking free from Chase and stumbling off the stage. She made it a few feet farther before having to lean on a camera stand. Hope felt her knees buckle, and it was as if a sheet of water were passing over her eyes before all went blank.

Still stunned, Chase watched as Hope swayed, reaching out to steady herself, and then went down. A cameraman caught her around the waist before she hit the floor. Tipping her limp body backward, he gracefully picked Hope up in his arms. People were screaming and rushing toward them.

The large, African American cameraman, a baseball cap perched on his big head, asked the director nervously, "What should I do with her?"

"I don't know. Take her outside?"

Chase crossed from the stage in two long strides, entering the ring of people surrounding Hope and the cameraman. "Take her into the dressing room. There's a couch there, and we can open the outside door to get her some air." Several people nodded, confirming this was a good game plan and seeming pleased someone had taken charge. "Do you know if there are any doctors close by?"

"The next building is filled with them. I'll get you one," a second cameraman offered.

Chase led the way to the dressing room. He went to open the door at the end of the hall. Leaving the outside door open, he reentered the room, leaving its door open as well to funnel in the fresh air. As he caught sight of Hope lying listlessly on the couch, he immediately flashed back to a similar scene.

It was a couple of months before prom. Chase had just finished baseball practice and was swinging his gear into the car when a man approached him. The man was middle age, with dark brown hair, and he wore jeans and a tan windbreaker.

"Hello there," he called out in a friendly manner. "I was wondering if you could help me, son? I'm looking for Hope Creswell. I think she goes to school here. Do you know her by any chance?"

"Yeah. I know Hope," Chase answered without offering any further information.

"Well, I'm Hope's uncle. I was just passing through town on business, and I thought I'd drop in and visit, but I didn't have my address book with me or anything—"

"Oh, hi! My name's Chase Hatton." He extended his hand. "I'm actually Hope's boyfriend."

"Oh, you are, are you?" The man appeared to be sizing him up. "I guess you can give me directions then, to their place?"

"I'll go ya one better. I was heading there myself, so why don't you just follow me?"

"Sounds great." He smiled, then trekked back to an old blue Ford.

Chase hopped in his Camaro and led the way to Hope's. When they got there, he found the door to the house open to let in the breeze. He stepped through the screen door, calling out, "Hey, Hope! I've got a visitor for you."

Hope came bounding down the stairs swinging around the newell post at the landing, all smiles, framed in the light of the window behind her. "Hey, Chase—" Her voice seemed to catch in her throat, and the blood drained from her face. "D-d-daddy?"

The man stepped in front of him, and Chase caught his expression in profile in a mirror to his left. The man's whole facial structure seemed to have changed. Replacing the open, friendly air it had held earlier, the face now looked hard and cold. "Yeah, Hope. It's Daddy. Bet you've been missing me, huh?" She stared at him, shaking her head a little from side to side as if in disbelief, but not saying a word.

"I see you've filled out," he said suggestively. Hope wrapped her arms around herself, seeming conscious of the tank top she was wearing, though it wasn't revealing in any way. "And I hear you've been messing around with this kid." Hope's father jerked a thumb in Chase's direction, his voice almost a growl. He didn't take his steely eyes from Hope. He took a menacing step forward, and then came to his point. "Where's your mom, Hope?"

Hope took a step backward, bumping into the window ledge, still shaking her head mutely. With a startling swiftness, the man lunged forward, pushing the couch out of his way and advancing on Hope. She turned to run up the stairs, but her foot slipped on the third step and she slid, falling to her knees. The man Hope had called Daddy was on her before Chase could get to them. She screamed as he pulled her head back by the hair. "You're gonna tell me where your mom is, Hope."

Chase sprang after the older man but it was hard to maneuver much in the tight confines of the stairwell. As he reached for the man's shoulders to yank him off of Hope, an elbow caught him right in the chin. Stunned, he staggered backward and lost his balance on the stair, falling down a few steps to the landing. He scrambled to get back up only to be met with a mule kick to his midsection. This time he flew against the wall, smacking his head on the window frame, knocking him senseless.

He groaned, moving his head a little. There was a ringing in his ears but he could hear conversation.

"Why did you come back?" Hope's voice was raspy, and she coughed. Chase's right temple throbbed but he forced his eyes open and turned his head a fraction to focus in on the scene before him. Hope was seated on the couch, her dad in front of her, his feet spread wide, hands on hips. How long had he been out?

"Why did I come back? I've been waiting eight years in prison, thinking of the two of you every day, and you're gonna ask me why?"

He kicked a chair over. "Tell me where she is, Hope, or things are gonna get real ugly," he snarled.

Chase raised up on an elbow. His ribs ached as he tried to push himself up. Across the room Hope flew off of the couch, grabbing the poker from the fireplace and holding it in front of her. "You n-need to g-go! Leave us alone!" Her voice pitched, almost as if she were begging. "We're happy here."

"Is that so?" Hope's dad leapt at her and she took a swing. He grabbed the poker in midair and wrenched it from her grasp. "I see your ma ain't taught you any manners."

Still holding the poker in his right hand, he backhanded Hope with his left, sending her flying into a coffee table. Momentum carried her across the table and a lamp toppled as she fell off the other side with a crash. She pulled up with a groan, moving quickly to drag herself away from her attacker. Chase reached for the stairpost to pull himself to his feet.

The big man stepped between the coffee table, which had been knocked askew, and the couch. He held the poker aloft. "I guess if you won't tell me where your mom is, then our conversation is over." So intent was he on his victim, he didn't see Chase as he launched himself from the stairs, taking them both to the floor. Hope shrieked as her father's body initially fell on her, but she scrambled out from under its weight. Chase had never been in a fight in his life but desperation was a good teacher. He rolled with the man until he came out on top, held him down with one hand and punched him with the other with all of his might. He pulled back for another punch but the man became still beneath him.

Where moments before there had been crashing and screaming and splitting of wood, the only sound now was Chase and Hope's labored breathing.

"Oh my God, Chase! You killed him! You killed him and it's all my fault," Hope sobbed hysterically.

He disengaged himself from his foe and scooted over to put a hand on the side of her face, which felt hot and was turning red already from the blow she had received. "It's okay, Hope. It's okay."

"Oh my God! Oh my God!" She reached a trembling hand toward her father's shoulder where he lay on the ground next to her, his nose bleeding.

Chase grabbed her hand before she could touch him. He shifted his weight and gingerly reached over to feel for a pulse. He kept expecting, like in some horror movie, for Hope's dad to reach up and grab his hand, but he remained still. As soon as he touched the man's skin, Chase felt him take a breath.

"He's breathing, Hope. Let's get out of here. We'll go to my house and call an ambulance." He lifted her to her feet and the two of them ran to his house.

As they pounded up the back steps and came rushing into the kitchen, Chase's dad entered through the swinging door to the dining room.

"Chase, what..?" Prepared to scold the pair for coming into the house so recklessly, he shifted gears as Chase immediately crossed to the phone, taking it off the base and punching in 9-1-1.

"Mr. Creswell attacked Hope and I knocked him out," he explained matter-of-factly, though his stomach was in knots.

"You WHAT?" Chase's dad looked from him to Hope and seemed to notice for the first time the swelling along her cheekbone and the stunned look in her eyes. He crossed to her immediately. "Hope, honey, are you okay?" He put his arm around her and she began to sob, burying her head into his chest.

By the time the police arrived at the Creswells' house, Hope's father had come around. After questioning all parties, and finding out Andrew Creswell was actually still on probation, they cuffed him and took him down to the station, first stopping at the hospital to have him checked out. Mrs. Creswell was called and she went down to the station to fill out paperwork, asking if Hope could stay at the Hattons' until she got home.

At 10:30, the phone rang. Chase got up carefully from the couch in the dark living room, shifting Hope's head from his lap to a couch pillow, as she had fallen asleep. His parents had gone up to bed a half hour earlier, so he hurried to answer the phone before it could wake them. It was Mrs. Creswell letting him know it would still be a few hours, the precinct was busy. As he stood in the doorway talking to her on the phone, the light from the kitchen spilled out over Hope as she lie on the couch, breathing rhythmically.

Chase hung up the phone, and watched her sleeping for a minute, glad she had finally calmed down enough to drift off. He let the door close and made his way over to her carefully in the darkness. He bent down to peer into her face where it was lit from the TV screen. He listened to her breathing peacefully, smoothing the hair away from her face, mindful of her bruised cheek. A wave of guilt hit him. *He* had brought the monster to Hope's home. Not for the first time that day, his jaw tightened at the thought of what Andrew Creswell had been about to do to her. How could he call himself a father? Chase knelt down and gently kissed her cheek. He had never felt his love for her more strongly. Then, he switched off the TV and stretched out on the hardwood floor in front of the couch, close enough to touch Hope should he choose to, and after a time, he, too, fell asleep.

Chase's heart was gripped in the same way as he observed her on the couch in the dressing room now. A woman entered the room from the bathroom with a handful of wet paper towels. Hope stirred when she pressed them to her head. Chase allowed a sigh of relief to escape him.

A voice from his elbow announced, "Excuse me, I'm a doctor. Where is the young woman who fainted?"

Chase gestured, letting him pass through the door.

Hope was trying to get up. "Nah-ah-ah, young lady," the doctor instructed. "You just lie down there a minute." He went to work quickly, taking her pulse.

Fifteen minutes later, assured of his patient's recovery, he left, ordering her to lie still for another fifteen minutes and drink a glass of water. Hal walked the man out, leaving Chase and Hope alone.

Hope looked up. "I am so sorry I caused all these problems."

Chase took a few steps forward. "Hope, you could hardly help feeling ill."

"I know, but all those people out there—"

"No need to worry about that," Hal answered as he reentered the room. "We got all we needed today anyway. They're all either gone, or on their way out." He moved in front of Chase. "How are you feeling?"

"Much better." Hope swung her feet off the side of the couch.

"The doctor said—" Both men began.

Hope smiled. "I know, I know. I'm just sitting up. I feel like such an idiot." As she said it, she realized for the first time that someone had partially unzipped her dress and parts of her black lingerie were showing. She snatched at her dress.

Hal didn't seem to notice. "Now there's no need to feel bad about anything. If anyone is to blame, it's me. I normally insist everyone get lots to drink before a production because the lights can really take it out of you." Hope doubted if that were solely the cause in her case. "You were a real pro out there," he added. "We were able to get everything we needed in less than fifteen minutes. That's unheard of."

"So the video's complete?" Hope asked in surprise.

"No." Hal glanced at Chase, but continued hurriedly. "That's what I wanted to ask you about. When you're feeling better," he added for Chase's benefit.

"I'm feeling much better," Hope interjected, looking from him to Chase. "Since I have to sit here anyway, we may as well discuss whatever it is you were going to say."

"Hope, you were fantastic out there. I don't know what it is about the two of you, but the camera loves you. But what we shot today is only a small portion of the video. We have ideas for a scene on the beach and were planning to shoot it back at Chase's place in L.A. I've already talked to your boss, and he said he thought it would be great for the story and that he could spare you for as long as we needed you." She wasn't surprised as she sometimes felt that Jack Delaney wouldn't mind to spare her entirely. "We would pay you, of course."

She considered the proposal. She had been ready to walk out on the story at one point that day; if she were stuck on the West Coast, it would make that a whole lot more difficult. *My gosh! Just being with Chase today made me pass out. I'd be a fool to say yes.* That was why she was so surprised when she did.

CHAPTER NINE

After getting out of the limo, Chase insisted on accompanying Hope up to her apartment. She stood at the door nervously. It would be rude not to ask him in after the effort he made to escort her to the door. She wished he hadn't been so unmoving on the subject of going upstairs with her.

"Would you like to come in for a minute?"

He studied her briefly. "Sure."

When they opened the door, Mr. Mewford came trotting over right away. The cat circled her, including Chase in his loop. She laughed. "This is Mr. Mewford. He's usually not so friendly with complete strangers."

"Hi, Mr. Mewford. Nice to meet you." He squatted and rubbed the cat under his chin.

She threw her jacket over one of the barstools sitting right outside of her kitchen underneath the countertop, which jutted out into her living room. She entered the kitchen. "Can I get you something: water, beer, soda...a glass of wine?" As she asked him, she quickly snatched an empty bottle off the counter and subtly put it into the trash.

"Wine sounds good." He took a seat on the couch, where Mr. Mewford immediately jumped into his lap. "Well, hey there, fella. You sure are friendly."

She entered with a bottle of wine and two glasses. "I'm sorry, Chase. He's usually not—"

"No, it's okay. I like cats. I'd have one if I weren't on the road so much." She handed him the glass of wine. "Thanks. This is a nice place."

"Oh!" she cried excitedly. "Let me show you the best part." She grabbed his hand and led him into the bedroom. Realizing her mistake, she blushed. "It's in the bathroom."

She hurried over to do her best Vanna White imitation in front of the tub, displaying it with a glamorous sweep of her arm.

"Wow! That's nice. I bet you enjoy taking a bath in there. Oh, I get it. That's where they got The Claw-Foot Condos."

"Yeah. Cute gimmick, huh?"

"Yeah."

"Are you hungry? I'm starved. I think I've got some snack mix."

"That sounds good. We didn't take a lunch break, did we? No wonder you were lightheaded. Man, I should have thought to get you something to eat."

"No. I'm a big girl, Chase. If I had wanted something, I would have asked. I don't think it was that, anyway." But she wasn't about to let him in on her emotional trauma. She returned with a bowl of snack mix, catching him holding a picture of Phillip that had been sitting on the end table.

"This your boyfriend?"

"Mm-hmm." She stuffed a pretzel in her mouth uncomfortably. There was a pause.

He returned the photo carefully to the table. "How long have you two been seeing each other?"

She felt her face getting red. "A few years." She was aggravated by the way her stomach was suddenly doing little anxious loops. *What do I have to be embarrassed about?*

"A few years. And I see no ring on your finger, so I take it you're not engaged?"

She stuffed a second pretzel in her mouth, wishing she could steer the conversation in another direction. "No," she said quietly. "We are not engaged."

He shook his head. "What an idiot!" he mumbled. The phone on the end table rang, making them both jump.

"I'll just let it go to the answering machine." Hope took a sip of her wine. "So, tell me about—"

Phillip's voice interrupted, "Oh, man! I missed you! The first chance I get—" She snatched up the phone.

"Phillip, hi."

Chase made a move to get up off the couch. "No, Chase, wait."

"He's at your apartment?" Phillip queried through some static.

"Yes. Chase, what time are you picking me up tomorrow?"

"He's picking you up?" Phillip's voice rose an octave.

Chase cocked his head. "How does nine sound?"

"Perfect. I'll have my bags packed."

"What the hell do you need bags for?" Phillip sounded angry.

"Oh, and Chase." She grabbed his arm as he slipped through the door. "Thanks for everything today." She gave him a smile and a squeeze, and then he was gone.

"Just what does 'everything' entail?" Phillip snapped.

"Oh, Phillip, nothing, nothing."

"It's not nothing when I call at...what time is it there...and Mr. Sexy-Rock-Super-Star is there in your apartment with you."

"It's two o'clock in the afternoon, Phillip, and he just drove me home is all."

"Something wrong with your car?"

"They were concerned about me driving because I got a little lightheaded, but it was no big deal."

"Oh, Hope! Are you okay?"

The concern in his voice made her feel guilty. *I have nothing to be guilty about,* she reassured herself. "Yes. I'm fine. It was really no big deal. Much ado about nothing."

"Are you sure? Have you seen a doctor?"

"Yes. There was one in the next building. Really, Phillip, I'm fine. This phone call is costing you an arm and a leg. Let's talk about something else."

"Well, it's costing Jack Delaney, but I do want to tell you how much I miss you."

"I miss you, too."

"Where are you going that you need bags?"

"Well, it's kind of a long story, but I'm going to L.A. To be in a music video."

"You're what?" He sounded distracted.

"Going to L.A. to be in a music video."

"Oh, geez! Sorry, Liz. Man-n-n! Hope, I just spilled coffee all over our notes. I'll call you back tomorrow. Email me the number when you get there. Shit, that's hot!"

"Okay, babe."

His voice sounded far away. "I love you."

"I love you, too."

"WOW, CHASE. THIS IS fantastic!"

The limo pulled into the driveway of his house in the hills of L.A. While a big house by most people's standards, for a celebrity of his caliber, it was extremely modest, definitely dwarfed by the homes surrounding it. The outside was a neat mixture of stone, glass, and light wood. Decorative beams formed a crisscross archway above the front door, giving it a sort of clean lodgy feel.

They had decided Hope and Hal would be staying in guest rooms as it would be more practical while recording the video.

"Thanks."

"Okay," Hal said, all business. "You have exactly thirty minutes to get settled in and change before the crew gets here. I'll bring you your outfit momentarily."

"Hal doesn't believe in wasting time." Chase added with a lopsided grin.

When they entered the house, she gazed around in admiration. The house was expansive, but not overwhelmingly so. "This is how I would build a house if I had sold...how many records do you have to sell to go platinum?"

"A lot." Hal sighed, immediately ensconcing himself at a glass table with his laptop.

"All work and no play makes Hal a dull boy," Chase whispered in her ear.

"I heard that," Hal said, not looking up from his work.

"And he's got owl ears, too. I'll show you to your room."

She followed him down the hallway, still taking in every detail of the décor. "Do you mind if I take some pictures?"

He grinned at her. "Would it matter to you if I said no?"

"Not really," she returned with a smile.

"Then of course you have my permission."

"Thank you."

He opened a door on the left.

"Ooh!" she squealed, rushing in ahead of him. "Oh, Chase! I'm running out of adjectives."

"Well, that's not good, considering your profession."

The room was decorated with the fresh whites and blues of the sea, and had some sand colors mixed in as well. The white, four-poster bed's headboard and footboard were slatted like shutters, and the matching end tables had bead-board sides and shelves containing white wicker baskets with white and blue striped canvas liners. The comforter was a textured white and the sheets were ocean blue.

Light, knotty floorboards completed the look. The far side of the room was all windows, with French doors in the middle that opened onto a faded gray deck. Chase hefted her suitcase onto a stand by the closet, which featured slatted French doors, similar to the bed's design.

Hope ran to the windows, whose airy white curtains were pulled back, to check out the view. "Wow!" she exclaimed in one long breath. A lengthy, winding staircase led from the back of the house, traversing over rocky terrain, until it reached the pristine beach below.

"Can I get you something to drink? Wine, flavored water, soda..."

"Sure," she responded absentmindedly.

He grinned. "Which one?"

"What? Oh. You choose."

He returned a few minutes later with two glasses of wine. As he entered the open door, he heard a loud squeal of delight.

"You found the tub."

"Chase, this is fabulous! I want to hop in it right now."

The tub, which sat up on a little platform, was huge and had jets situated throughout. The bathroom was quite roomy, half the size of her apartment, Hope guessed. Wainscoting covered the bottom of the walls, up to a thin chair rail. Light shone through a series of skylights overhead, and again, the far wall was made up of windows, so you could gaze out over the ocean while you bathed, if you were so inclined.

"Man! I feel a little foolish now making such a big deal over my little tub. My apartment must have felt like a cage to you."

"No, Hope, not at all. I loved it. And your tub was a thing of beauty. These kinds of monstrosities are a dime a dozen," he said, casually kicking the light-colored woodwork surrounding it. He paused, adding softly, "It's nice having you here."

Her cheeks flushed and she turned to gaze out of the window. After a moment of awkward silence, she commented, "I saw a series of pictures in the other room. Were they taken by a local artist?" She wandered back into the bedroom, taking a drink of her wine and studying the photos again.

"Umm...no. I took them."

Her eyebrows shot up. "You took these?" They were all beach scenes. A sunset, a pair of footprints in the sand at the water's edge where he had captured the bubbles left by the waves, a view from atop the cliff of several brightly colored umbrellas gracing the beach, a sandpiper, his distinctive footprints following behind him in the shiny, smooth, wet sand; all were spectacular. "You're really talented."

Now it was his turn to blush. "That means a lot coming from you. But I just mostly fool around. These were just luck."

"Luck is what photography is all about...when you happen to catch the right light for your subject that, five minutes later, would be gone..." she trailed off, still captivated by the photos.

Chase watched her face as she considered his pictures. It was at times like this she was almost magical. Her ability to completely give herself to the moment was a wonder to him. Her sense of rapture was something he wanted to hold on to, something he wanted to re-create over and over again. Had they missed capturing something special all those years ago? Did they have a chance of grabbing hold of it now? Suddenly, Chase knew he no longer cared about why she had left him. Being with her had made him realize what had happened between them in the past no longer mattered to him. He knew he wanted her back. The question remained, was it too late?

HOPE WAS AMAZED BY the number of people needed just to take shots of the two of them playing on the beach. The makeup artist and hairdresser were there, as well as the producer and several cameramen, and various people whose function she hadn't quite figured out yet. A dressing area had been set up under a tent in the sand, which boasted a table with a mirror. The makeup artist and hair designer fussed over her, finally putting a big white flower in her hair and calling it quits.

She had been relieved when the swimsuit turned out to be more substantial than others she had seen. It was red with white flowers and came with a matching wrap, which she loved. She was glad they told her she could keep her suit and wrap. Chase had on a loose white shirt, which buttoned up the front, and beige trunks that looked more like cargo shorts than a suit.

He stood on a small crest above the waterline, digging with his feet in the sand for the tiny shells that had been abandoned there, his hands stuck in pockets. She joined him, waiting for instructions from those in charge. A single seagull flew past them with a loud screech, drawing their attention seaward. The air smelled salty and fresh, not heavy with the wet fishy smell the ocean sometimes had.

"It's beautiful here," she murmured quietly. "I can see why you chose this spot to live. It's quite a bit different than dirty, old Chicago." The breeze lifted her hair, which today had tumbling curls, as she spoke. It ruffled his shirt, tugging on the fabric playfully as if it wanted to undress him.

"Yeah, but they both have their charms. Chicago has the aquarium, theater, museums..." he trailed off, turning his head to peer at her. "You look beautiful."

"Thank you," she replied softly, wondering why he kept saying things that unnerved her so. She could not return his gaze, but instead stood turning over a shell with her foot to capture its brilliant colors in the sunlight, wishing idly she had brought her camera with her. They became aware the crew had been filming them.

"Go ahead down and frolic in the waves," the producer called out.

They strolled toward the water together, Chase smiling and commenting to no one in particular, "Frolic?"

"I haven't had a good frolic in a long time."

He chuckled. "Me neither."

After a few seconds, she glanced over her shoulder to make sure they were well out of earshot of the producer. "What exactly, do you think, frolicking entails?" She giggled.

Laughing, he responded, "God only knows!"

They entered the water and she scooted a little bit away from him.

"Do you suppose," she began with a grin, "I would be frolicking if I did this?" She kicked water on him, and then stood brazenly laughing. He scowled and she started backing up.

"Hope Creswell, you are...TOAST!" With the last word, he took off after her. She tried to escape, but shorter legs were a handicap in the higher water and he caught her by the waist. She laughed and fought him, but he picked her up. As the tide receded, he swung her in a circle. He set her down but started dragging her deeper into the water.

"Oh no, Chase." She sensed his purpose. "Andre will kill you. He spent fifteen minutes curling my hair."

But heedless of her warnings, he lifted her. "I'll take my chances," he retorted, smiling widely. "I think I can take him."

As he taunted her, she continued to squeal in protest and tried to kick her way free. He pitched her into the heart of a wave. Her ears, so full of his laugher and her shouts seconds before, filled with the peculiar silence of water, which muffled all noise as she sank down. She let the water slow her, then, planted her feet, springing from the ocean like a discharged missile. Bobbing in the water she pushed her wet hair back and laughed. Not to be outdone, he let out a loud cry and dove into a wave, coming out the other side and rising from the depths a few feet away.

"Now, that's some damn good frolicking, by God!" he roared, spurting out salt water like a fountain. He turned and spotted the crew. Shrugging his shoulders with a wide grin he waved. After a moment, a few hands raised and tentatively waved back, as if they were unsure of why they were even doing it.

Hope had turned to watch their response, and he suddenly grabbed her legs, lifting up as if to throw her again. Her hands pushed against his wet shoulders as she struggled to get free. His mood changed. As he gazed up, the sunlight dancing off his wet hair, she was reminded of another night, another body of water, when they had been together, just as they were now, about to kiss. Her hair was dripping onto him and somehow, miraculously, the flower had managed to stay in place. He gradually loosened his grip, but kept her close as she slid down in the circle of his arms.

Hope was mesmerized by the dangerously compelling desire she saw in his eyes. As he slowly lowered her, her laughter became stuck in her throat; her mouth, which had been open wide in a smile, wavered uncertainly. As if beyond her control, her fingers glided along the muscles of his shoulders and chest, her eyes following their journey. Her heart suddenly remembered the way to him and hammered in her chest. She knew now, with conviction, whatever he asked of her she was powerless to deny him, and at that moment, she truly had no wish to deny him anything. Her hands on his shoulders went to the sides of his face. A sweet pain seemed to fill her every pore. She lowered her lips gradually onto his waiting ones. The first kiss was hesitant, the next more sure, and the next simply a yearning for more.

A movement drew their attention. A cameraman had waded into the water and was zooming in on their impassioned moment. Chase released her and she dropped back down into the water, her feet touching the sandy bottom, but he continued to gaze deeply into her eyes, hoping to find something there. But, he saw only fear and confusion.

"That was hot, man!" the cameraman called, blind to the feelings stirred up by the kiss. Hope turned her face to the sea and Chase, realizing that she was embarrassed, played along with the idea it was all for the camera.

"Yeah, how's that for frolicking?"

The cameraman laughed and turned around, not noticing Chase had reached back to gently take her hand as they waded ashore.

"That was fantastic!" the director called excitedly as they came out of the water.

Hope dropped his hand and rubbed her arms, looking uncomfortable.

"Should we do the beach-walking scene next?" the director was asking Hal.

Hal nodded. He was studying him and Hope intently as the producer took over.

"I just want to film you guys strolling along the beach hand in hand. Not as steamy as the last scene."

Hope didn't raise her head, but nodded slightly and the director raced off to holler at someone about a camera angle. They stood for a minute or two in silence, then Chase held his hand out to her. She hesitated, then slipped her hand into his and turned to walk up the beach with him. They padded through the surf, beginning with their hands stretched out, fingers just touching, walking some distance from each other. The crew hung back, using zoom lenses to get the footage they needed, perhaps knowing it was difficult to be intimate with someone when you have a movie camera in your face.

She looked straight ahead, and he could guess she was formulating something to say to him in her head. Unable to wait for her to speak, he broke the silence. "Hope, I'm sorry if I made you feel uncomfortable."

"No!" she almost shouted. "Let's not talk about it."

Why? Because that might make it real? But he closed his mouth out of deference to her feelings, and they continued meandering through the sand without speaking.

"It's only natural to get caught up in the moment," she continued quietly a few minutes later, seeming more in control of her emotions now. "But when this video is over, I'll return to Chicago and write a nice little piece for the Sunday paper, and you'll go on being a rock legend, or whatever. Nothing's changed." She murmured the last even more quietly, almost as if to herself.

He felt as if he'd been shot through the heart. His mind replayed the scene in the waves, the way her face had been full of longing and pain, the way she had responded to his kiss. He knew she cared about him, so why would she deny her feelings? Was it this boyfriend, this Phillip guy? Or was it something else?

The pair alternately looked at their feet, watching the sand ooze through their toes, and then at the sun setting in front of them. From time to time, they glanced furtively at each other, but kept their thoughts to themselves. Eventually, the footprints they left in the sand that had started off far apart, drew closer.

The director called for them to change direction and head back toward Chase's house so he could get a shot of them as the sun poured over their shoulders. The wind picked up, she shivered and he put his arm around her. For a moment she remained stiff, but eventually she leant into him, slipping her hand around his waist. Their faces seemed reflective, serious...but this would make a good contrast with the sillier scene they had filmed earlier the director said, so he was content.

CHAPTER TEN

When they got back to the house, Chase and Hope changed out of their wet clothes. When Chase came out to the living/dining room area, he found Hope across the table from Hal, looking as if they were part of a dueling laptops show. She had pulled on a plain pink t-shirt over a white tank with black and white yoga pants; perched on her head was a black ball cap, which she had somehow stuffed the majority of her hair into. It was about the most understated outfit she could have put on, but he still thought she had somehow managed to make it look sexy. He longed to knock the cap off her head and let all that gorgeous hair free, to touch the delicious curve of her full breasts, which the t-shirt couldn't hide, and to slide his hands up the smooth hips the yoga pants glided over. At the same time, the outfit reminded him of the girl he used to know, the girl he had fallen in love with. In that light, she simply looked adorable.

Lifting her head and catching him observing her, she explained, "I thought I should do a little of what I actually get paid for on a regular basis."

"I suppose I should, too," he responded clumsily. He left but came back in a few minutes with his own laptop and guitar. "This won't bother you, will it?"

"Are you kidding?" She grinned. "Besides, it might be good for the article to actually study the way you create your music." She got up and came over behind him to gaze at his computer screen. "You can actually write music on a computer?"

The sound of her voice so close was exhilarating. He had to re-focus to remember what she had asked him. "Yes, in just a second, the program will open. I've been working on a song called, 'Lost in a Memory.'"

The notes and lyrics splashed onto the screen. "That's cool!"

"Yeah. It is pretty cool. But, every once in a while, I have to get out a pencil and paper. There's something about the smell of eraser that stimulates the creative process. Besides, it's much more satisfy-ing for me to viciously rub out a mistake than simply hit a delete but-ton."

Hal snorted and shook his head, but said nothing. He often stat-ed that he could not function without his laptop and couldn't under-stand Chase's reliance on writing things out by hand.

"Well, I don't want to disturb your creative process by snooping over your shoulder—" he was just about to comment that he didn't mind, when she added, "—and if I don't start showing some sign I'm not just out here lying on the beach, I might just get my walking pa-pers from my boss." She returned to her place, curling her feet under her cross-legged while she worked. "Oh, Chase, would it be okay if I received a phone call on your landline? Most people will call my cell, but, well, Phillip is in Afghanistan, and I don't think there are enough cell towers between here and there. He asked me to email him the number."

He stiffened at the sound of her boyfriend's name. It was one thing to see his face in a picture frame, another thing altogether to have a living, breathing Phillip calling her on his phone. But, before he could say anything, Hal had rattled the number off and she had typed it in and sent it.

For the next half hour, the room was full of the sound of key-strokes and guitar chords, although he and Hope were getting little accomplished. She was staring out the window. He was remembering the feel of her lips on his, the sweet taste of salt and sunshine on her skin, the way his body automatically reacted to hers, bending toward her so they touched at as many points as possible.

Chase, for his part, spent much of the time peeking over at Hope and wondering over the fact that after all these years she sat six feet away from him, staring at her laptop, oblivious to the effect she had on him.

After a while, she seemed so disappointed in the paragraph or two she had written that she slammed her laptop closed. "Do you mind if I check out that bathtub of yours?" She began to smile in anticipation.

He grinned. "Quite frankly, I'm surprised you haven't already." He reached up and closed his computer. "I'm not getting anything done here. How 'bout I start dinner?"

"Sounds fantastic! I'll make it quick then so I can help you."

"No. Take your time. I'm going to take a quick shower, too, before I start."

AS CHASE LET THE HOT water pour over his body, taking with it all the salt and sand that had been deposited on his skin, it dawned on him that just on the other side of the shower wall, Hope was naked. His movements stilled and he stared at the marble as if he could bore a hole through it with his eyes. On a whim, he reached out with both hands and touched the wall, then leaned his forearms against it, letting the water flow over his back. He could just make out her voice over their combined water use, singing. Since she hadn't turned on the jets yet, he was able to make out the melody of "In Your Eyes," the song they were shooting the video for. It hadn't even been picked up yet by many stations, but obviously she had heard it. Had she guessed the lyrics had been written with her in mind?

All I want is to forever be lost in your eyes,

To sing you my love, and to hear your reply.
I strum in the dark, put my heart on the stage,
To the roar of the crowd, but it's your voice I crave.
I pace in the shadows and wait for my cues,
All the while wondering why I must pay these dues...

He pushed his arms back out straight and raised his head to let the water tap dance on his eyelids and flow over his lips and chin. Then, he hung his head between his arms and let it pound into his shoulders, losing himself in the sensations. He reached down and finally turned off the shower, and then stepped through the open marble doorway to grab a towel from the bar.

He rubbed his hair briskly, and then patted the moisture off his body, finally wrapping the towel tightly around his waist. He moved over to the mirror, veiled in steam, placing both hands on the marble counter and leaning, his head down, still hearing the sound of her sweet singing, if only in his head. He grabbed a hand towel out of a basket and rubbed an oval in the steam, peering into his reflection. Why the hell had he ever agreed to let her do this story? Her nearness was like poison running through his bloodstream, burning him from the inside out.

He heard the phone ring in his bedroom. He thought about Hope's email message and rushed to pick it up before the second ring. "Hello?" He noticed the jets turn off in the next room; she must have heard the phone, too.

Over the static, he heard a male voice reply, "Hello? Is Hope Creswell available?"

He hesitated only a second, moving in the direction of the door. "Um...she's in the tub. Just a minute." He hurried into her bedroom and up to the bathroom door. "Hope, you have a phone call."

"Oh, just a minute." She sounded flustered. She opened the door, looking surprised to see him standing there with a towel wrapped around his waist, holding out a receiver. Her eyes grew wide, and she quickly reached up to secure her towel with one hand and grasped the phone with the other. Then she waited, pointedly, until he left.

He knew he shouldn't be listening in on their phone conversation, but he had to get dressed, didn't he?

"Phillip! How are you? Do I have my own room?" Chase smiled. His plan to make Phillip nervous about the accommodations had worked. "Well of course I have my own room. What sort of a brazen hussy do you think I am? Oh! That sort of brazen hussy. Oh my! You have been away too long." She laughed in that low, sultry way that gave him goose bumps. "You're in London? That's fantastic! No kidding? Tomorrow? Sure, let me get a piece of paper to write this down." He heard her rummaging through a few drawers before she, evidently, discovered a pad of paper and something to write with. "Go ahead. The Sunset Astoria Hotel. Isn't that expensive? Well, of course I'm worth it. I never questioned that," she teased. "But can you afford it? What do you mean something special? All right," she said with a sigh. "I guess I'll just have to wait then. I'll see you tomorrow night. You, too. I will. Goodbye."

He listened carefully for any type of reaction to the phone call—an excited squeal, happy humming, Hope throwing the phone against the wall—but he heard...nothing. *So, it sounded like What's-His-Name is on his way back,* he thought, though he knew perfectly well his name was Phillip. *It's not like the two are engaged. And I'll be damned if I let her walk out on my life again. So, I've just got tonight.* He got ready carefully, wanting to look his best.

CHASE KNEW HIS WAY around the kitchen and soon had a linguine with shrimp underway. He knew he could hire a cook, but he liked to keep his life simple. Besides, he found he enjoyed cooking. Hope came into the kitchen wearing a white floral halter top tied behind her neck and tan shorts. He noticed the sun had loaned her skin a soft glow, and that she had twisted and swept her hair up in the back, giving it a carelessly elegant appeal.

"I'm sorry about the whole coming in your room dressed in a towel thing. I just knew you'd want to talk to your boyfriend as soon as possible, and he was calling long distance and all."

Hal made a snorting sound, staring at him with raised eyebrows that said, "Just who are you trying to kid?"

"Well, uh, thanks." She seemed like she wanted to steer clear of the subject. "Can I help with the salad?"

"Sure." He moved to give her room. Over the countertop where he was working was a wide cutout opening between the kitchen and the dining room.

"I'll do you both a favor," Hal called from the dining room, where he was again waist deep in paperwork, "and stay out of the kitchen. I'm a miserable cook." He added the last under his breath.

Chase grinned. "I'll just throw in some French bread. Toss in whatever you want from the fridge or pantry."

Hope combed the state-of-the-art refrigerator and played around with the sliding shelves of the pantry. "Boy, I wish I had these in my apartment. There are probably things in the back of my cabinets that have been there for decades." She returned to her salad bowl, gently ripping apart the lettuce leaves. Hal,concentrated on a document's fine print with the thoroughness of a car-detailer. Chase came over to check her progress and she leaned in conspiratorially. "Does he wear a suit to bed?"

"Only on special occasions," he joked.

"I heard that." Hal sighed, thumbing through a planner now without looking up.

They both chuckled.

"So," he queried, peeking over her shoulder and checking out the assortment of items she had found on the shelves, "what ya got there?" He leaned in, inhaling her fragrance. He couldn't believe the way she still smelled like a pear, freshly picked from the tree.

"Do you mind a raspberry vinaigrette?" she responded tentatively.

"No. That sounds good. Just let me know if you need anything. Wine?" He offered her a glass and she took it, their fingertips brushing for a second. She looked up at him with an indecipherable expression, and then turned back to her work.

When she had finished the salad, she asked if she should set the table, and he directed her to the linen drawers.

Hal had taken his cue and cleared his things off the table, going to his guest room to wash up. Chase reached up and turned on some soft music, his attentive eyes following her as she moved around the table. Unaware of being watched, she swayed to the music as she straightened utensils and refolded napkins. When at last all of the food had been brought in, he held her seat out for her.

Hal cleared his throat. "So, Hope, you said you moved to Chicago with your mother. Is she still living there?"

She swallowed a drink of wine, setting the glass down on the table carefully. "No, actually, she passed away just a few months after we moved there. She had lung cancer. She was a secret smoker, and it caught up with her." Talking about her mother obviously moved her. She took another long drink of her wine.

Chase's face must have registered the shock he felt. He thought if something like that had happened in Hope's life, he would have known about it somehow.

"Oh. I'm so sorry to hear that." He hesitated. "Were you in contact with your dad at the time?"

She chortled derisively. "No. I tried to avoid all *contact* with my dad." She took another drink, draining her glass. "He found *me*, though." She sighed, looking up at Chase meaningfully.

He suddenly wished Hal would become violently ill and have to leave and stay in his room for the rest of the night. He wanted so badly to ask her about it all. He had always imagined her happy somewhere, and to hear she had suffered, without his being there to help, pained him deeply.

"Chase," she stated with forced lightness, "this linguini is absolutely delicious. Where did you learn to cook?"

"My mom taught me, mostly, I guess."

"That's right. I remember what a fabulous cook she was." She smiled, the memory evidently warming her. "I would sometimes sneak over to Chase's house after our supper and eat there, too. My mom was a horrid cook. But she tried. Too hard sometimes." She chuckled. "Remember that time she had you over for dinner?"

Chase laughed. "I've never had Chicken Cacciatore since!"

"Ugh! And I burned that Tater Tot Casserole recipe she had, but then she just made it from memory, and it turned out even *worse*!" They all laughed.

"Listen," Hal said after a while, "you two cooked, so I'll clean up. Why don't you go out on the porch? It's a beautiful evening."

They rose, thanking him, and took his suggestion. Chase held open the door, and they stepped outside into a night that still retained much of the daytime heat, but countered it with a soft breeze. She didn't move to sit, but stood instead, leaning her forearms on the top railing of the deck. She twirled the wine glass in her hand by its stem and stared into its depths. He touched her arm, and she turned to give him a curious look.

"Hope, I'm so sorry about your mom. She was a neat lady. I always liked her."

She nodded silently, again studying her wine glass, then gazing out over the water. He could see the tears collecting in her eyes in the moonlight. "Damn!" she murmured, swiping a tear that had escaped. She turned away from him slightly, struggling with her emotions.

He laid his hands on her shoulders and gently turned her around to face him. "Hope," he said, his voice almost a whisper. She ducked her head, but he cupped her chin in his hand and tenderly lifted it to raise her eyes to his. She was crying noiselessly and she looked so sad and lost, his heart caught in his throat. "Hope, tell me about it."

She nodded, her voice strained. "Okay." She crossed to a wicker settee and sat down, curling her legs to one side, leaning on the arm as he took a seat in a rocker close by. "I think she must have been sick for awhile, but too afraid to do anything about it. By the time I got her to the doctor..."

Her voice faded away. She looked down into her lap and he let her gather her thoughts without interrupting. She sighed. "It was pretty bad at the end. The cancer whittled away at her until she was next to nothing. It took her strength, and finally it took her hope. She couldn't eat because of the mouth sores from her chemo." Her voice caught, but she pressed on. "She used to pray to die." She glanced up. "We ran out of what little savings we had. We lived in this horrible place." She shuddered and stopped talking, lost in thought. "We moved to Chicago so my dad couldn't find us, to sort of melt into the crowd. And it worked, until the night before her funeral."

She played with the hem of her shorts. "I came home after making some final arrangements, and my apartment was dark. I don't know how he got in." She seemed to be getting more emotional. "He blamed me for her dying, said I didn't take good enough care of her." A small sob escaped. "He was *really* angry." She shook just remembering it, but then her face contorted, as if another thought had crept into her mind. "I had always wondered how he, without fail, could find us, but my Uncle Tim, he came to the funeral. When he saw what my dad had done to me, he broke down crying, saying he never thought my mom's stories were true. And if he'd known, he would have never told my father anything. Tim was a cop, so he had access to a lot of information, and my dad always knew just how to wheedle it out of him."

Even though he knew all about her dad's temper, he was shocked. "Your dad, he...hit you?"

"Ohhh yeah. He did a real number on me. I *never* hurt like that." She bit her lip, looking off into the distance, trying to compose herself.

"Hope, I'm sorry. If I could have been there—"

"Yeah," she said with an edge, jumping up. She moved again to the railing, spreading her arms wide and leaning on it. He wondered what he had done to set her off, why she suddenly seemed so distant. She took a deep, shuddering breath, turning at last to face him. "Do you have any more wine?" she said, holding up her glass and beginning to laugh through her tears.

"I think we drank all we have in here, but..." Sensing she needed a break, he added, "I'm building a wine room. Do you want to see it?"

"Yes." She hesitated, laughing at herself. "Do you have a lot of wine in it?"

He chuckled, putting his arm around her as they moved toward the door. "I think I have enough."

CHAPTER ELEVEN

Chase led her away from their bedrooms. A large, open room spread out to their left.

"I'm also redoing my exercise room right now."

"So you do the work yourself?"

"Yeah, the heavy labor stuff anyway. I don't fool around with electricity or plumbing much. It's great for when I'm struggling with a song. Using my body physically seems to loosen up my mental self, too. Maybe the sweat oils the cogs or something. And here..." he said, opening a door just beyond the weight room with a flourish, "is my wine cellar."

She stepped through the doorway and into a large closet. The walls were lined with cubbyholes big enough for a bottle of wine. In the middle of the room was a pair of sawhorses with a board stretched between them, and a saw sat on the wooden floor, which had been covered by a tarp.

"Wow!" she gazed around in awe. "You must have had a lot of problems with your songs."

He laughed. "Well"—he ran his hands over a shelf—"I have been keeping busy." *Maybe I'm taking out my sexual frustrations,* he thought, chagrined.

"I'd say!"

"Oh, and here's the cool part. When the electrician gets this hooked up"—he indicated a keypad by the door—"the door will seal shut and this room will be climate controlled with just a touch of a button." To emphasize his point, he tapped the keypad. There was a sudden hissing noise. "What's that?"

"Uh...I think you just hermetically sealed us in here."

"Oh my gosh! I thought he hadn't hooked it up yet."

"What do you do to get out?"

"Enter a code."

"Okay."

"I don't know the code."

"Okay," she replied slowly.

"Do you think that Hal could hear us from this far away?"

"I don't know if noise will escape very well through a sealed door, but it's worth a try."

They screamed in tandem and Chase tried various combinations on the keypad, but after twenty minutes, he turned away with a laugh. "I guess we'll have to wait until Hal notices we're missing." He walked over to a mini-fridge, which was plugged in, nested in the far corner of the room.

"But what if he doesn't miss us?"

He shrugged. "He'll miss us eventually. And besides, we have this," he commented, pulling a wine bottle out of the fridge.

"Oh, great! So we can get drunk," she said sarcastically. "Chase, what if there is a fire?"

"We pray the seal will keep it out? I don't know, Hope, I guess we're going to just have to sit here and wait."

She sighed resignedly. "So how are we going to get the wine bottle open?"

He smiled and pulled something out of his pocket, which turned out to be a Swiss Army knife complete with corkscrew.

"How very Boy-Scoutish of you."

He retrieved a mostly clean coffee cup from the end of one of the saw horses, cleaned it off with the bottom of his shirt, and poured her some wine. "*You* should be thanking me."

"For sealing me in this room?"

"Well, gosh, when you put it that way..." He stretched his long legs out with his back to the wall, patting the ground beside him.

She smiled. The patented Chase Hatton ease, incredible. She took the cup and he clinked the bottle against it before taking a swig straight from the bottle. She sat down next to him, drinking wine from her coffee cup.

"Chase, you should really be proud of all you've done here," she gestured widely.

"What, this room? It really isn't that hard to—"

"No, no. Your whole life. You saw what you wanted and you worked hard to achieve it." He wondered if that were true. "Not many people can say that."

He peered into her eyes, wanting to tell her she was wrong; the one person he had really wanted in his life had walked out the door when he was eighteen. But he found he had lost his voice. His eyes traveled from her eyes to her lips and back. He set the bottle down on his opposite side purposefully. She remained motionless, engaged by his actions. He reached over and put his hand behind her neck, rubbing his thumb across her cheek gently.

"What about you, Hope? Have you found what you wanted?"

He pulled her in and kissed her, his lips pulling hungrily with each kiss, wanting to bring her closer, wanting to go deeper into her.

At first Hope froze. But then, she didn't know if it was the wine or something else, but she just felt helpless to resist. It felt so good. Her life had been without this sort of passion for so long. Sure, she had Phillip, but he had never had the pull on her Chase did. She kissed him back, releasing her heart a little more with each kiss until she felt like she had given him her all. Her body was molten, hot and liquid, and she imagined him gently pulling on a beautiful golden ribbon running through her core, releasing her with a steady power that flowed from him through her.

He sat on her right, turned toward her with his right knee up. She reached out and touched his leg. "Oh, God, Hope," he moaned. She knew that even if the door had been open, she would still want to be making love to him here, now, in the middle of sawdust on a painter's cloth. His hands ran down her bare arms to her legs and slid underneath the thigh, pulling her closer. His kisses became harder, wilder, more impassioned, crushing her with his need.

Shivers slid through her as his hand moved ever so slowly across her stomach to the bare skin of her upper chest. He took her bottom lip into his teeth and nibbled, forcing a groan from her. His hand slid under the cloth of her halter top, where she was already aroused and cupped her flesh. Changing course, he moved his hand to her back to ease her down to the floor.

Panicked seized her and she pushed against him, struggling to get away. "No! No!" She scrambled to her feet and turned away from him. "I'm sorry," she cried out. "I can't!"

He jumped to his feet behind her, seizing her by the shoulders. "Hope." He spun her around to face him. She tried to back away and tripped over a wrinkle in the tarp. He reached out and quickly snatched her around the waist, saving her from toppling over. "Hope." He searched her eyes. "Don't do this to us again!"

Her hair had come loose when he grabbed her to stop the fall. He took both of his hands and frantically, almost roughly, began brushing it away from her face, as if desperate to get through somehow. "Can't you see I still love you? I've always loved you. Why can't the past just stay in the past?" He kissed her again and she tasted the salt of her tears. "I know you want me."

She shook her head, trying to deny it and pull away, but he grabbed her arms. "I can feel it. But Hope, do you love me? Isn't there any part of you that still loves me?"

The thought rang through her head so loudly she was sure he could hear it. *Of course I love you. That's the problem!*

"Chase, I can't do this again," she sobbed. "I just can't!"

"Why?" He released her arms. "Why?" he said more quietly. There was a loud thump on the door. They both jumped, startled. She instinctively flew back into his arms, their hearts racing.

"Chase? Hope? Are you in there?" Hal's muffled voice came through the door.

Hope began to brush at her face, wiping away any signs of tears. He let her go and took a step toward the door. "Yes," he called out tiredly. "We're in here."

"How do I get this open?"

"There's a code," Chase replied halfheartedly. "Could the man have any worse timing?" he mumbled under his breath.

"Would it be ten numbers? There's a sticky note on the wall out here with some numbers on it."

"Yes, I suppose so."

They heard the beeping of buttons being hit and the hiss of the door releasing. Before Hal could even look up from the keypad, Hope burst out of the room.

"Thanks, Hal," she said, keeping her head down. "I'm going to bed," she called over her shoulder.

He stormed out wordlessly and followed her down the hall. He glanced back to catch Hal staring in the room as if it could give him some clue as to what went on inside it. Then Hal turned and simply followed the pair to bed.

THE NEXT MORNING, CHASE was in a foul mood. He ate his breakfast in silence, staring out at the rain pouring into the ocean, the gray day suiting his frame of mind. Hal sat opposite of him, reading the newspaper.

Hope came in dressed in a black, sleeveless, lightweight sweater with a squared neckline and tan shorts. "Good morning," she said brightly, although her eyes showed she had gotten little sleep. "So, Hal, what's on the agenda today?"

He lowered his paper with a smile. "Well, we *were* going to do some shots of the two of you hiking—" his eyes shifted to the window, "—but the rain has put that out of the question. So instead, I thought we'd head to the studio and get some shots of Chase singing. We'll intersperse them in the video. We'll shoot a few where Chase is actually singing—it gives a more realistic impression—and a few where he is lip-synching as it has to match the actual recording we put out. You're welcome to tag along."

Hope glanced up, perhaps to see if he would form any kind of objection. His lips were set. "Okay, I'd like that."

She continued to make small talk as she ate some yogurt and granola, but after being met with curt answers, or in some cases, no answer at all, she gave up and sat stirring her half-eaten yogurt around. "Umm, I'm going to be spending tonight at a hotel, but you'll be able to reach me and I'll be available to you any time you need me."

Hal peeked over his paper to catch his reaction to the news. He kept his face as rigid as stone. "Okay," Hal answered for him. "That'll work just fine."

"I think I'll just go then and pack. I'll be in my room when you guys are ready to go."

After she walked out, Hal folded his paper in half. "So just how long are you going to make things miserable for her?"

"Stay out of it, Hal!" he growled.

"Damned if I will, Chase!" Hal rose and stood behind his chair, his hands gripping the top rail. "If you have feelings for the girl, Chase, you need to tell her about them."

He glanced up quickly, and then sighed, placing one hand over the bridge of his nose and rubbing his eyes. "I did, Hal. That's the problem." The rain began to beat down harder, thudding loudly on the roof of the deck.

"Chase," he said quietly, "Hope has feelings for you. Yeah, maybe she keeps trying to push them down for some reason, but they're still there. You need to be patient with her." Hal turned and padded softly down the hall, leaving him to stare out at the rain pouring from the gutters and onto the deck.

CHAPTER TWELVE

Hope thought about how excruciating the limo ride to the studio had been. Chase brooded and cursed the electrician who had caused them to be locked in the room together. She fluctuated between distracted and close to tears. And Hal shuffled through papers that didn't need to be shuffled through.

At least when they got to the studio, Chase came out of his stupor a little. Here, he was in his element. By the time he sat down on the stool in front of the mike and donned his headphones, he was even joking around with some of the crew. She breathed a huge sigh of relief, and her smile felt less strained.

But when Chase began singing, the mood changed again. She was totally caught up in the music, hardly daring to breathe; and for his part, Chase had never sung more beautifully or with more emotion. He looked up and caught her eyes in the booth, and it was as if he were pouring his soul out.

All I want is to forever be lost in your eyes,
To sing you my love, and to hear your reply.
I strum in the dark, put my heart on the stage,
To the roar of the crowd, but it's your voice I crave.
I pace in the shadows and wait for my cues,
All the while wondering why I must pay these dues.
Why don't you come back, I would beg you to stay
So I could get lost in your eyes, if only just for the day.
Your eyes once led me down paths of desire
In their reflection I could see my soul on fire

And now your eyes haunt my dreams at night
And I wonder just why we couldn't get it right. So,
I pace in the shadows and wait for my cues,
All the while wondering why I must pay these dues.
Why don't you come back, I would beg you to stay
So I could get lost in your eyes, if only just for the day.

Someone came in from an outside door and the light shifted causing her to see the reflection of her eyes in the glass separating her from Chase. The mirrored version of her eyes widen as a thought rammed into her with the force of a Mack truck. It jarred her so much she staggered backwards, losing the reflection altogether. Chase had always told her how beautiful her eyes were. Now, as he watched her and they again connected through the glass, she knew. Her hand flew behind her as she fought to seek her balance, stumbling backwards a few more steps. She turned and bolt out the door.

HOPE HEARD HAL BURST through the exit door behind her. She stood just a few feet away, her back to him, trying to control her trembling. She brought a hand to her mouth in order to stifle a sob, the other arm wrapping around her waist as she tried to even out her breathing. The sky had cleared and the only sign left of the early morning rain was the humidity in the air and a few dried worms on the concrete.

"Hope," he said tentatively.

"Oh, God, Hal, I'm sorry. I just can't do this anymore. I've tried because I knew he needed me, but this is tearing me up inside. And what's worse, it's tearing him up inside and I *really* can't bear to see that." She started sobbing uncontrollably.

Putting his arms around her, Hal led her over to sit on the curb. She put her head in her hands, trying to calm down. "I'm sorry. I know you don't need this. You're always so professional, I'm sure you must think I'm a complete fool."

"No, Hope. No. I don't think that." He rubbed her back soothingly.

Chase left the studio by another exit and was searching for them in the parking lot. He rounded the corner of the building and saw them at a distance: Hope, sitting on the curb, obviously distraught, and Hal, comforting her.

This is an impossible situation, he thought. *It's killing Hope, and it's not doing wonders for me, either.* He had tossed and turned all night, still feeling his lips on hers, the way she had touched his leg, the warmth of her sun-kissed skin...and knowing she was only a room away didn't help matters much.

He wondered what she must be saying to Hal. The only thing he knew for sure is that he would only make matters worse. He turned around slowly and headed back inside.

Hope had begun to regain some of her equilibrium.

"Hope, I know this is none of my business. But, what's going on with you and Chase?"

She sighed. "It's a long story."

"Well, I've got all day," Hal said kindly.

She squinted at him through her bloodshot and swollen eyes. "Okay. Okay, I'll tell you. I've never told anyone this except my mother. As you probably guessed, Chase and I dated in high school. He was my first, and only, love. Until the day I caught him...cheating on me."

"That just doesn't sound like Chase! I don't believe he could do that to you."

She got choked up again. "I wouldn't have believed it either, but there they were. He had gotten her pregnant and they were discussing it." She sprang up, agitated, pacing back and forth in front of him. "I know this sounds ridiculous. It was eight years ago. And

I had gotten over it, I swear! Well, sort of. I had moved on anyway. But then my boss gave me this assignment, and I really tried to stay professional, I did. But Chase...has this...power...over me. He moves me when I want to stand still. And that song. I just couldn't take it! I'm sorry, Hal, I really am."

"Hope, quit apologizing. I know you are doing the best you can do under the present circumstances." He sat quietly, contemplating the next course of action. "We can just make do with what we've filmed already."

"No, Hal. I don't want you to change anything because of me. I think I'm just tired. I couldn't sleep last night. If I could just go back and sleep for an hour."

"Of course. I'll get Tom to take you back to Chase's. If you're up for it, we'll film tomorrow. But if you're not, it'll be just fine. I'm sure we can make a video out of what we have." He turned to leave, but she reached up and grabbed his hand.

"Thanks, Hal, for listening."

"You got it." He smiled at her, giving her hand a squeeze before heading indoors.

CHASE WRAPPED UP THE studio work as quickly as possible. All the way home he thought about Hope and how he wanted to apologize to her. When they walked into the house, it was stone quiet. He immediately headed toward the bedrooms, but when he got to Hope's, he found the door was open, the bed was made, and all signs of her had vanished as if she had never been there at all; all except for a note propped against the pillows. He plucked it off the bed, and read.

Thanks, Chase (and Hal), for letting me crash here. Your home is beautiful. If you need me, you have my cell.–Hope

He crumpled it in his fist, and threw it across the room.

HOPE LUXURIATED IN a bubble bath in her posh hotel room. She heard a key in the lock outside. *It can't be Phillip, because his plane doesn't get in until...oh my gosh! Is it really that late?*

"Phillip?"

"Hope!" His voice sounded good. He rushed into the room. "Why, you little vixen! Waiting for me in a bubble bath. I'll be right in." He yanked on his tie.

"No, silly! Come here." He came over and knelt on the soapy floor to kiss her. She ruffled his hair, which had gotten a little bleached; she liked it. "You look good."

"Uuum! So do you," he said, swatting at the bubbles that were covering her body. He kissed her again, deep and passionately.

He's a good kisser, she thought matter-of-factly. "Tell me about your trip."

"It was long and boring, and I'm glad I'm back."

"Long? You weren't even gone long enough to get there. What happened?"

Phillip sat crosslegged on the floor, pulling his tie and shoe off as he spoke. "We got as far as London and they closed off entry to the country, so we came back."

"Why to L.A.?"

"Because we're covering the People's Choice Awards tomorrow."

"You and I?" She flew up.

"No, me and Liz, silly. But don't worry. You'll get to go, as my guest."

"Oh!"

"You sound disappointed."

"It's just...I wish I could get pieces like that."

"Well, it's just because they knew you were on this Chase Hatton thing. How's that going by the way?"

"Don't ask." She sank lower in the tub.

"That bad, huh? Is he a real ass or something?"

"No, not at all. It's just... Hey, wait a minute, my invite to the People's Choice Awards, that was your big surprise, right?"

"Not exactly." Phillip raised an eyebrow, his blue eyes twinkling. Without another word, he stood and walked out of the bathroom.

"Well, what then?" she called after him.

"You'll see."

CHASE PULLED UP IN front of The Sunset Astoria Hotel. He had told Hal he was going for a drive, but he went, instead, to check on Hope, expecting to arrive before Phillip's flight did. As he pulled into the wide drop-off loop in front of the famous hotel, he saw her waiting on the sidewalk. She was dressed in a simple but curve-hugging black dress and her hair was arranged with soft ringlets which were swept up on top of her head. She held a little black purse in her hands by a gold chain strap and appeared to be waiting for something. He was about to get out of his car when he saw a black sedan pull up in front of her. The driver got out and walked around to open her car door for her. He recognized the face from the photo on her end table. Phillip grabbed her around the waist and kissed her. She giggled, glancing around to see if anyone had noticed.

Chase closed his car door and started his engine, speeding away before she noticed him sitting there.

IT HAD BEEN A PLEASANT evening for Hope. They enjoyed an excellent dinner followed by a little dancing. Now she and Phillip were walking to their car from the restaurant. She had a sheer wrap around her shoulders over her sleeveless dress, and Phillip looked as always as if he had been cut out of the cover of fashion magazine. There were times when she took great pride in being his date; tonight wasn't one of those times. Her mind kept drifting to Chase.

The night was mild, and people were out enjoying it: families with dripping ice cream cones, people in-line skating, young couples in love. Being with Phillip had been so...uncomplicated. Like the route you take home from work every day, she could be with him with her eyes closed and still arrive in one piece. Phillip held her hand as they walked, and they were in the midst of a comfortable break in conversation when he halted in front of a huge water fountain. It was lit with a variety of lightbulbs in different hues as geysers of varying heights danced up and down in random order, as bright and welcoming as the candles in the windows at Christmas time.

They stopped to take it in. "It's really spectacular, isn't it?" she commented. Catching his sly sideways glance, she asked, "What?"

He kissed her sweetly, then slowly bent down on one knee on the sidewalk. She heard someone gasp and out of the corner of her eye she could see people nudging each other, drawing others' attention to them.

"Hope," Phillip began, "we have been together for two years now, on this very day." She hadn't even realized it was their anniversary. "And as far as I'm concerned, this is way overdue, but..." He cleared his throat. "Hope, honey, you make me so happy, and I was wondering"—he pulled a ring box out of an inner pocket of his coat to another round of gasps from the crowd—"would you do me the great honor of becoming my bride?"

Her head was spinning. A marriage proposal? Phillip gazed up at her fondly, seeming sure of her decision and proud things had come off as he had planned them. The crowd held its breath. "Phillip, I love you—" Her statement was drowned out by the thunderous applause of those around them.

Only Phillip seemed to realize no acceptance had been given. He looked stunned for a beat, and then got up and hugged her. Perhaps feeling loose from the champagne he had drunk earlier, he dipped her elaborately, and planted a huge kiss on her. The people applauded, and she felt like she had suddenly been thrust into some sort of "play in the park" performance. Phillip beamed at everyone and took her hand in a proprietary way. He led her through the ring of bystanders who were still cheering as he opened the car door for her and she got in.

She sat stunned in the car, suddenly submerged in silence as the door closed off the crowd noise. She watched Phillip walk around the front of the sedan, and then wait for a break in traffic before sliding into his seat. His door slammed shut, and he stared straight ahead. Seconds ticked off and she noticed his jaw twitching. He turned to her, taking her hands.

"I noticed you didn't say yes."

"Phillip, I was just so surprised..."

"And now that you've had a few minutes to think about my proposal, your answer is?"

"Phillip, I love you..."

"Yes. I heard that out there. What I didn't hear was 'yes'!" He didn't bother to hide his anger now.

"I...I..." She had never been so glad to hear a cell phone ring.

"God damn it!" Phillip nearly tore the flip phone apart opening it. "Yes?" he growled. "Liz? Calm down! You what? Shit, Liz, how did you do that? Oh, all right. I'll be right there." He slammed the phone shut and started the engine, glancing into the side-view mirror for a break in traffic. "Liz thinks she may have erased our notes on her lap-top, the ditz!"

"I thought there was no story."

"The boss gave us some stupid assignment in London while we were waiting to see if the Afghani borders were going to reopen or not," he explained, speeding down the road. "This is great! This is just great!" he muttered.

She wasn't sure if he was still angry with her, or if Liz was now the subject of his rage. He didn't say another word until they pulled up to the hotel. He shut off the engine, but when she moved to get out, he put a hand on her arm.

"Listen, Hope. I'm sorry I kind of sprung this on you. But we've been going out for two years; I thought maybe the idea had crossed your mind."

In truth, it had. She made a list of all the reasons he would make a wonderful husband, and the other column didn't have one detraction except for the big one...she didn't love him, not in the way she was supposed to.

"You take all the time you want. Just do me a favor, and wear the ring until you've decided, okay?"

She nodded, stretching her neck to kiss him on the cheek. He smiled, satisfied for the moment.

When he came to bed later, she pretended to be asleep.

CHAPTER THIRTEEN

Chase stared at the ceiling in the darkness, his arms folded behind his head. He flipped over roughly on his side, grabbing the pillow from the other side of the bed and punching it a couple of times before laying his head on it. All he could see was Hope in that hot dress, giggling, with Phillip's arms around her waist. It made him want to punch something more solid than his pillow.

But the more he thought about it, the more he realized what bothered him most was not the kiss, but the giggle, the smile on her face, the fact Phillip had made her happy, where all he seemed to do was make her cry.

And why? What exactly had he done to make her react to him in this way? He went over that night for the gazillionth time in his head. One minute things were peachy, and they were dancing. She looked so pretty in that floral dress of hers...like a Hawaiian princess. There was a twisted scarf tied under her bosom in a tantalizing way. The ends hung loosely, taunting him as if to say, with one gentle tug, this could all come off, though he knew it was only a belt. Still, they floated behind her, whispering to him as they danced.

He remembered how it was with her then, so easy. They were always having fun together, but if for some reason he had had a bad day, a hug from her could make it all go away. And he liked to be the one to comfort her, too, if she'd had a bad practice or was plagued by some memory of her father. And that night had been no exception. They joked and laughed, until he had to leave and talk to Susie McNamara.

Susie had been upset because Chip Carter had gotten her pregnant and was now denying any responsibility. Not only was Susie frightened to death about being a single parent, she also loved that loser, for some reason, and was distraught over him turning his weasely back on her.

Chase had to recall every detail of that evening so he could discover where things went wrong. He had told Hope he was going to talk to Susie, and she was fine with it, so that couldn't be it. He talked to Susie for a long time, so long Susie had been worried Hope would get mad. He had assured her Hope would understand and she and the baby came first. Then, seeing how lost and alone she felt, he had reassured her he would help her through this. Then, she had kissed him. The kiss surprised him because it wasn't a thanks-for-being-a-good-friend kind of kiss, it was more of an I'm-lonely-and-scared-and-I-want-to-do-you kind of kiss. He had pulled back and said firmly, "I need to go back to Hope now," in a way, he hoped, made it clear he loved Hope, but didn't make Susie feel too bad about having kissed him.

Chase had walked away from the cafeteria shaking his head, feeling bad for Susie and half-hoping to run into Chip Carter so he could knock his block off. When he got back to the table, Hope's soda was half-drunk, but she was nowhere to be seen. He sat down to wait for her, trying to let Susie's problems fade into the background so he could enjoy the rest of the evening with Hope.

After twenty minutes, he started to get worried about her. He left the gymnasium and ran into Kyle Stockwell, a basketball teammate, in the hall. "Hey, Kyle, have you seen Hope?"

"Uh..." he replied nervously.

"Dude, it's pretty much a yes or no question."

"Y-yes," he returned hesitantly, but offered no further information.

"And that would have been"—he gestured widely—"where?"

"Listen, man, I saw her in the parking lot, going at it hot and heavy with Chip Carter in the front seat of his pickup truck. Sorry."

"Y-you must have been mistaken," he sputtered. "It must have been someone else," he added with more confidence.

"Didn't she have on a white, crinkled-looking dress with flowers on it?"

Chase paled. "Yes."

"Then it was her."

He rushed out to the parking lot, only to see Chip Carter's red pickup truck speeding out onto the street. The next day, Hope and Chip were gone. It didn't take a rocket scientist to figure out they had left town together.

He remembered his pain anew. All summer he had thought of her, wondering why. He had missed her company, missed her kiss, plagued by all of the wonderful memories they had made together. He would have gone after her, if he had known where to go. If she had a cell phone, maybe they could have spoken and cleared the air, but she didn't.

When fall came, he wondered constantly if she had gone to journalism school like she had intended to. Finally, unable to handle his doubts anymore, he drove to her campus. Thankfully, when he saw the list of dorm names, he remembered which one she had gotten into. When he strode past Hope's first floor room, he glanced in the window and saw her. She was sitting on the floor with a textbook open on her lap, and a guy was sitting on the bed she was leaning on, also studying, but at the same time, slowly stroking her arm. They seemed so cozy it had made him want to puke. She may have moved on from Chip Carter, but it was to someone else. He hopped in his truck and drove the long way back to Lincoln, planning to never make the trip again.

While Chase was lost in his memories, he heard a rap on the door to the deck. Was the storm blowing something against the door? He got up to investigate. He opened the door just as a bolt of lightning lit the sky to find Hope standing, dripping, on his doorstep.

CHASE THREW HIS ARM around Hope and ushered her in as the storm raged on outside. She sat, shivering, her pretty black dress plastered against her body like wet papier-mâché.

"Geez, Hope! You're a mess. Let's get these wet things off." He escorted her to the bathroom, glancing at the clock. What the hell was she doing knocking at his door at two o'clock in the morning?

He didn't care.

In the bathroom, she froze in his arms. Slowly, he reached behind her to unzip her dress. She made no move to stop him, just stood like a zombie, looking utterly confused. He brought both hands to the side of her neck and waited for some reaction. Getting none, he pushed the dress off her shoulders and she shimmied a little, the dress falling to the floor with a wet *plop*. She stood in front of him in just a strapless bra, her panties, and thigh-high hose, still trembling. He put his hand under her chin and lifted it an inch, kissing her, but holding his desire in check.

"You should get under some blankets." She nodded mutely, like a child.

He tucked her under the blankets and made a move to go sleep in the guest room.

She held out a hand to restrain him. "No! Don't leave!" It reminded him of the night she hurt her ankle in the cornfield. Her voice was desperate, and her eyes begged him to stay. Weakened by the need he saw in their depths, he relented, sliding in beside her. He lifted an arm, and she laid her head on his chest. He rubbed her side, afraid to break the silence, the magic, by asking her why she had come. All he knew was she had stepped out of his dreams and into his bed, and he didn't want to ruin that.

IN THE MORNING, CHASE snuck out to make breakfast. Minutes later he heard his bedroom door open, and Hope came carefully out, tiptoeing in an exaggerated way like a cartoon wolf sneaking up on his prey. She was wearing one of his t-shirts, nearly as long as a dress, adding to her odd appearance.

"Is Hal up?" she whispered hoarsely when she saw him at the counter.

He shook his head, amused.

She tiptoed to the front door, pulling the hem of her t-shirt down. He wondered why she bothered, seeing as she had lain next to him last night wearing far less. She opened the front door and retrieved her bag from the stoop. She crept back in, closing the door quietly and heading back to the bedrooms, smiling first at him. He sat and observed her actions, contemplating what a mysterious thing a woman could be. He watched, interested in seeing whether she returned to his room. She, instead, entered the guest room she had used before.

He continued to flip the scrambled eggs over, wondering if she and Phillip had a fight, or was Phillip simply waking up now to find her gone? In a few minutes she came back, wearing the black v-neck sweater and khaki green shorts the director had approved for their hiking scene. He came around the corner with two plates of eggs and bacon and toast.

"Good morning," he murmured, kissing her on top of the head. He set the plates on the table and they sat down side by side. She reached for her napkin and his hand came quickly down to grab her wrist. The diamond ring she wore on her finger sparkled brightly in the new morning sun. He looked up in shock and saw her staring at the ring as if, she, too, was wondering where it had come from.

"Chase—" she started to say.

"Good morning," a particularly perky Hal announced.

Chase released the hand he held, and Hope stuck it under her leg, still staring at him, an excuse poised on her lips. Chase turned from her coldly. "Good morning, Hal. Do you want some eggs? I just lost my appetite." He swatted his napkin down on the table and pushed away, rising and going to his room.

FROM HIS ROOM CHASE could hear her cell phone ringing. He stormed out of his room and into hers. Finding it on her bedside table, he snatched it up and stepped over to yank the door to the deck open. "You have a phone call!" he barked. Dropping it into her hand, he noticed how red her finger was from where she had obviously been trying to get the ring off.

He plopped down on the settee behind her. So that was the problem. She couldn't get it off. Had she been able to, would he have ever known? *Dammit! Why did you come here?* his head screamed. She redialed the number of her missed call. *Why did you leave his side in the middle of the night and hop into my bed? True, nothing happened between us, but it could have. Lord knows I wanted it to!*

"Hello." She spoke into the phone but looked directly at him. "Yes, Phillip, I'm fine. I couldn't sleep." There was a long pause. "I'm sorry. I didn't intend to alarm you. I'm going to stay here tonight. No, no. You and Liz will be working on your story anyway, and I have a lot of work to put in on mine. I'll see you before The People's Choice Awards. Yes, you, too." She hung up.

She looked at him earnestly. "Chase, please believe me, I haven't given him an answer yet."

He jumped up and paced in front of the couch a couple of times. "You know what, Hope? You don't owe me any explanations." He threw his hands up and stormed away from her, stopping with a hand on the doorknob to his bedroom. "You can stay here tonight," he said frostily, without turning to look at her, "but you'll be staying in *your own bed*." He left, slamming the door behind him.

Chase entered his bathroom and saw the wet dress lying where they had left it on the tile floor. He grabbed it, ready to launch it into the tub, but he stopped in mid-motion. Instead, he tromped over to the tub and squeezed the excess water out of the dress, hanging it over the shower curtain rod and smoothing the folds of the fabric.

He sighed, sitting on the side of the tub, steering clear of the dripping dress. *Was she toying with Phillip and me? Could she really do that?* He thought about the Hope he knew before prom, always forthright, truthful to a fault. She was the type who would make an extra trip back to the grocery store to tell them she hadn't been charged for one of her gallons of milk. She was loyal to her friends and not free and easy with others' feelings. *Maybe she's just confused. Maybe I should be patient like Hal said.* He took a deep breath, and got ready for the shoot.

CHAPTER FOURTEEN

Chase and Hope were climbing in Los Flores Canyon, at the foot of Mt. Lowe, a camera crew several yards below them. The trail was much rougher and more rigorous than expected, but the physical workout was welcome, forcing them to put other thoughts on a back burner, at least while hiking. The weather had turned out to be the best so far of the season, seventy degrees with a light wind and the sun shining benevolently down on them through the trees.

Hope was keeping up with Chase, despite her much shorter legs, her natural athleticism working to her advantage. In fact, in some areas she had less trouble than he did—her litheness and agility making her a mini-Spider-Woman. At times when she did struggle, though, he would reach down to lend a hand, each time having to push away the thoughts about the ring she wore on hers.

At one point, he ran into a section of deceptively loose rock and sent a small avalanche down on her. She ducked, but still received several blows to the head with fairly sizable rocks.

"Hope!" he called, concerned. "Are you okay?"

"Yes," she grimaced, running a free hand over her head to feel for injuries. "I thought it was bleeding. But I think it was the rush of blood to the spots where I was hit giving me the sensation of bleeding. "I'm fine." She smiled up at him.

He acknowledged the little cartwheel it gave his stomach, and then continued up the slope. He hadn't gone much farther when the whole slab of rock he was on broke away and he slid down the steep grade rapidly.

She must have heard his boots scraping against rock and debris falling as she looked up quickly. "Chase!" She scurried along the rock face, trying to angle over to intercept him. She reached out as he was sliding by, and together they were able to stop his descent.

They sat breathing heavily for several minutes, hugging the cliff. "You know Hal is screaming at the director right now." She panted. Hal had been fit-to-be-tied when he saw the terrain they were expected to traverse, questioning the director's sanity, but they had assured him they could handle it. "By now he's probably telling him he'll never find work again if he kills off a rock icon."

He laughed, blowing dirt off the cliff face with each exhale. He closed his eyes, his face contorting for a minute.

"Are you all right?" she asked, her worry evident.

"Yeah, yeah. It's just a side-stitch." He raised his head and canvassed the territory ahead. "I think if we could just angle over and hit that little ledge over there, the rest would be a piece of cake."

She nodded her agreement.

"The camera crew gave up, didn't they?"

Hope followed his gaze below. "About twenty minutes ago, I think."

"So it's just us two idiots up here, then."

"Yep." She smiled.

"I still think we need to get up top so we can find a safer way down."

"I agree."

"All right." Chase began climbing to the right, carefully choosing his footholds and handholds. They were silent until they both stood on the ledge. Now, they were able to give their hands and toes and knees a rest, and lean with their backs against the wall, catching their breath. Hope peeked over the edge, but then threw herself back against the cliff, squeezing her eyes shut.

"That's right," he said with a chuckle. "You're afraid of heights. You're an even bigger fool than I am, Hope Creswell."

When she opened her eyes to respond, she stared at the blood dripping down his leg. "You're hurt!" she cried, zipping open her waist pack and seeming to forget her fear instantly.

"Yeah," he said absentmindedly, watching the blood drip toward his sock. He saw she was getting out first-aid supplies. "Hope, its okay. I don't need that."

"No. You have to clean it. You don't want to have to deal with infection." She poured a generous amount of antiseptic spray on the abrasion, stopping the flow with a cotton ball.

He winced, sucking in his breath through his teeth, feeling like a big baby. *But that stuff stings!*

She grinned at him, applying a bandage. "There, that's better."

"Okay," he said hurriedly. "We can go now."

"Let me see your hands."

"What? No. They're fine."

"Chase! Let me see them."

"All right, here. Are you happy now?" He turned over his hands to show her. They were scraped raw.

"Oh my gosh! That must have hurt like hell."

"Not as much as that stuff hurts."

"I'll blow on it first."

"What?"

"I'll blow on it. It's supposed to help."

"Okay."

She held the back of his hands firmly. Bending her head, she gently began to blow over the surface of his hands. A tingle ran up his arms, which had little to do with his injury, and everything to do with the way she was puckering her lips and the way her warm breath felt on his palms. Thankfully, she was concentrating on her work and had not noticed how turned on he was. She poured a small amount of the liquid over his hands.

"How's that?"

"Not bad," he commented, surprised.

"Good." She smiled. "This will take care of the dirt that was imbedded when you slid, but I really can't bandage these, and you're bound to pick up more dirt, so we'll have to wash them again when we get down to the bottom. But don't worry; I'll blow on them again."

"All right," he agreed, showing more enthusiasm than he should have.

They started off again. The rock to their right was practically stair-stepped and they reached the top in less than five minutes.

"Whoooo!" he whooped, raising his hands in the air in victory and listening to his voice echo back from the surrounding hills. Instinctively, he put his arm around her and hugged her to his side. As they stood taking in deep breaths, they began to survey their surroundings. In front of them they could see all of Los Angeles, all the way out to the ocean and even Catalina Island. Behind them were the hills: Mt. Markham, Mt. Disappointment, and San Gabriel Peak. It was an interesting contrast between the man-made "mountainous" skyscrapers of downtown L.A., and the God-made, awe-inspiring canyons and valleys and hills that dwarfed them.

She gazed out over the sweeping vistas. "It's beautiful."

He peered down into her smudged face. "Yes it is," he murmured. He battled his urge to kiss her, reminding himself she wore another man's ring on her finger. "This is what I think the director wanted to capture, us overlooking some breathtaking vista. Not the sweaty, dirty, bloody couple we are now, though."

She laughed.

He glanced ruefully at his cut up hands. "Hal is gonna be so pissed. What do you say we find a way down off this piece of rock?"

"I say, lead the way." She placed her hand in his.

They had not gone far, Chase searching this way and that for a gentler slope, when he stepped on a rock, twisting his ankle. He lurched and lost his balance, stumbling, his feet sliding over the edge of the cliff. He grabbed desperately at some grass as he fell, which held him only for the briefest of moments, but it was enough time for Hope to lunge and catch his arms. She lay on her stomach, staring down into his shocked face.

"Oh my God, Chase! Don't let go!" she screamed, her face panic-stricken.

"I wasn't planning on it," he replied. The ridge below him was too far to fall to without injuring himself. His sweaty hands began to slip.

"Chase! Chase! Hold on!"

"I'm trying to!" He had already decided if he were to start to fall, he would immediately let go. She would fall headfirst if she came over the edge and would no doubt be killed.

The veins on both of their arms were taut, and Hope grunted as her muscles began to shake. "What I wouldn't give right now...for Hal's...cell phone."

As if in response to her statement, they suddenly heard, "Ms. Creswell? Ms. Creswell?"

"Yes! Yes! Over here!"

Seconds later the rotund face of a Mexican man peered over the ledge. Chase recognized him as part of the studio crew.

"Oh my!" he said in a highly understated way. He got down on one knee and reached down to grab Chase's arm. Using his weight and strength he leaned back, pulling him up a little. Chase's feet hit something solid and he was able to take some weight off, allowing the two above to pull him up completely with one great heave. Hope and their Latino savior sat down as he rolled to his back, all three panting heavily.

"That was not good," the man said.

Chase and Hope looked at each other and began laughing, relief fueling their amusement, making them nearly hysterical.

"You two are loco," the man commented, whirling his finger in circles by his temple, but smiling.

Turning from him, Hope leaned her head down and kissed Chase. Her hands on either side of his face, she stayed close, whispering, "God, Chase, don't ever do that again."

He smiled up at her. "Not in my game plan."

Within minutes the rest of the crew had found them, taking a Jeep most of the way up on the opposite side of the hill. The director, not to be defeated, had the pair cleaned up and took pictures of them standing on an overhang, Chase's arms securely around Hope.

"See," the director said to Hal, "the day was not a waste."

Hal just rolled his eyes.

Hope and Chase decided to ride in the Jeep on the way back to the studio. With the sun, just beginning its descent, and the wind blowing their hair, she leaned against him, laying her head on his chest and falling asleep as she had the previous night.

WHEN THEY RETURNED to the house, a late dinner was decided upon so everyone could rest and/or wash up. Later, Chase put some steaks Hope had marinated on the grill, along with baked potatoes and little packages of seasoned vegetables she had thrown together. Hal went to get wine out of the storage room/cellar, telling them he would be careful not to seal himself in.

During dinner, Hal announced they wouldn't need any more footage; he and the producer were sure they had enough to put the video together. With his statement the mood turned sober. Chase felt his stomach drop.

"Do you have enough information for your article, Hope?"

"Hmm?" she replied distractedly. "Oh yes. More than enough. I'll email you a copy for your approval before I submit it."

"I'd appreciate that, Hope. It's not that I don't trust you, it's just I've been in the business long enough to understand how something innocent can be turned into something ugly."

"Oh no, Hal, I want you to look it over. I would never want to write anything that could possibly hurt Chase." She and Chase locked eyes.

"Well," Hal said, raising his glass, "it's been a pleasure working with you." He clinked glasses with her.

Chase raised his glass as well, and she slowly brought her glass to meet his, again staring into his eyes.

Hal cleared his throat. "I've been feeling like a third wheel for so long now, I figure my tire needs to be replaced." He rose and waved off Hope, who seemed about to protest. "I think I'll just excuse myself and go do some paperwork in my room. Good night, all. Leave the dishes. I'll get them later."

Hal left, in his wake, an awkward silence. Chase twirled his wine glass on the table. "Hope, we need to talk."

"I know. Let me clear the table and we'll talk on the deck."

Together they cleared the dishes. She suggested they just wash up the few dishes to save Hal the trouble. Chase wordlessly grabbed a towel, letting her know, in his own way, he knew she was stalling, and he could outlast her. The inevitable was going to happen. They were going to have to rehash things painful to her, and she probably dreaded the conflict it would bring between them.

He chuckled quietly as he dried a plate and put it in the cabinet. "What?"

"Do you remember our first date?"

"At the golf course?"

"Yeah. Boy, I sure was one smooth operator!"

"Yes, you were," she agreed with a smile.

He set his towel down on the counter. "You know, you aren't doing the dishes right."

"I'm not?" she said in surprise, looking down at the soapy dish in her hand.

"You're supposed to do it like this." He stepped behind her and brought his arms around, sticking them in the water to grab her hands. He meant it as a joke at first. But when their bodies touched, and he could smell her sweet fragrance...

She appeared caught off guard when he moved behind her. She froze in his arms at first. He manipulated her hands, simulating wiping the dishes with her. The feeling of his hands touching hers in the soapy water was unbelievably sensual.

"Like this," he whispered in an ear.

"Chase," she breathed. She turned in his arms. Her cell phone rang, disrupting the quiet. They reacted as if they'd been splashed with cold water. "Oh, I got you all wet." She grabbed the towel off the counter and tried to dry him off.

"Never mind." He laughed. "Go. Answer your phone."

She ran into the living room, snatching up her phone. "Hello...Phillip? What? You did research on me, l-like I was some piece you were writing?" she sputtered with outrage. "Yes, I dated Chase in high school." There was a pause. "Because it was irrelevant." She tromped toward her bedroom, but her voice carried back to Chase. "Whatever is between me and Chase has nothing to do with you and me. No! I didn't mean something was going on...you have no right to call me that!" Her voice sounded shocked. "Phillip, have you been drinking? NO! You are not coming over here. I'll come to you, do you hear me? Don't get in a car. Promise me. Okay, I'll be there in fifteen minutes. Stay put!"

She came out of the bedroom, visibly upset.

"Chase, can I borrow your car?"

"Of course, you can. But do you really think you should be driving?" She was flinging stuff out of her purse. "Hope." He grabbed her by the shoulders. "Slow down, honey. What are you trying to do?"

"Find the damn car keys!"

"But sweetheart, I haven't given them to you yet."

She collapsed into his arms, sobbing. He closed his arms around her, pulling her closer with one hand on her head. "I just can't do this! He's mad at me! You're mad at me!"

"I'm not mad at you."

"Well, not anymore."

"Hope." He pushed her away so he could peer into her face. "You can't let us influence you. You need to make a decision, but it has to be your decision."

"I know," she replied, her voice small. "I'm better now." She reached down and found a pack of tissues she had thrown onto the floor. She wiped her face and blew her nose.

"Are you sure? I can drive you—"

"No! That would be the worst thing that could happen. You two might end up in a fight."

"What if I promise to behave myself?"

"No, Chase. This is something I have to do myself."

"Okay," he said reluctantly, fishing the keys out of his pocket. He pulled her close one last time and kissed her head. "I'll wait up for you."

She nodded and was gone.

CHAPTER FIFTEEN

Several hours later, as Chase watched, her headlights lit the driveway. He heard her enter below him and trudge up the steps.

"Hey, babe," he said softly so as not to startle her in the dark room.

"Oh, gosh, Chase, have you been up this whole time?"

"No, I snoozed on the couch. Come here."

She dropped her keys on the sofa table and plodded into his arms.

He kissed her head as he had done before she left. "Are you okay?"

She nodded, but didn't elaborate for a moment. "I calmed him down. He was traaashed! Then the concierge and I put him to bed." Chase didn't say anything, just continued to stroke her hair. "He's not a bad guy, you know. I mean...he is a jerk sometimes, but underneath all the bullshit he has a good heart."

"I'll have to take your word on it," he said wryly. He was rewarded with a small chuckle.

Her voice came, muffled, from his chest. "I have a raging headache."

"Come on. We'll get you an aspirin." He escorted her to her bedroom. "Just stay here and I'll be back in a second." He went back to his bedroom and rifled through the medicine cabinet. He went to the kitchen to get a clean glass for her water.

When he returned he found her lying on the bed. She had changed into a white, linen, eyelet nightgown with wide straps, buttoned up the bodice, and simply flopped on top of the covers, falling fast asleep in minutes, her face turned away from the door. He knew immediately she had fallen asleep. He set the glass of water and the pain relievers on the bedside table. He went around to the other side of the bed and climbed up carefully, stretching out next to her. Resting on his elbow, he peered into her peaceful face. *Poor thing*! *You're exhausted!* He brushed the hair back from her cheek and bent to feather a kiss along her lips, then laid his head down on the pillow, and watched her sleep.

Around two in the morning, Hope awoke. Chase was lying beside her, asleep, fully clothed. She pulled up on one elbow and peered at him. She had to smile. Gazing into his face, she saw the boy with the model airplanes she had first met, the handsome teenager she had fallen in love with, the rock star whose face had been splashed across numerous magazine covers, and the friend who had been with her the last couple of days.

Taking care not to jiggle the mattress, she rolled out of bed and reached to turn off the light. She circled around the end of the bed, pulling a thick, pale blue cardigan out of the top of her suitcase. Throwing it around her shoulders, she continued to watch him sleep peacefully. How could this be the same guy who lied to her and snuck around behind her back? It just didn't jibe. She finally moved to the other side of the bed and switched off the lamp there. Some light still spilled in from the bathroom. She crossed to the door and opened it as quietly as she could, going out onto the deck.

WHEN CHASE WOKE, HOPE was gone. For one irrational moment he thought Phillip had come and spirited her away. He swung his legs over the side of the bed, and sat up. Ignoring the head rush this gave him, he checked the bathroom. Not finding her there, he was about to check the living room when he noticed the deck light was on. He opened the door and stepped out onto the gray planks. He leaned on the railing and scanned the beach below where his shadow stretched out across the sand like a giant. He saw her sitting near the water, knees drawn up, arms wrapped around them. The reflection of the moon on the water gave her an ethereal glow, just around the edges, defining her shape.

He reached her, and then stood beside her for several minutes, his hands dug into the pockets of the white shorts, his blue shirt fluttering in the breeze. In the full moon, the waves shined like a sequined evening gown.

"What are you doing out here?" he said quietly, without looking at her.

She didn't answer immediately. The only sound to break the stillness was the constant roar and swish of the waves. It pleased him, the commanding thunder of the water, followed by the gentle murmur. He knew they were heading for the crest of the wave, and dreamed of the promised peaceful swish that always followed.

"Just thinking." She peered up at him and moved to stand. He reached down to lend her a hand. "I hope I didn't wake you. You were sleeping so peacefully."

He shook his head. He clasped his hands behind his back and watched the waves rise and swell, full of power, and then crash onto the sand. They stood that way for several seconds. He wriggled his toes into the cool sand, watching the grains fall skittering down the slope he had created trying to cover his foot. "What were you thinking about?"

She thought for what seemed like eternity before answering him. "You," she said looking straight ahead.

He stared at her for a minute in surprise, and then turned back to study the waves again as she was. He debated whether he should ask more, but he knew she would offer more if he waited patiently.

As if on cue, she breathed out, "About you and me. Times we had in the past, good times."

He studied her profile, seemingly so serene. "I've been thinking about that a lot lately, too." She looked so beautiful as she hugged a sweater around her, the breeze pressing against the nightgown underneath, making it flap loudly, like a flag on a pole. Her skin was luminescent, her eyes reflecting the swirling motion of the waves. He knew then he would not back down, would not let her go without a fight. He stepped toward her, touching her arms.

She turned to him, looking him fully in the face for the first time. "Chase," she said against the wind, "I feel so confused."

"I'm sorry," he replied. "But what I'm going to do next isn't going to help you any." He slid his hands up her arms and kissed her, letting her feel all of the desire within him, his tongue searching for hers with sweet need. Then, he simply let her go, turning to retrace his steps through the sand.

She kept her eyes closed for a moment, wanting not even sense of sight to detract from the singular sensation his lips created when they touched hers. She opened them slowly, expecting to find him there. Bewildered, she turned to search for him, and saw him, already far off, near the stairs, trotting briskly away.

She was furious at herself for being indecisive. One thing she knew for certain, she couldn't marry Phillip; she simply didn't love him, and he deserved better than that. She knew, just as certainly, she did love Chase. Every breath she took when she was with him told her that. But she just couldn't get past the fact that he had cheated on her. The pain it had caused was forever etched inside her core. *Why?* she asked herself. *People make mistakes. It was years ago. He was young. So, why is it so hard for me to put myself out there? To try again with Chase?*

Without precursor, the answer reverberated from deep inside her soul—the realization becoming so crystal-clear it shocked her. It was because she felt unworthy of his love. She always had, and the cheating was just confirmation of it. Her father had so completely warped her way of thinking, she wasn't sure if she could ever trust in his love.

But Hope knew if she was to ever try, she would have to be free of Phillip. Having at least made the decision to break it off with him, she felt somewhat better. She climbed the staircase to the house and went to the kitchen, to search for some butter. She would get this ring off one way or another.

When she returned to her bedroom, Chase wasn't there, but he had turned the sheets down on the bed for her. This small gesture of love nearly melted her heart. She climbed in, switched off the light and pulled the covers up with a sigh of contentment. Her life hadn't seemed so full of promise in a long time.

CHAPTER SIXTEEN

When Hope opened her eyes, she was lying on her stomach and the first thing she saw was a piece of paper that was shoved under the door. With a slow smile, she hopped out of bed, grabbed the note, and got back in under the covers. On heavy, gray paper Chase had written:

Hope—

Thought you could use some space today, so I headed to the studio with Hal to work on the video. I didn't want to put any more pressure on you. The keys to the car are where you left them on the table. Spend your day however you want, relax on the beach, work on your story, or, of course, you're welcome to join us at the studio. I'll be thinking of you all day. If I don't

see you before, I'll try to find you
at The People's Choice Awards this
evening.

I love you (okay, maybe a little pressure), Chase

She smiled at his last comment, hugging the note to her chest, feeling it warm her all over. She flipped over and peered out the window. She could tell by the way the light slanted in, and by how refreshed she felt, it was late. Wasting no more time lying in bed, she got into the shower. She decided to skip breakfast and have an early lunch. By the time she sat down to her laptop, it was after eleven.

Once she got started, the story just seemed to flow out of her. She read it and reread it, fine-tuning the language. At three-thirty, her phone rang. Hoping it was Chase, she rushed to answer it.

"Hi." Her heart sank.

"Phillip. How are you feeling?"

"Like hell. How 'bout you?"

"I'm okay."

He sighed. "I need to be there early tonight. Can you get ready and meet me there by five?"

She glanced at the clock. "Yes, I think I can do that."

"Thanks, Hope. Sorry I was such an ass last night."

"That's okay. I'm used to it."

"Very funny," he said, but she could tell he was smiling. "I'll see you in a little while. I love you, you know."

"I love you, too, Phillip." She hung up the phone and stood thinking for a minute. She hated to see him in pain. He meant a lot to her, and there were so many memories of times they had shared together. He had always been so good to her; he didn't deserve the pain this would put him through. She fiddled with the ring in her pocket. She dreaded the conversation they would need to have, but she knew it was necessary.

WITH HER PRESS PASS, Hope was able to be part of the pack of photographers taking shots of celebrities on the red carpet. Her pictures were no doubt different than the others were taking, because she took shots of chauffeurs trying to appear dignified, and fans ecstatic over seeing their favorite star, or caught photos of the celebrities themselves, which were more candid. She enjoyed being part of the frenzy, but was glad when it was time to take a seat with Phillip.

When she approached the table, Phillip rose, his mouth falling open. "My God, Hope, you look fantastic!" They hadn't had many opportunities to play dress-up, so to see her like this was a rarity. She wore a floor-length, red satin dress that was cut on a diagonal, leaving one shoulder bare, hair a mass of curls piled on top of her head. She'd even been pleased to find she had thrown appropriate jewelry in her travel case at the last minute. She'd actually been asked by a young man for her autograph, much to her embarrassment.

"Thanks."

Phillip made a move to kiss her, but she turned to offer a cheek.

The evening was entertaining, with many famous people performing, and she was enjoying herself immensely, despite the fact that Liz McPherson also sat with them. Phillip was up and down a lot doing various backstage interviews. Each time he came back, he seemed a little less put together, his voice a little louder. At one point, Phillip excused himself to go to the bathroom, but hadn't returned twenty minutes later. Concerned, she went to find him. She discovered him sitting on some sound equipment backstage, guzzling a glass of champagne. He was following the onstage show and didn't see her approaching.

"Phillip!"

He jumped, spilling some of the champagne down his shirt. "Shit!" he yelled, setting the flute down on the floor and brushing off his pants and shirt. A few people turned their heads.

She whispered, "Phillip, I think you've had enough to drink."

"You're right, hon. I'm sorry." He reached over, pulling her close and running his hand over the back of her dress, stopping at her tush.

"Phillip!"

He swung her back against the stage wall so fast that it took her breath away and pressed his lips to hers aggressively. She pushed against him, angered. "Phillip! This is inappropriate."

Phillip banged his fists on the wall on either side of her, his face inches away, so distorted with rage, he didn't even look like himself. For a second, she was actually frightened. "Dammit, Hope! You never thought it was inappropriate before."

Her eyes were wide with shock, and then she glanced around. A big, Asian man, who was obviously a part of the security staff, started moving menacingly toward them. As her eyes continued to travel around the backstage area, she saw people shaking their heads and staring at Phillip disapprovingly, and then she caught Chase's eyes. He had on a black suit with a scarlet shirt underneath and a scarlet handkerchief sticking out of the pocket, which someone was fussing over. He had been talking but his jaw fell open when he saw her.

He had been talking to the person straightening his attire when Phillip yelled at her, and heard the commotion, but was not aware of who was causing it or why. Now, looking over and seeing her pinned against the wall, he stopped in midsentence, his mouth hanging open.

Hope seized Phillip by his lapels, and started dragging him away. "We need to get out of here, NOW!"

He glanced around and seemed to sense he had made a mistake. He broke away from her grasp and stumbled over to the security guard. "Everything's okay, man," Phillip said, patting his expansive chest. The guard, who had his arms crossed, displaying his large biceps, actually *growled* at him.

She wedged herself between them, and keeping her eye on the guard, grabbed Phillip's arm. He finally fell into step with her. She glanced back over her shoulder and saw Chase being pushed into the footlights, still looking at her and arguing with a man who wore a headset. A few seconds later, as she sped Phillip away from the scene, she heard the audience erupt in applause and knew Chase had taken the stage.

They moved in silence, their heels ringing on concrete, until Phillip began to beg for her forgiveness. "I was way out of line. I don't know what I was thinking. Please, Hope..."

They reached the door that allowed access to the backstage. The security personnel there had obviously been alerted to their presence by walkie-talkie as they were greeted with unconcealed glares as they passed into the hallway outside the auditorium.

Phillip still rambled on with his apologies.

"Phillip, it's all right. Shhh!" She hustled him through a doorway to the theater so she could maybe catch a glimpse of Chase on stage.

"Aw! Great!" Phillip muttered.

She was so preoccupied she didn't notice him wander off. After Chase left the stage, she turned around to discover Phillip missing.

"Aw! Great!" Hope echoed unintentionally. She made her way back to their seats, but he wasn't there. Not only that, but Liz and the few other newspaper reporters they knew were gone also, so she couldn't even ask them if they had seen her runaway. She went back into the hall.

"Hope! Hope!" Chase came running breathlessly from the backstage area. He grabbed her arms and bent down to peer into her face, still panting. "Are you okay?"

"I'm fine."

"If I get my hands on that jackass...!"

"Uh, Chase, I'm grateful and all, but I could do without the male testosterone right now. Phillip's missing and I'm afraid, in his condition... Well, anything could happen."

He raised an eyebrow. "And that would be a problem because...?"

"Chase, please."

"All right." He sighed. "I'll do it for you." He rubbed her arms up and down. "But if he ever lays a hand on you again—"

"You can wail away."

"Okay." He glanced up, studying their surroundings. "Well, I didn't pass him, so he's not back there. I'll go straight down the hall, and you can check out these banquet rooms."

"Thanks, Chase." She smiled.

"You're welcome." He took off trotting in the opposite direction.

She began opening doors into banquet rooms. The first two were empty. The third had a handful of waiters smoking.

When she opened the fourth, she stared in shock. Liz McPherson sat on the edge of a table with her dress up, her legs wrapped around Phillip's waist. Phillip had his hands on top of the table and was thrusting his hips back and forth. Liz heard the door open, but when she glanced up and saw Hope, she relaxed and even smiled at her.

Hope covered her eyes, stumbling backward, not wanting to see anything more. "Oh my God!"

Phillip followed Liz's line of vision. "Oh, God, Hope!" He pulled away, struggling to be free from the circle of Liz's legs, hopping up and down and frantically trying to zip his pants.

Hope turned back into the hallway, crossing to lean against the far wall, feeling like she was going to be sick.

Chase entered from the other end of the hallway just as Phillip ran out of the banquet room.

"Hope!" Phillip stopped, and began pacing back and forth with his hands on his hips, finally stopping to throw them up in the air. "Oh, come on, Hope. Like you weren't sweatin' up the sheets with your big rock star here?" He gestured to Chase who was now within earshot.

She rounded on him heatedly. "*I never*...I would never...I c-can't believe this!"

Seeing the stark sincerity and incredulity on her face, Phillip began to falter. "Well, I needed you in London—"

"This has been going on since London?" she cried in shock.

"Aw, shit!"

"Here." She began to rifle through her purse. "You can have this." She held out the ring. "Take it! I'm through with you!" she shrieked hysterically, her tears evident now. He took two steps backward, shaking his head. "Take it, dammit!" When he still refused to take the ring, she threw it at him and it pinged off the wall, ricocheting out of sight.

She turned to leave and Chase put a hand on her arm. "No!" she screamed, shaking with fury. "I'm through with both of you!"

He stood, stunned, watching her march away.

"Chase, where have you been? Your category is up!" Hal yelled from the other end of the hall.

Chase watched as Hope hit the metal bar to open the exit door at the end of the hall and disappear.

"Chase?" Hal called anxiously.

He turned around, moving toward Hal. He glared at Phillip with loathing. He was leaning against a wall, looking ill.

Chase entered the backstage area just as they announced he had won the award for Best Male Vocalist of the Year, and the crowd roared with applause. He strode out on stage, receiving the award with a smile and taking the mike at the podium.

"Wow!" he started when the crowd settled down. "This is great! Well, first of all, I'd like to thank my fans—"

A teenage girl shrieked from the balcony, "I love you, Chase!"

He turned in her direction. "Thanks." The audience chuckled. "Umm...I'd like to thank my manager, Hal Westbrook." He held the award up, gesturing in his direction backstage. "He keeps me focused and organized and out of trouble, for the most part." Hal nodded and smiled.

"Uh...I'd like to thank my crew." He looked out in the direction where he knew they were sitting in the audience. "You guys are the best, and I couldn't do it without you."

"And finally," he paused, wanting to get this right. "I want to thank the woman who was the inspiration for every love song I've ever written—I pray you're in the building somewhere—Hope, I love you. I have always loved you, and I will always love you. Thank you."

He left the stage to more applause. The backstage was abuzz. The World's Most Eligible, Sexy Rock Star had a girl? He handed Hal the award and dodged microphones.

"But Chase, you've got four more categories."

"You'll just have to accept for me." He was already flipping his cell phone open to call his driver as he headed for the backstage exit.

CHAPTER SEVENTEEN

C hase climbed into the back of the limo.

"How was your night, Mr. Hatton?"

He rubbed his eyes, feeling a headache coming. "I've had better."

"I thought I heard you won Best Male Vocalist?" he asked, his eyes widening in the rearview mirror.

"I did," he said simply, staring out the window. Alternately the streetlights lit his face and then it was left in shadows. He sat with his elbow on the sill, his fingers curled, resting against his chin.

"Where to?"

Where would she have gone? As upset as Hope was, she could have gone anywhere, but his best guess was she had gone home.

"If you could please take me home, Terrence. As fast as you can."

"We're not going to one of those all-night parties?"

"Not tonight," he responded vaguely.

Fifteen minutes later the chauffeur was laying on the horn and cussing. "I'm sorry, Mr. Hatton. I forgot all about the basketball game tonight."

Chase sighed restlessly, studying the long line of traffic ahead, feeling like a rat caught in a trap. "That's okay, Terrence. You did your best." He just prayed he hadn't missed her.

When he pulled into the drive, the house was dark. He hopped out, not waiting for the garage to open, and ran up the sidewalk to the front door. Finding it locked, he remembered, *I never gave her a key*. He put his hand on his forehead, shading his eyes from the glare outside so he could peer inside the window running parallel to the door. Whether it be a moonbeam shining through the skylight, or light filtering down from the kitchen, he was able to make out the car keys on the hall table. He had forgotten there was a house key with them. So, she was here. He pulled a set of keys out of an inner pocket, struggled with the lock and opened the door.

Stepping into the darkness, he called her name. The sound of his voice dissipated in the stillness. He ran up the few stairs to the main level and into her room. When he didn't find her there, he opened the door to the deck and stepped out, almost imagining seeing her there on the beach where she was the night before. But all he saw was sand and shimmering water. He stretched his hands wide on the porch railing, and hung his head, exhaling loudly. "Shit!" She was gone. He had known it all along, but kept hoping, maybe.

He ambled back to her room, closing and locking the door behind him. He ran a hand over the bedspread, half-expecting it to still be warmed by her body. There was no sign she had ever been there. Her shampoo was gone from the bathroom, her brush from the dresser.

He left her room, turning off the light and closing the door softly behind him. He wandered into his bedroom aimlessly, and it was as if he could see her there, lying asleep in his arms; he, watching her in the early dawn light.

He went to the bathroom and found it, the dress, still hanging from the shower curtain. She had forgotten it. He pulled the black dress down and buried his face in it, finally losing his control. He sat on the edge of the tub and cried, wondering why she had ever come back into his life.

VAGUELY CHASE HEARD Hal come in the front door. Chase sat on the couch upstairs in the dark. Hal set some awards one by one on the hall table, and climbed the stairs. Chase didn't even look up.

He slouched on the sofa, still wearing his suit, though his shirt was semi-unbuttoned. He held a glass of scotch in his hand and swirled the ice, watching it as it clinked against the sides.

"You won three more awards," Hal offered hopefully.

Chase nodded. Hal moved to go to his room.

"Hal?"

"Yes?"

"Thanks."

"Sure, Chase." He was about to leave, but turned back. He came around and sat down on the couch across from him. "What happened tonight?"

"Hope's asshole boyfriend decided to screw somebody on a conference room table, from what I gathered."

Hal's jaw dropped. He knew he had shocked his manager. He didn't usually talk like that, but after tonight...

Hal lowered himself into a chair. "I heard rumors backstage. So they're true?"

Chase nodded.

Hal rubbed his chin, thinking, then looked up. "Where is she?"

Chase took a long drink of his scotch, draining the glass. "Gone." He poured another drink from the bottle, which was left out on the table.

"Well." Hal sighed. "I can't say I blame her, having gone through the same thing with you."

Chase tilted his glass back. It took a moment for his words to sink in. "What?"

"I mean, all those years ago. Back in high school."

"I never cheated on Hope!"

"Well, she said you did."

"She...I *never* cheated on Hope! Why would I? I loved her."

Hal seemed confused. "Well I didn't think you would, but she said she saw you with the girl."

"What?" He sat up quickly. "That's impossible!"

Hal stood. "I believe you, but I'm not the one you need to convince." He walked off towards his bedroom.

Chase sat in the dark, thinking. Then, he called his pilot. It was late, but he needed the jet to be fueled and ready to go first thing in the morning.

HOPE TOOK THE REDEYE back to Chicago. All she wanted to do now was turn in her article and be done with Chase Hatton for good. First thing in the morning, she waltzed into Jack Delaney's office with a rough copy.

"I still need to get approval from Hal Westbrook, but I'll send him an electronic copy right away."

"Hope, close the door."

Her heart skipped a beat; the editor had never wanted to talk to her in private before.

"Take a seat, Hope." Jack Delaney rose. He came around the desk and leaned against it near her, his legs stretched out in front of him. "When we first hired you, I saw a lot of raw talent in you. But to be frank, I've never seen that potential fulfilled. You...hold yourself back too much. Don't take risks. In your writing, and I daresay, in your personal life." He put a hand on her shoulder kindly, something so totally out of character she almost had to check the nameplate on his desk again. "If there is one thing I've learned in my"—he cleared his throat—"fifty-some-odd years of life, it is life isn't worth living if you're not willing to take a risk now and then." He returned to the other side of the desk, putting his reading glasses on and picking up her article. He peeked at her over the top of the glasses. "I'm afraid this is the last article you have written for *The Chicago Globe News*," he finished. He returned his attention to the paper in front of him.

"You're firing me?" She was stunned.

Delaney continued reading, not looking up. "Yes."

She slowly rose and left the office. *What a week!* she thought morosely.

HOPE ANSWERED THE KNOCK, opening the door to her apartment.

"Chase!"

He stood in a t-shirt and jeans, a small, leather duffle bag slung over his shoulder.

He craned his neck around her at Phillip, who laid on his stomach, one arm dragging on the floor, eyes closed, mouth open.

"What the hell...?" Chase began.

"Hope, honey," Phillip drawled. "I think there's somebody at the door."

Frowning at him, she stepped into the hall, closing the door behind her. "He's drunk," was all the explanation she offered.

Chase lifted his head. "We need to talk."

"Well, we can't talk out here."

He grabbed her hand, dropping his bag in the hall and then led her toward the stairwell. They climbed to the top, opened a door and stepped out on the roof. She paced over to where a low brick wall defined the building's edge. Staring down from the dizzying height, she felt her stomach lurch and her knees go weak.

"I can't believe that s.o.b. came back here after what he did," Chase muttered.

She spun around in fury, tears blinding her. "Don't be a hypocrite, Chase!" she spat.

He actually nodded his head. Not like he agreed with her, but as if she'd proved something to him. "What do you mean?"

"You know exactly what I mean." She rushed toward him, heading for the door to the stairwell. "I can't do this!"

He grabbed her arm as she passed and spun her around. "Dammit, Hope, we're going to talk about this!"

"Okay. Okay!" she screamed, hitting him and pushing away. "We'll talk about it then." She walked over to the low wall again and leaned her arms down on it, this time oblivious to the drop-off below.

The conversation with Jack Delaney replayed in her head. "You...hold yourself back too much. Don't take risks. In your writing, and I daresay, in your personal life... If there is one thing I've learned in my fifty-some-odd years of life, it is life isn't worth living if you're not willing to take a risk now and then."

She whirled back around, taking a deep breath and looking him straight in the eye. "I'm talking about you and Susie McNamara."

"What?"

"Dammit, Chase! Do you need to hear me say it?"

"Yes, I guess I do."

"I heard you, all right? I heard you that night!" Her eyes blazed with anger and tears ran down her face.

"I don't understand what you are talking about."

"Ahhh! I don't know why you have to do this to me!" She bit her lip, again fighting an urge to turn away. "Chip Carter told me. He told me that you had been seeing Susie behind my back. Dropping me off nights and going to her." A sob escaped. "And, you g-got her pregnant."

"Hope!" He made a move to comfort her, but she stepped away.

"No! Don't touch me!"

He turned his back on her. After a few seconds, he asked her, "And you just believed Chip?" His anger was evident in his voice..

"No! No, of course not. I'm not an idiot." She took a shuddering breath and her eyes took on a distant look. "But then I saw you. You were with Susie. You told her 'Hope wouldn't mind' 'she and the baby came first,' and that you'd be there for her. And then, and then...you kissed." She staggered two steps backward, spinning around and covering her face with her hands, shoulders shaking.

He froze, silent as seconds ticked by. "Wait! I remember now! Susie was concerned you would be mad because I stayed away so long talking to her at the dance, so I told her you wouldn't mind, she and the baby came first and I'd help see her through it, as a *friend*. The baby wasn't mine; it was Chip Carter's."

She whirled around. Her mind struggled to grasp what she had heard. She stared at him, speechless for several seconds. "Y-you didn't cheat on me?" Her mind was slow to comprehend. "You never cheated on me?"

He moved forward, touching her arms. "No," he answered definitively. "I could never have done that to you. I was in love with you." His words were like a cool salve for all the old wounds she had carried with her since prom night. Without warning, she broke down, and he held her, both of them sinking to their knees.

"Oh, God! I'm sorry. I didn't want to believe him, but when I saw the two of you kissing..."

"She did kiss me. And I told her in no uncertain terms you were the only girl for me. And then I left her to find you."

"And I was gone."

"Yeah," he said dryly. There was a pause. He pulled away a little, looking her in the eyes. "So, that's why you left town with Chip? Because you thought I had gotten Susie pregnant?"

"I didn't leave town with Chip."

"What? Come on. We need to be honest with each other. You're not going to tell me you weren't making out with him in the parking lot, and it's just coincidence you both disappeared the same night without explanation?"

"That's exactly what I'm saying, yes. I didn't leave town with him. My gosh, Chase, I still hated him for making my life so miserable with all those rumors he spread about me. And as far as making out in the parking lot goes, I was upset and he offered me a ride and then he..."

"Made a move on you?"

"Yes. And I, well, I...kicked him...in the crotch, and walked home."

He laughed. After a beat he questioned, "You walked home from the high school?"

"Yes."

"That's a long way!"

"Yeah. Especially in high heels. Though, as I recall, I ditched those pretty soon and walked the rest of the way in my panty hose." They shifted to sit on the rooftop, Chase with one knee up and his arm around her, who had her knees curled to one side and was leaning into him.

"And no one stopped to offer you a ride home?"

"Oh, sure. I got offers. All from guys. And I'd had enough of guys that night."

He snorted and then they sat in a daze, absorbing all the new information they had learned and reexamining the night in its new context. After a few minutes, he put his hand under her chin, lifting her face and gazing into her eyes. He asked softly the question she now knew he had been asking himself for eight years. "So why *did* you leave me, then?"

She cringed, hearing the hurt in his voice, the hurt he had been living with for so long. "I didn't leave you." She paused, remembering. "When I got home that night, there were movers everywhere. My mother was packing everything. She had it planned all along. She had talked to my teachers and everything. She was worried about my dad coming after us again, so she waited until I had my senior prom, not telling me anything for fear of spoiling it for me, and we moved that night. She was especially ready to go after she had heard...my version...of what happened at the dance."

He squeezed her to his side, closing his eyes and sighing. "I can't believe this!"

"All this time..."

They sat for several minutes in silence. Then, she pulled away to turn and look at him. "You thought I left with *Chip Carter?*"

He laughed. "I know, it doesn't make much sense, but none of it did. You were there, and then—"

"I was gone."

"And Kyle Stockwell told me he saw you going 'hot and heavy' with Chip in the parking lot."

"Chase," she murmured, touching his face, "I am *so* sorry."

He took her hand from his face and kissed it. "No, Hope. We are both to blame, and both blameless, in a way. Man, if I ever see that Chip Carter..."

"I remember now!" Hope sat up, excited. "Chip told me his parents had made him join the Army. He was leaving the next day."

"They probably wanted to get him away from the whole Susie mess."

"Yeah. And he told me he was giving me my last shot at him. I have never met anyone with such a high opinion of himself."

He laughed, hugging her to him again. They sat in the quiet on the roof, the sound of traffic distant, alone in a city filled with millions of people. "So that's why you were so upset with me last night. The whole Phillip thing—"

"Stirred up a lot of bad memories for me." She was quiet. "What Phillip did upset me, made me feel angry and hurt. But when I thought you had cheated on me, I was devastated."

He turned her to face him again. "You left before I won my award last night. When I was up on stage I thanked Hal and the crew and you."

"Me?"

"Yes. I thanked you for being the inspiration for every love song I've ever written, and I told everyone listening that I loved you. I always have, Hope. And I always will." He leaned in and kissed her in a way he had never kissed her before, as if giving her all the old wounds of the past along with all his hopes for the future.

She was stunned. "You said that on TV?"

He laughed. "Yes, I did. Didn't you see a newspaper today?"

She shook her head, thinking about the day she'd had. After getting fired, she'd come home to find Phillip on her doorstep. The day had gone from miserable to one step beyond miserable.

"Well, everyone wants to know who 'the mystery woman' is who inspired my music. I'm afraid you will be hounded for awhile."

They sat in silence again. She spoke what was in both of their hearts. "So, what do we do now?"

He helped her to her feet. "We start over." He took her hand in his. "I heard you want to be a pilot, or a photographer."

"That's right!"

He chuckled, and then pulled her in to kiss her once more, passionately.

When he pulled away, she said, "My, you're fresh! We just met a minute ago."

"Are you complaining?" He grinned, raising an eyebrow.

"No way!" She stood on her tiptoes to kiss him. "I love you."

He sighed happily. "Gosh, I've been waiting a long time to hear you say that!"

They stood in the comfort of each other's arms for awhile, until he heard her muffled voice from his chest. "I want to be alone with you, but we can't go down to my place. Phillip's there."

"And we can't go to my penthouse. I heard it's already being staked out for signs of 'The Mystery Woman.' I could get us another hotel room?"

"Ooh! A clandestine meeting, sounds interesting."

"No. If this is going to be our first time...alone together—"

"You mean making love?" she queried with a wicked grin.

"—then it needs to be special. Intimate, not—"

"Tawdry?"

"Exactly."

"Hum." She pretended to pout.

"Come on. I'm being serious."

"I'm sorry," she said with a chuckle. "What about putting Phillip in a cab?"

He seemed to contemplate this briefly, then grinned. "Let's pack him up."

When they got inside the apartment, Phillip was snoring loudly.

"Now that's just pathetic," he muttered without sympathy.

She called a cab, and then paged through the phone book again.

"What are you doing?"

"Looking up Liz McPherson's address."

"Who's Liz McPherson?"

She jotted something down. "The slut who was with Phillip in the conference room." She ripped the page off with a sense of satisfaction. "Here, give this to the cabbie."

"Ohh!" he chortled. "You're bad."

She kissed him on the nose. "Yes, but that's what attracted you to me in the first place."

CHAPTER EIGHTEEN

Chase thought about her the whole way down in the elevator, and as he assisted the stumbling Phillip into the cab. He liked the grown-up Hope. Now that she was feeling comfortable with him again, and was able to joke around more, he found her to be even sexier than before. The elevator ride back up, anticipating being with her, was exquisitely painful.

He knocked on the door. She opened it.

"Hel-l-l-o," she purred, her hand running up the doorframe beguilingly. She had changed into a sheer black blouse over a silky black camisole and jeans. He could feel his willpower flying out the window.

"Hel-l-l-o!" he answered in kind. He grabbed her by the hips, a huge smile on his face.

She backed into the room, dragging him with her, and closed the door. She pressed him against the door, playing with his long hair seductively.

He cleared his throat. "I've never seen this side of you."

"I'm not sure she existed before tonight." She sauntered away, and he watched the tantalizing sashay of her hips without moving. "Do you want some wine?" she asked over her shoulder.

"Not really." The words carried a suggestive tone.

She smiled at him. "I think I need some. I'm nervous," she confessed.

He laughed in surprise. "You don't seem like it."

"I'm weird that way."

"Good to know."

"Oh my gosh, Chase! Does Hal know where you are?"

He snorted. "Of course, he does." He reached over the arm of the chair and rubbed a sleeping Mr. Mewford behind his ear. "I think the man had a tracking device embedded somewhere on my body so he can know where I am at all times. Actually," he said more seriously, "he sends his love. He...encouraged me, with some rather strong words this morning, to come out here and make things right with you. What he didn't know is I had already called a pilot and had my jet fueled."

She smiled, raising her glass of wine. "To Hal," she murmured. She took a gulp and then brought her glass to the table and sat on the couch, patting the seat next to her. He came and sat down, now suddenly feeling nervous himself. She took a long sip of her wine, and then set it down again, touching his hand lightly. They both studied their hands while she talked.

"This is strange, isn't it?" She rubbed her fingers over his hand; her voice was tender and sweet. "First, you were my childhood friend. Then, you were my teenage crush. Then"—she sucked in her breath—"we were a pair of idiots. And now..." She raised her eyes to meet his, and a charge of electricity arced between them. "Now we're adults who have always loved each other, but spent years apart." He turned toward her and rested his elbow against the top of the couch, cheek in his hand as she spoke. She reached up and touched his face, her hand trembling. She continued talking, as if to herself. "I dreamed about this, about you..." Her thumb brushed across his lips, and he closed his eyes, sucking in his breath. Without seeing her approach, her lips were on his. They explored, experimenting. He noted each sensation, both familiar and long-missed.

Just as abruptly as her kisses had started, they ended. He opened his eyes slowly, and she stood and took his hand. He followed her wordlessly, fascinated by her, as she led him to the bedroom. When she dressed earlier, she must have lit candles; now they shimmered about them. She still had the white, wrought iron bed he remembered her having as a child. She shut the door on Mr. Mewford, who had followed them, with a soft, "Go on, now." She continued to lead him to the side of the bed, and then turned to him, looking unsure about what was to happen next.

Taking his cue, he brought his hand to the back of her neck, and tilted her chin up. He kissed her, running his hand slowly over her exposed neck. To have her here, finally, awakened everything in him. His heart raced, and his head swam with desire. The physical need radiated from his core, gripping him and setting his nerves on full throttle. The candlelight played on her hair, making its golden highlights sparkle. He pulled away and started to unbutton her shirt unhurriedly. When it was loose, he pushed it off, running his hands down the smooth skin of her shoulders and down her arms. He kissed her neck slowly, as if he didn't want to miss any inch of her. As he started to slide the strap of her camisole down, he felt her shiver. He stopped.

"You're shaking."

"I'm scared," she admitted.

"Of me?" he said in surprise.

"You are the only one I'd be scared with. Doing this with you...you are the only one who has ever meant so much. I don't want to mess up."

"Hope." Suddenly, he didn't want to hurt her; she was so fragile. "Maybe we're rushing this. We've only known each other a short time as adults." He started to move his hand, and she covered it with her own.

"No, please, Chase." Her voice was almost hoarse. "Don't stop. I've waited so long. I want you so badly."

Her words pushed him over the brink. *She wanted him!* How many times had fans screamed they "wanted" him? But he had longed to hear it from only one woman, this woman. And he knew there was no turning back for him now. He lowered his mouth to hers. With each kiss he claimed more of her, drawing her up and into him.

They took things slowly, finding each other again, finding each other for the first time.

They both appreciated they would never have this again, this first time together. They took off their clothing piece by piece, and viewed with their eyes, touched with hands and mouths, appraising, approving, wanting, but trying to hold down desire, until restraint was no longer an option. He caught their reflection in the mirror and was turned on all the more. He lifted her and laid her on the bed.

She was more beautiful than he had ever imagined. He lay with her and let his hands travel over her taut stomach to the luscious curve of her hips, his own body responding with each sensation his hands offered. Her feet were delicately shaped, and the calves were a wonder in and of themselves, their muscles rounded, but firm. She bent supple knees, drawing him upward, moving him to her center.

Chase's touch was liquid fire, a prairie fire, sweeping along her, racing out of control. Her body anticipated where his fingers would go, trembling with impatience. Wherever he touched her, the next inch beyond his fingertips begged for him to roam there, too. Her hands ran over his wide, solid chest, over broad, hard shoulders, and along his back, clutching with desperation. It had never, *never* been this way before. She had never felt this overwhelming need to be closer to someone, to melt together so that the lines became blurred, to form each other as one. Being pressed together, flesh against flesh, was not enough, not nearly enough. She wanted to take him into her, to offer herself up willingly to whatever need he had. She wanted to please him more than she had ever wanted to please a man before.

What started out slowly, with respect and wonder, ended up in wild abandon, each completely trusting in the other's ability to fulfill them, to value and to cherish them. It was the first time either had made love with both their bodies and their whole hearts, and the experience was mind-blowing.

As he journeyed over her body, he discovered unexpectedly erotic places, like when he kissed her delicate ankles or pushed his tongue between the flesh behind her curled knee, arousing them both. She was ready for him, wanting to be complete, but he wasn't finished yet. His strong hands flipped her onto her stomach. He explored the flesh of her rear, and then pressed his palms into her hips, allowing his fingers to venture to her front side, grasping her along her pelvic bone. She tightened. He was in control of her there and she wanted more of it. Instead, he slid his fingers over the curve of her butt and down the slope of the small of her back. He spread his hands out as they trailed up her back, along her shoulders.

She felt his tongue trailing along her shoulder blades, nipping at her as he brought himself down on her, his weight pleasant, his hardness, the feel of his skin against hers, the heat, sending yet another spasm of delight through her. She lifted herself on her arms, throwing her head back to reach him. He moved her hair to one side and brought his mouth to her neck, applying pressure with his teeth in a primal way that forced a moan from her lips. His hands slid to feel the fullness of her breasts, the hardness of her nipples as he pressed them between his fingers. She was surprised by the strength of her desire and drunk on his power to sway her. He lifted himself suddenly and she took the opportunity to turn over.

They stopped all movement, staring into each other's eyes, wild with the passion of their bodies and the ardor of their hearts. His hair fell forward and she could see his muscles bulging as he held himself above her. Her hands rested on his chest, waiting for him. He brought himself down and into her while gazing on her face. She closed her eyes, and they both released the pressure of wondering what it would feel like when, at last, he was inside her.

They savored the sensation momentarily, and then he began moving. Her hips rose to meet him, her hands slipping down to his rear to pull him in with each potent thrust. Her face contorted and her breathing came quickly until she let out a gasp of ecstasy. Her body relaxed and she ran her hands along his back, barely letting them touch as she soaked in her pleasure. He let her enjoy the feeling before he moved again, and she let out a gasp of surprise as another silvery shiver stirred within her.

He drove deeper and deeper, until their passion peaked and they collapsed together. Her nails raked gently along his sides, holding him close, without the will to release him. Reluctantly, after a time, she loosened her grip. He kissed her on the forehead tenderly before falling beside her on the mattress, letting his breathing return to normal.

In the moments right after their lovemaking had ended, Chase lay with her in his arms, enveloped in utter bliss, unable to speak.

"You are...*incredible!*" he breathed finally.

She rolled on top of him impetuously, her arms crossed on his chest, her head on top of her arms. She smiled brightly. "I'm so glad you said that, 'cause there is nothing to make you doubt your...abilities...like having someone cheat on you."

"Hope, your sexual prowess isn't that important to me."

She frowned. "I'm not sure that is a compliment," she teased.

"You know what I mean. I mean...if you could never make love again, I'd be okay with it."

"Again, not sounding like a compliment."

"What I'm trying to say is I love you for more than just your body."

She pouted.

"Not that there is anything wrong with your body, your body is fantastic, it's just there is more to it than that."

She continued to stare at him, enjoying the way she made him squirm and watching his backpedaling spiral downward. "I'm just saying—"

"If you couldn't do me at least once a day, your life would have no meaning?" She walked her hands up his chest as she said it in a most beguiling way.

He smiled. "Okay, I'm going with that. That's my answer."

"Good!" she cried cheerfully, kissing him on the nose.

He grabbed her around the waist and flipped her so it was he gazing down on her beautiful face in the candlelight. She laughed, and he kissed her happily. Then, he became serious. He leaned on his elbow, rubbing her smooth skin, not able to get enough of her.

"You know, I came to find you at Mizzou."

Her eyes flickered with surprise. "You did?"

He nodded. "I wasn't able to get away until about a month after school started. I had started a daytime job at Mr. McCoy's. You remember Mr. McCoy's?"

"The candy store across from the school? Of course! How did you land that sweet job? No pun intended."

"I don't know." He shrugged. "Maybe because Mr. McCoy was always sweet on me."

"Oh, that was bad!"

"And yours wasn't?" He tweaked her nose playfully. "Anyway, I worked days there, and nights I was wrapped up singing. But, I finally had a day off and I went to find you, to straighten things out between us. But, as I went to climb the stairs into the dorm, I saw you in the window...with a guy."

"Oh!" She felt as though she had the wind knocked out of her. "I'm sorry. I'm so sor—"

He put a finger to her lips. "Sh-sh-sh! No, no! That's not why I told you. I didn't want you to feel bad." He gazed at her. "I just wanted you to know, I didn't give up on us easily. I came for you."

"Thank you." She reached up to pull him in for a kiss. Tears trickled down her cheeks.

"I shouldn't have walked away," he added regretfully. "I should have stayed and we could have talked things out like we did tonight. I should have fought harder."

"We can't undo the mistakes we made in the past. I'm just so thankful we have a second chance. And I'm glad you told me I mattered enough to you that you tried to find me. I always wondered," she ended quietly.

He took her hand and kissed it. "I don't know if I can ever explain to you how much you mean to me, Hope. After you left, it took me a long time to get my head on straight, and even then, a day didn't pass without me thinking of you." Tears began pouring down her face. "Oh, honey! I didn't mean to make you cry."

"No," she answered, choked up. "It's just...I'm so happy. I had kind of given up hope that I could ever love anyone again. And the idea of making my way back to you...well, it was too much to hope for." They kissed, and then snuggled closer together, their fingers intertwined, almost afraid to sleep for fear it might all slip away.

"Chase?"

"Hmmm?"

"I'm sorry I didn't believe in us more. I should have at least given you a chance to explain."

"Hope, like you said, it's all in the past. And besides, I've been thinking about that. Do you think maybe it is because of how your father was, the things he told you constantly? Maybe he made you feel, I don't know...undeserving of love. Maybe that made it easier to believe Chip's lies?"

She couldn't believe how well he knew her, perhaps better than she knew herself. "I thought about that, too," she responded slowly. "I think he kind of messed me up in a lot of ways. He made me afraid to reach too far, to stray too far from my comfort zone..." she trailed off, deep in thought.

He squeezed her and turned so they were both on their sides, his arms wrapped around her, and eventually, they fell asleep.

CHAPTER NINETEEN

When Chase woke up, he found his arms still around her. It wasn't a dream. His mind flashed back to the night before, remembering all the confessions and promises it held. Then, as he breathed in the sweet fragrance of her hair, he started remembering more, a rapid fire series of sensations—the way she had looked as they stood naked in the candlelight, the sound of her moan as his tongue traveled along her thigh, her hands clenching the iron bars of the headboard in her ecstasy, and her warmth as she had finally melted into his arms and fallen asleep.

He carefully sat up on his elbow so he could peek at her peaceful face. He played with a few stray hairs that fell along her neck. Then, unable to resist, he kissed her there.

She stretched languidly beside him. "Chase, tell me that's you and not just a wonderful dream I had," she said sleepily, without turning over.

He kissed her more along her neck, then nuzzled her ear, whispering seductively, "It better be me."

She turned over slowly, and he felt her breasts brush his chest. She peered at him for several seconds, her eyes seeming to soak in each detail of his face. Then, impulsively, she threw her arms around him and squeezed him tighter than he thought she could, holding on until her arms grew tired. "Oh, I'm never letting you out of this bed."

"Sounds good to me," he responded, his cheek against hers, his eyes squeezed shut with emotion. All of a sudden, he sat up, taking the covers with him. "Oh, geez! You're going to be late for work."

She clutched at the covers. "No. Come back. I don't have to go in today. I was fired."

"You what?"

"My boss fired me yesterday."

"But...why? Did it have anything to do with Phillip?"

"No. He told me I didn't 'put myself out there' in my writing, or in my personal life."

He thought about this. "Well, do you think that's true?"

She sighed. "I think he was pretty much right on the money. Until last night." She reached up and stroked his face, and he smiled.

He lay back down, and she snuggled next to him again. "Actually, this is great. You can come on tour with me now, if you want. It's just a short one, three months." She didn't respond. "Don't you want to come?"

She sat up, leaning on his chest. "Oh, babe, I want to come. Nothing in the world sounds better...but I have some things I have to take care of here first."

His face clouded. "Does this have to do with Phillip?"

"No. As far as I'm concerned, everything with Phillip is long over."

"I'm not so sure he knows that."

She thought about this. "No. I think he will move on now. He's a smart guy. I think he's probably figured out I'm in love with you and he has no chance."

"I still don't like the idea of him being here, and my being gone."

She lay across his chest, putting her head down. "It'll be okay, Chase, I promise."

"Okay. Well, I just don't like the idea of my being gone, then. I've finally got you back, and I have to leave. It sucks! Maybe I'll just call Hal and cancel the tour."

She lifted her head. "You can't do that! We can wait a little longer to be together."

"Honestly, Hope, I don't know if I can. Besides, you said you were fired. What could you have to do?"

She rolled back over into his arms. "I just have some...unfinished business. Something I have to do for myself. By myself."

He frowned. "You're being awfully mysterious."

"I'm not meaning to be. I'm not sure I even understand it myself. I just need to take one more shot at proving myself to my boss. Then I can walk away." She looked him in the eye. "I'll come as soon as I can. It's just something I have to do."

He squeezed her head, kissing the top of her hair, feeling the heartache beginning. He pushed it away. He would not let it ruin the time they had left together.

"When do you have to leave?" she asked quietly.

He sighed. "Tomorrow morning, at the latest."

"Oh!" she breathed, and he could hear the surprise and extreme disappointment in that one short exclamation.

"We'll just have to make the best of our time together."

She exhaled.

"Hope?"

"Hmmm?"

"I'm starving."

Her laugh sounded like bells ringing. "Well, I guess we'll have to do something about that." She flounced out of bed, completely naked, and headed to the kitchen.

He sat up and watched her through the doorway as she started the coffee, and then came back to pull on some clothes. "Do you always walk around your apartment naked?" he asked, amused.

"Not always." She smiled. "But, I figure I'm too high up for anyone to see me from the street, and no one can see over from the building across the way because it's too far." She had pulled on a pair of sexy red panties and an over-sized t-shirt he thought must belong to Phillip until he saw the symbol on it.

"Hey! Isn't that my t-shirt?"

"Uhhh...maybe?" she answered with a guilty look on her face. "One time we got caught in the rain, and you let me borrow it...and I kind of"—she rushed the rest of her answer—"purposefully didn't give it back."

"Why you little thief!" He grinned widely. "It looks better on you than it does on me anyway. Come here," he growled.

"Uh-uh! Not yet." She scurried into the bathroom and he could hear the water running. A few minutes later, she returned. She smiled. "I had to brush my teeth first."

"Not fair." He swung his legs out of bed. He grabbed his underwear off the floor and pulled them on. "Just wait there." He disappeared into the bathroom for a few minutes, then rushed past her and jumped into bed, pulling the covers up. "Okay. Now you can come."

She ran over and jumped playfully into bed with him. He grabbed her, kissing her deeply, rubbing his hands over her legs, to the back of her thighs and slipping a finger or two underneath the elastic of her lacy panties.

"What...about...breakfast?" she asked between kisses.

He pulled away and grinned at her wickedly. "To hell with breakfast!"

With a suddenness that made her gasp, he rolled them over so he was now straddling her. He began kissing her neck and let his hands wander under her t-shirt. The skin was soft as he slid his hands along her sides tantalizingly, not yet touching her breasts, but letting her know wordlessly that he intended to. His lips were on hers, and she picked her head up off the pillow in a reflexive effort. Taking advantage of her positioning, he pulled the pilfered t-shirt over her head.

He left her lips with a teasing pull, sucking on her lower lip before releasing it to slowly move down her body. She gripped the bedposts, tense with withheld passion. His mouth reached her panty line and his hands pulled gently, slowly on the lace, removing her panties and tossing them aside.

"Oh, Chase!" She moaned.

The way she called out to him made him come unglued. He loved the feeling of having her pleasure in his control. Millions of women had called out his name, giving him unsolicited kisses, offering any variety of sexual pleasures, but all he had ever wanted was for Hope to desire him.

He came up abruptly to lie on top of her, catching her biting her lip. Her arms were taut as she squeezed the wrought iron above her head. She stilled, allowing herself to relax into the bed momentarily.

"Tell me you want me, Hope." His voice came out husky and commanding and he knew it gave away his need for her, held the memory of the pain of having lost her once. He gazed into her eyes, liquid with desire.

"Oh, do I want you, Chase!" She grabbed the back of his neck and pulled him down, kissing him feverishly, recklessly, with animal-like intensity.

After a minute, he pulled away to stand beside the bed, both of them breathing heavily. She watched him take off his underwear, and then he came back to her, taking the pace down again. He kissed her stomach and trailed his tongue over her skin to her breast, sucking her nipple into his mouth and applying subtle pressure with his teeth.

She arched with pleasure and he closed down harder. Her nails dug into his back and he came up to seek her mouth. He pulled away to watch her face. Her eyes were, at first, squeezed shut. He slid inside her and her eyes opened, the unusual sunbursts of her irises seeming to glow, searing him with a burning intensity. He felt her hands slide down to his rear, and her hips begin to move beneath him. He stilled, spellbound by her movements and the feelings they sent rocketing through him. And then, they were moving in tandem, driving forward until they were jointly released from passion's hold and lay sweetly spent.

"You..." He gave a low laugh; there were no words to describe what they had found together. "Wow!"

She laughed, still panting, "Yeah!"

They fell apart, only their hands touching, breathing in the calm after the storm of their lovemaking. Hope drifted peacefully off. He stroked her arm gently, each pass extending beyond the last in a rhythmic way. After a few minutes, she stirred, opening her eyes. "Mmm. I almost fell back asleep. I'm sorry."

"No, I was just watching you. You're beautiful when you sleep."

She smiled and reached her hand up to stroke the side of his face. He brought her hand to his mouth and kissed the inside of her palm.

"I never knew love could be like this."

He gently pushed the hair from her face, noting how fresh and innocent she looked in the morning light without any makeup.

"I should get you that breakfast."

She moved to get up and he pulled her down for one last kiss. "We'll do it together."

CHASE STOOD BY ONE of the four long windows in the living room finishing his cup of coffee. They had enjoyed a breakfast of French toast and fresh fruit, and he had grabbed a quick shower. Hope was in the bathroom now; he could hear the water running in the next room. Suddenly, his keen eyes sighted a man on the roof of the building across the street. He was peering into a telescope lens. When Chase saw him, the man straightened and looked in his direction with his naked eye. Chase calmly finished drinking his coffee, and then took his cup to the sink.

Knowing he was now out of sight of the telescope, he grabbed his jacket and slipped out the door. He ducked into the stairwell and flew down the stairs, hoping to catch the culprit before he decided to leave. He came out of the door of The Claw-Foot Condominiums and didn't waste time getting to the street corner. Ignoring honks and hand gestures, he dodged cars and taxis to get to the building on the opposite side of the street. Once inside, he stood panting with his hands on his hips, impatiently watching the dial above the elevator door as it showed the elevator's slow descent. When the doors opened, he waited, with growing irritation, for all the riders to get off. Luckily, no one else was waiting for the elevator, and he was able to make a nonstop trip to the top of the building.

Once there, he quickly noted the separate staircase to the roof. He hit the door and burst out onto the roof breathing hard. The person at the telescope jumped at the noise, but, to Chase's surprise, didn't run.

"So it *was* really Chase Hatton," he said, almost to himself.

Chase stared at the stranger in surprise. This was not what he had expected, a teenager with bushy red hair and glasses wearing a Cubs jersey and jeans. He decided to switch gears. He wanted to get near enough to the telescope to confirm his suspicions.

"Yes." He stepped closer, extending his hand with a smile, although part of him wanted to beat the kid's face in. "Hi, I'm Chase."

The kid stepped forward and shook his hand eagerly. "My name's Kip Taylor."

"Nice to meet you, Kip. What grade are you in?"

"I'm a junior."

Chase angled even closer to the telescope. "Go to school near here?"

"Yeah, Independence High. It's a dump."

"Is that so?" Chase bent down to peek in the telescope. Even though he saw what he thought he would, he still was shocked to look in on Hope in her bedroom in the middle of getting dressed. What was most surprising was the clarity and detail with which he could see. He might as well have been in the room with her. He couldn't help but notice how hot she looked. He was suddenly furious.

When he lifted his incensed eyes to meet the young teen's, it was readily apparent the latter had come to an epiphany of sorts, realizing the rock star might not be too keen on him checking out his girlfriend when she was in the buff.

Kip backed up. "Uh-h-h...listen, Mr. Hatton..." He turned to run, but Chase's rage catapulted him across the rooftop. He grabbed the teen's jersey and shoved him against the door to the stairs. He wished he was a grown man, because intimidating a high schooler wasn't nearly as satisfying. He turned the youth around to talk to him, still keeping a tight grip on his jersey.

"Listen, man! Like when you were young, you didn't look at pretty naked girls?"

Chase remembered their early morning activities. "You w-watched us..." he sputtered.

"What? Gettin' it on? Yeah. It was much hotter than when she was with that other dude," he added. "She's much more into you. I can tell." He chuckled coarsely.

At any other time Chase would have taken a warped sort of pride in the kid's statement, but now he was concerned that he was looking in on Hope. "How long have you been watching her?"

"Uh...since my birthday last June. Gr-r-reat birthday present! Huh-huh." He chuckled again.

Either this kid is dumber than a bag of rocks, or he just doesn't care if I pulverize him.

"Listen, dude, if you're worried about me telling reporters or something where the 'Mystery Lady' lives, don't worry. I respect your guys' privacy." He nodded his head up and down knowingly.

Chase almost laughed out loud. *Respects our privacy? Is he for real?* But then it dawned on him, the kid was right. He could put the press on to them and make their lives miserable. He knew it was bound to happen anyway, but he wanted to forestall it as long as possible. He'd put something over Hope's windows; he couldn't do anything about what the kid had seen thus far anyway.

"Listen, *dude,*" he said through clenched teeth. "I don't want to see you looking in her window anymore. You got that! ANYMORE!" He banged the teen against the wall again for emphasis. The kid's disappointment was evident on his face. "I mean it. If I so much as suspect you're ogling her, I'm gonna come back here and launch your telescope over the ledge, and you after it, got it?"

"Okay," Kip replied begrudgingly, lowering his head.

"Can I get your promise, Kip?"

"I promise, Chase." He hung his head. "Hey, do you think I could get some concert tickets?" he asked, brightening and lifting his head.

"You've got to be kidding me?" Chase released him with a sigh. He shook his head, and started down the stairwell, slamming the door behind him.

"MY GOSH, CHASE! I THOUGHT you'd run out on me already," Hope cried when he walked in the door.

"Sorry, baby," he said, grabbing her hips and kissing her neck playfully. "I had to take care of something."

"What?" She arched a brow in suspicion.

"Come here." He led her to the windows, standing behind her with his arms around her waist. He pointed to the opposite rooftop. "See that telescope."

"Uh-huh."

"It's pointed at your apartment."

She paled. "Pointed at my... Can he see anything?"

"Oh yeah!" He felt the hair rise on her arms and he caught her frightened reflection in the glass. "Now don't worry. I went over there and explained a few things to him. He won't be looking this way anymore."

"How can you be sure?"

He could tell in her voice this was really upsetting her. He squeezed his arms around her harder, reminding her nonverbally he was there to protect her. "We had a gentlemen's agreement, or more like, a gentleman-to-teenager agreement."

"Teenager?" she asked weakly. "I don't know if that makes it better or worse." She jumped a little with a gasp. "Did he see us...?"

He nodded and she moaned, leaning into him. "But he said it was way hotter than what he'd seen in here before," he couldn't help but add.

Her body tensed. "He saw Phillip and me? How long has he been watching us?"

Chase ignored the question, whispering in her ear, "And he said you were way more into me than Phillip."

"Your voice sounds so sexy in my ears." She melted again and made a little purring noise in her throat before laughing. "Do I hear a note of pride?" He chuckled. She turned in his arms, touching his face. "That must be one hell of a telescope!"

"It is," he acknowledged.

She paused a minute, seeming to absorb this information. She sighed. "I guess I can either choose to be upset by this situation or let it go." She looked up into his face. "Did you see me?"

He nodded, grinning widely.

She moved her fingers in little circles on his chest, then lifted her head, batting her eyelashes. "And did you like what you saw?"

"Uum-hum," he answered, kissing her.

"Mmm. We need to put something over the windows."

He nodded and she sprang from his arms, running into the other room. She called over her shoulder, "I'll get some beach towels."

CHAPTER TWENTY

Hope had explained to Chase she had only one thing she needed to do today and that was clean out her desk at *The Chicago Globe News*, so the pair headed to the building in a cab. Riding the subway would be impossible with him along, and he insisted on coming, if only to wait in the parking garage for her. As soon as they were underway, he grabbed her hand and they sat in comfortable silence, each thinking about how lucky they were and how strange it was fate had brought them back together.

Leaving him in the cab to make some phone calls, she collected a box from the mailroom and proceeded to her desk, only to find a staff meeting was going on in a glassed-in office directly across the hall from it. As she approached, she happened to catch Phillip whispering something in Liz's ear in an intimate way, until he glanced up and saw her. His face, which had been animated, froze in midsentence for a second, and then he completed his conversation and turned away.

She tried to ignore what she had just seen, placing personal items in the box one by one, thinking about how strange it would be not to come back here after all these years. Hearing thunderous footsteps, she looked up to find the fast-striding figure of Jack Delaney barreling down the hall toward her.

"Hope. Good to see you." He stopped by her desk. "I heard some inner-office gossip; Phillip Rutledge is seeing Liz McPherson..." She studied his face to judge whether or not this was meant to be hurtful. He looked warm, even...kind. He sat on the corner of her desk. "I also heard Chase Hatton's acceptance speech at The People's Choice Awards." He leaned in and spoke confidentially, "I see you're taking my advice." He winked and stood up, giving her arm a squeeze and chuckling quietly. "Good luck."

She stared after him in wonder. The man seemed hurried and oblivious, but in fact, he was well aware of everything that was happening around him, not to mention, his wizard-like ability to see inside her. He reached for the knob on the conference room door, but then turned back to her. "Oh, and Hope, I trust you haven't given up on your writing completely?"

"No." She smiled warmly. "I'm hoping to do some freelancing."

He opened the door, speaking loudly. "I expect you will give me first crack on any pieces you write?" All the faces in the conference room turned toward them.

"Yes, Mr. Delaney"—her blue eyes danced with delight—"I'll do that."

He winked and turned to enter the room. She felt certain he had wanted the others to hear their conversation, especially Phillip, she decided. She grinned and shook her head as she turned back to her task. As she worked, Jack Delaney's usual blustery words carried out to her.

"Okay, people, this'll be a quick one. I have a source telling me Antonio Vasculli, who has long been rumored to have mob ties, has had some unsavory dealings with our own city councilman, Robert Mulrooney. I don't need to tell you all if we could crack this story, it would be huge. So keep your ears to the wind. Also..."

Hope tuned out the rumbling voice. Antonio Vasculli and Mulrooney? This was it! This was her story. If she could get this story and prove herself, she could walk away from this life and start her new one with Chase. She glanced up and saw no one was looking her way. She moved over to a neighboring computer someone had left on. Her fingers began to fly over the keyboard, pulling up article after article on Vasculli. The society pages showed him with a number of women, at every social event under the sun. On paper, his money appeared to come from his monstrous shipping business, but he had been accused in the past of everything from drug running and money laundering, to murder for hire. She was so caught up in digging through the paper's files, she almost didn't notice when the meeting adjourned. Out of the corner of her eye, she saw her former boss eating up carpet with his long strides, and she quickly emailed the information to her home computer and wiped the screen blank. He nodded to her briskly and proceeded down the hall without stopping. She sighed in relief, then gathered the rest of her things and left as fast as she could to avoid contact with Phillip.

She entered the elevator and was just congratulating herself on avoiding a scene when, without warning, a hand appeared between the narrowing crack of the closing doors. Phillip jumped in.

They stood awkwardly for a beat, both trying to foresee what was to come next. "Hope, how are you?"

She shifted her box, uneasy. "Fine. And you?"

"I'm good," he said hastily. "Listen, Hope, I'm sorry about last night."

"No need to apologize."

"No, I really am sorry." There was an uncomfortable silence that she filled by mentally moving the elevator down the shaft. Abruptly, Phillip turned to her. "This is all a mistake, us breaking up, I mean. I love you. Liz was just, well, there, and I was weak. I needed you and you were half a world away with Mr. Wonderful."

"Phillip, I don't want to hear—"

He grabbed her behind the neck without warning, and with the box between them, pressed his lips to hers. She was shocked to realize his breath tasted like alcohol; it was only ten o'clock in the morning! He forced his tongue into her mouth, and she was violently repulsed. She brought a hand up to push him away, and lost hold of the box, dumping its contents just as they hit the bottom floor. They both bent to pick up her belongings, Phillip muttering apologies.

She glared at him. "Phillip, it's over between us. Okay. *Over!*"

The doors slid open and they both glanced up to see Chase leaning against the cab with his long legs crossed in front of him, talking on a cell phone. He lifted his eyes, saw the two of them, and stopped in midsentence.

Chase's voice drifted back to them in the hollow space of the garage. "Yeah, um, can I call you back in a few minutes?" He closed the phone, barely giving the person on the other end time to respond, and frowned, his brow furrowed.

"Oh, great!" Phillip groaned. "Just great!" He threw up his hands. "We're barely broken up and you've already hopped into bed with him. Haven't you? Haven't you?" he shouted.

She marched away from him, not looking back.

"You think you're just gonna ride off into the sunset with your little rock star, do ya?"

Chase straightened and took the box from her, but kept his eyes on Phillip. "Everything okay?"

"Fine," she said evenly, giving Phillip a meaningful look.

Phillip turned around and kicked a metal trash can over, spilling fast food containers and soda cans across the floor of the garage, but headed back into the elevator and punched his floor number, albeit much harder than necessary. Chase had just turned back to her when they heard the rough clang of the elevator doors reversing again and Phillip came charging toward them. Chase handed the box back to her and took a step or two away from the cab.

"Oh shit!" she murmured, shoving her box into the back of the cab as fast as she could. She knew Chase had come to an end of his patience with Phillip and asking him to stop now was like asking a teenage boy not to eat the last slice of pizza, but she tried anyway.

"Chase, he's drunk—"

Before she could finish her thought, Phillip rushed at Chase, grabbing him around the midsection, his momentum carrying both of them into the cab with a loud metallic crunch. This finally caught the attention of the cabbie who cursed in a strong Bronx accent and exited the cab, coming around to check for damage. Hope screamed as Phillip and Chase slid down to the ground, grappling with each other and trying to get the most advantageous position. Both men were big, but Chase had a slight advantage in both height and musculature. The cabbie ran his hand along the side of his vehicle and, seeming satisfied, straightened up to watch the fight with interest.

Hope glared at him but then stepped forward. "Come on, cut it out!"

"You son-of-a-bitch!" Phillip yelled. He was now in a place where reason was a stranger.

"I said, CUT IT OUT, YOU MORONS!" she shrieked, her voice reverberating throughout the parking garage. Both men stopped and stared at her in a way which might have been comical, if she hadn't been so pissed off. She hit Chase on the shoulder. "Get off him!"

He let go of Phillip's shirt, and lifted himself from on top of his opponent's legs. Phillip scrambled up, straightening his clothes and brushing dirt off them, while trying to retain his dignity.

"Okay." She tried to bring her breathing back to normal. "Phillip, I'm sorry, but I love Chase. I always have. I was just trying to convince myself I didn't. Even if Chase hadn't come back into my life, I could not have loved you the way you deserve because I'd already given my heart to him long ago. I'm sorry, but no amount of fighting or kissing is going to change the way I feel."

Phillip stared at her oddly, as if the concept had just clicked in his mind. His face said it all. This wasn't a fling. This wasn't revenge. She truly loved this guy. She would never be his. This appeared to hurt more than any punch could. He stood there with his mouth hanging open for a second, stunned, then turned around and walked away without saying a word.

His pained expression had been like a dagger through her heart. She hung her head for a second, and then spun around.

The cabbie was giving Chase a congratulatory pat on the shoulder. "Way to go, Mack."

She scowled at the driver who held his hands up in a defensive position. "Okay, okay!" He walked around to his side of the cab and got into the front seat.

She looked at Chase. "Are you okay?"

"Fine." He turned and got into the back seat.

She sighed and climbed in behind him, uneasy with his mood. Imitating his position she stared at the cracked vinyl seat in front of her. She turned to say something to him, and then thought better of it, closing her mouth and facing forward again. The driver started the motor and put the cab in reverse.

The car began its downward spiral, staying close to the outer wall already marked with car paint and scrapes, the cabbie unusually quiet. She worked up enough courage to speak. "Chase, I'm sorry about—"

He interrupted her. "You said no amount of kissing or fighting was going to change the way you feel. Why did you mention kissing?"

She contemplated this question. Or, rather, contemplated possible ways she could avoid answering this question. She could pretend she didn't hear it, but they were sitting right next to each other. She could cause an accident...

"Phillip kissed me in the elevator."

"I knew it!" he screamed. "And I'm just supposed to get on an airplane tomorrow and leave you with that guy?"

She glanced up into the rearview mirror. The cabbie quickly averted his eyes, as if he hadn't been listening. She dropped her voice.

"But you forget," she answered tentatively, not sure if he would appreciate humor at this point, "I'm way more into you than him."

He turned to stare at her, and step by step his features brightened, the jaw relaxed, the fire went out of the eyes, and finally a grin stole over his face. "That's true," he responded smugly. He reached over and squeezed her hand. "Hope, I'm sorry. It's just—"

"Never mind. Let's not let Phillip ruin our day together."

"You're right." He pulled his cell phone out and flipped it open, hitting redial. "Hey, Rudy. Sorry about that. Yes. That's the address. And you got the credit card number, right? Perfect. That's fine. I owe you." He laughed. "Okay. Bye."

"What was that all about?"

"You'll see." He clapped his hands. They had reached street level. "So what do you want to do now?"

"Hmmm... What about making-out in front of the monkeys in the primate house?"

"Good idea." He grinned and leaned forward. "To the zoo, my good man."

CHAPTER TWENTY-ONE

The day turned out to be a glorious one, sun shining, seventy-five degrees. It was as if the whole world were celebrating their reunion. Chase and Hope strolled through the grounds of the zoo, just reveling in being together. They both wore baseball caps to keep from being recognized, and it worked, for the most part. Fans either didn't realize who he was, or if they did, they were polite enough not to disturb them, most just commenting, "I love your music!" and going their way.

An older man struck up a conversation with Chase when he was buying some hotdogs, though. After the preliminary compliments, he asked Chase, "So, is that Hope?" The man turned to stare at her as she crouched down to talk to a little boy who had commented on her Cardinals hat. "I can see why she inspired you."

Chase peered over at her shapely legs and her huge smile as she tugged on the youngster's Cardinal hat bill. He could just see a bit of her hair trying to break free in the back and he spent a second imagining it spilling out when he removed the cap back at her place. "Yeah," he said with a contented sigh.

He strolled over to her and she rose, waving at her new friend. "I leave you for a second and find you carrying on with some new guy," he teased.

"Oh, you!" She pulled the bill of his cap down with a giggle, making it hard for him to see. She led him to a bench and they sat to eat. She wolfed down her hotdog and was raring to go.

He watched her childlike face as she rambled on about one of the animals they had seen. Leaning his elbow on the back of the bench, he faced her. "Don't you ever get tired?" he asked with a smile.

"Never." She grabbed his shirt and pulled him in for a kiss.

"Ooh! That could be a *good* trait to have." Her lips were so soft, and she had a way of kissing him that was instant foreplay. She had just hooked him in with one of those kisses, when she took her lips from his.

When he tried to pull her back in, she shook her head playfully. "Nah-ah-ah! This is clearly not the primate house." She waved her hand in the direction of the elephant house directly across from them.

Looking chagrined, he snatched the map from her hands. "Give me the map!" He searched frantically for anything with even a slight resemblance to a primate. Glancing around to get his bearings, he yanked her up off the bench. "This way."

They headed down a hill, and she begged him to stop to watch feeding time for the seals. Next they watched the polar bear swimming. It had a glassed-in tank, and they could watch the huge beast dive into the water, swim toward them, arch his body as he neared the glass, plopping onto his back, and starting all over again. They could see him approach under water, and marveled at the enormous paw pads, which sometimes hit the glass with his backward somersaults. They continued on, spotting and identifying birds in the aviary, laughing at the waddling penguins, and admiring the sleek animals in big cat country. He spotted a house up a hill and dragged her forward.

"The reptile house," he said, disappointed, when they reached the top. He consulted the map again. "Where's the damn primate house?"

Her laugh bubbled out like the water from the nearby drinking fountains, where parents were lifting their kids for a drink. She pulled him in and kissed him with fervor.

"I thought you had rules?" he protested weakly.

"To hell with the rules." She laughed, taking the map from him and tossing it in a nearby trash can.

He laughed with her, lifting her off her feet and swinging her around as he kissed her. They stumbled over to a bench in the shade, and she sat with her legs bent over his, kissing in relative privacy. It reminded him of the first night they had kissed on the dock in the pond behind his house. "Do you have any idea how much I love you?" he asked.

"I think I finally do," she responded quietly.

"How would you like to go to see *Wicked* this evening?"

"*Wicked*? The *Wicked* that's perpetually sold out *Wicked*?"

"That's the one."

"You know I'd love it."

"Maybe we'd better get back to your place and change then."

"You're kidding!" she squealed.

"No." He chuckled.

She grabbed his hands excitedly and jumped up. "Really?"

"Really," he assured her, standing as well.

"Oh, Chase! Do you know how long I've wanted to see that?" She sprang into his arms, hugging him tightly.

"Well, come on then." He laughed, throwing an arm around her shoulders and heading for the entrance. A few minutes later, he commented, "Well, I'll be damned! The primate house!" It had been right inside the entrance; they had passed it coming in without even noticing.

CHASE WATCHED HER FACE in the dark as it was illuminated by the stage lights. To his thinking, this was a better show than what was going on in front of them. Once the theater lights had dimmed, her eyes had been focused on the stage without once looking away. A smile played on her lips whenever there was humorous dialogue; tears filled her eyes with moving scenes.

When Glinda and Elphaba sang their song about how their lives were changed by being friends, he silently reached into his pocket and handed her a package of tissues he had brought, knowing she would need one. Her face was such a window to her feelings. He could see fear hollow and then spark her eyes. Her sensuous lips parted, and her body jumped even though he was sure she was unaware of it.

During the suspenseful parts, he wasn't quite sure she was breathing. He could have been on an entirely different planet for all she was conscious of him, but it didn't bother him; he was into her being into the play. She clapped wholeheartedly when the actors made their curtain calls, her eyes aglow with her appreciation for their art.

When the lights came up, she finally turned to him, squeezing his hand. "Oh, Chase! Wasn't it fantastic?"

He chuckled. "It was fantastic, all right."

She seemed disappointed. "You didn't enjoy it as much as I did?"

"Sweetheart, I don't think even if the actors had family members in the audience, they could have enjoyed it as much as you did."

"Oh!" She rose and swatted him on the arm in feigned annoyance. "Like you weren't crying, too." He stood, shaking his head. "You weren't?" She turned to walk away. "Well that's just because you're a heartless bastard," she said, just loud enough for him to hear.

He roared and grabbed her around the waist, kissing her neck. She spun in his arms, grabbing his face and kissing him. "Seriously. Thank you so much for bringing me. I'll never forget this."

Her eyes were damp with the passion of her emotions, and he felt the familiar squeeze of his heart only she had the power to give him. She wore a long, black dress, with a straight cut that draped across her curvy body beautifully. Her hair was up like it had been in the video, and despite her tears, she looked perfect to him. He felt like he couldn't breathe.

"My God, you are gorgeous! Do you have any idea what you do to me?" His voice husky, he gathered her into his arms, kissing her in the virtual seclusion of their booth. Eventually, he took his lips from hers, laying his forehead against hers and still holding her close by the waist. "Let's go home and have dinner."

"Okay," she agreed. "I'm not sure what I have in the refrigerator, but I'm sure I can throw something together."

"Throwing things together is my specialty. Let's get out of here." He took her hand and led her out the back exit the manager had let them use, the same man who had supplied their tickets. Chase had wanted to hire a private driving service, but that could have drawn unwanted attention to Hope's location, so they had taken a cab.

When they got back to her condo and were sauntering down the hall together, she gestured to something ahead on the carpet. "What's that?" It appeared to be right outside her door. When they reached it, they discovered a tray with dishes on it. "What is this? Did someone leave this here?" She glanced around at the neighboring doors as if searching for a clue. He took the key from her hand and opened the door.

"I think it's our dinner."

She smiled, seeming to catch on at last. "Our dinner?"

"How do beef tips in a burgundy wine sauce and garlic mashed potatoes sound?"

"Scrumptious! You did this?"

"I knew we'd be hungry and"—he brought her hand to his lips and kissed it—"I wanted you all to myself. No fans, no interruptions." She blushed prettily and seemed at a loss for words. "I hope everything is still warm enough. Traffic took longer than I anticipated."

"I can't believe you planned all this."

"Hope, I just wanted to give back to you just a little of the magic you give to me every time we're together."

"Oh, Chase!" She was obviously choked up.

"Now, no more tears, we've had enough of those tonight," he teased, kissing her cheek. "It's so nice out, though. Do you think we could take this out on the roof? I should have ordered a table..."

"No, that's okay. We'll just take a blanket and eat it like a picnic."

"Are you sure? You might get something on your dress."

She shrugged. "That's what black dresses are for. They hide every stain. I'll go grab a quilt."

She carried the quilt and champagne bucket; he got the rest. Luckily no one else had had the same idea, and they had the rooftop to themselves. The food was delicious, the champagne delightfully cold and bubbly. He stretched out on his side, talking to her about his upcoming tour, and for a little while, they were able to forget that in the morning he would be leaving. They had chocolate mousse for dessert, and then she fed him strawberries and whipped cream while he lay with his head in her lap. After a while, feeling full and a bit tipsy, they stretched out together on the blanket, staring up at the stars, still visible tonight, despite the bright lights of the city.

"Chase, this was an absolutely wonderful day." She sighed.

He intertwined his fingers with hers. "I hope we have a lot more of these days, Hope," he returned softly.

"Will you take me miniature golfing?" she asked after a pause.

"Of course."

There was another long pause. "I haven't been miniature golfing in a long time. I might need some tips," she said slyly.

He smiled at the stars. "I think I can manage that." He rolled over on his side and kissed her.

When their kisses became more impassioned, she pushed him gently. He stared down into her sultry eyes and she said, "Let's go to bed."

He helped her to her feet, and they gathered their belongings in silence. They left the dishes at the door for the caterer, and took the remainder of the champagne, strawberries, and whipped cream to the bedroom. Once again in candlelight, their heads light from the champagne, they gradually disrobed. He reached up and pulled the clip from her hair and it fell down, the curly ends bouncing seductively at her shoulders, taking his breath away.

Perhaps seeing his reaction, she dipped her head back and closed her eyes, swinging her hair freely behind her, then bringing her head forward quickly so the ends cascaded over her shoulders, landing just above her breasts. She raised an eyebrow and gave him a come-hither smile, which left him weak in the knees. He scooped her up and threw her on the bed. He fed her strawberries, and then trailed them down her body. Their coldness sent erotic shivers through her. He kissed the sweet juice away and made love to her with a terrible slowness, drawing their pleasure out, until they lay quietly together.

They didn't speak; the pain of his impending departure another player in their bed. They wanted to lie together for as long as possible, not giving into the sleep that would steal away the hours, but exhausted from their day, they were soon breathing in rhythm with each other, her head on his chest.

CHAPTER TWENTY-TWO

C hase stood on the tarmac, his hands on Hope's shoulders, peer-ing into her eyes. It had rained overnight and the temperature had dropped dramatically. He shrugged in his dark brown leather jacket, thankful he had packed it along with jeans, and a thin black sweater. She wore a short, chocolate brown sweater and jeans with a blue jean jacket, which wasn't nearly heavy enough. A chilly breeze made her shiver. She had her arms around his waist, hands stuck in his back pockets.

"Are you sure you can't come with me?"

"Babe," she said, torn, "I promise, it'll only be a few weeks."

He nodded his head soberly, glancing toward the plane, but he seemed not ready to leave her yet.

"You promise you'll call when you get there?" She played with the zipper of his jacket. "Now that you're back, I have an irrational fear that you'll be taken away again."

He nodded. "I"ll call, I promise." He gazed into her face as the wind blew a few strands of her hair across her forehead. He bent down and kissed her tenderly, and then he left. He watched her from the window as the jet taxied away, seeming small as she hugged her arms to herself, the wind still beating against her mercilessly. He felt the knot in his stomach twist tighter.

HOPE PROMISED HERSELF not to fall apart until she got home to her apartment. She filled her mind with work. How was she going to get close enough to Antonio Vasculli to find out about his connection to Robert Mulrooney? She mulled this over as she drove through the streets and into her parking garage and then thought about it all the way up to her twelfth-floor apartment.

When she opened the door, she immediately spotted the huge bouquet of roses on her coffee table. Chase must have asked the landlord to put them in her apartment when they arrived. They were spectacular. Their petals were white in the center with a light pink that bled out to the dark-pink-tipped edges. She inhaled their fragrance deeply. She plucked the card out from their midst, and read it: **Miss you already. Love, Chase.** She ran her fingers over the words, as if they could make her feel his skin, know his touch.

Not totally understanding why she did it, she threw herself down on the couch and sobbed. All the emotions she had been going through since Jack Delaney uttered Chase's name came rolling up from deep inside her. Her anxiety over seeing him again; the passion he stirred when she had first laid eyes on him, when they had danced, when they had kissed; the doubts and fears; the anger over the past and over catching Phillip with Liz; her confusion over which road to take; her shock on discovering everything she believed to be true on prom night was false; the ecstasy of making love to him; and finally, the pain of watching him leave on the plane—all these things took possession of her and shattered her into a thousand pieces.

Her apartment, which had been so full of him hours before, now seemed too empty. She could still smell him, but not feel his arms around her. The ache she felt now seemed familiar, bringing her back to the time after her prom night. Her heart cried out for him, but there was no answer. She had never felt so alone.

HOPE BLINKED OPEN HER eyes. She was lying on the couch on her stomach, an arm trailing the ground. Her eyes were stinging and there was a ringing noise somewhere. What was it? She heard Chase's voice on the answering machine. She dove for the phone, knocking it to the floor, then falling off the couch as she scrambled after it.

"Hope? Hope? Are you there?"

"Yes, Chase! I'm here. Are you okay?"

"Yes." His voice sounded happy. "We just touched down, so I called you as per your instructions."

"God, you sound sexy over the phone."

"Don't toy with me, Hope. I'm two thousand miles away."

"Oh, Chase! This is so much harder than I thought it would be."

His voice was soft. "I know, babe, but we'll be together soon."

There was a long pause.

"I got your flowers. They are breathtaking!"

"Just like you."

"They made me cry. It was so thoughtful—" Her voice caught.

"They're not supposed to make you cry."

"I know." She reached for a tissue and dabbed at the corners of her eyes.

"I'm looking forward to that game of miniature golf."

"Me, too."

"Hal's here. I better go. Good night, Hope. I love you."

"Will you call me tomorrow?"

"Every day."

"Okay. Good night." She listened until she heard the phone disconnect, then hung it up. She sat, simply breathing in and breathing out for several minutes. *I will get this article. I will get it done quickly. I will see Chase soon.*

She marched over to the bar between the kitchen and the living room, and snapped open her laptop. Her fingers clattered over the keyboard as she pulled up every scrap of information she could access on Vasculli and Mulrooney. She needed an in somehow. Picture after picture splashed across the screen of Antonio Vasculli with one beautiful woman after another. So, he was a womanizer. Maybe she could use that to her advantage.

But how to meet him? She had met Chase in school, Phillip at work; she didn't know much about picking up men. She studied the pictures and stories over and over until her eyes burned from being in front of the computer screen. She got up and poured herself a glass of wine. It was well after midnight and her brain hurt.

She wondered what Chase was doing right then. It was ten something out there... Had he turned in early? He had already sent her his tour itinerary by email. Tomorrow he would be in Seattle. *Hang in there, Hope. You've waited eight years. You can wait another couple of days.*

With determination, she sat back down at the computer. She scrolled over the pictures again. After a few minutes, she sat up excitedly. Two of the pictures were taken outside of the same hotel. She scrolled down some more, there was another one. Over half of the pictures turned out to be in front of the same hotel, The Del Murrow. She sat back. She would go there tomorrow. She would go there and...and...she would pray for inspiration.

She shut down the computer and peeled off her sweater, throwing it carelessly on the couch and ambling into the bathroom. She washed her face, slipped out of her jeans, and fell into bed without even changing into pajamas. She inhaled deeply. She could smell Chase here. She reached over tiredly and turned off the lamp. An hour later, after tossing and turning, and turning and tossing, she got out of bed. She switched on her compact disc player. Chase's voice filled the room. She laid down her head, and fell asleep.

At six o'clock, the phone rang.

"Hey!"

"Chase!"

"Were you up?"

She sat up, rubbing her eyes. "Yes." She took a glimpse at the clock. "What are you doing up? It's like 4 a.m. there."

"I couldn't sleep."

She slid down in bed. "Gosh, it feels good to hear your voice! Although you sang me to sleep."

"I did?" He yawned. "I don't remember."

"No, silly! I played one of your albums."

"Oh!" He yawned again. "Maybe you should sing to me," he mumbled.

"Oh no. Singing is your thing."

"Then just talk to me. Tell me how much you love me."

She smiled. "I do love you, Chase. I love the way you make me laugh. I love the way I feel with you. It's like I've found my home." She closed her eyes. "I love the way you look at me. And the way you touch me. Chase?"

"Hmmm?"

"When do you have to get up?"

"In a few hours."

"Go to sleep, honey."

"I think I can now. Hope?"

"Um-hum?"

"I love you, too."

"Good night, Chase."

She heard the soft click of the connection being cut off. She hung up her phone, and tossed it carelessly on the bed next to her. She turned over, letting the sunlight bathe her face. The beach towel had slid off the curtain rod in the night; she would have to fix it later, but right now, the sunshine felt glorious. She slid out of bed, taking the sheet with her, just in case her nosy neighbor was on the roof next door. She filled up her beloved claw-foot tub, and soaked her body, thinking about Chase.

CHAPTER TWENTY-THREE

S he ate breakfast, lunch, and dinner at The Del Murrow's upscale restaurant, 5 East, for three days, but didn't see Antonio Vasculli. It was killing her to continue to pay those outrageous prices for food, but she put her time in, hoping against hope he would show up one day. On the fourth day, he walked in at lunchtime. Her heart skipped a beat as he sauntered past her table. She was racking her brain for what to do next when a young man approached her.

"Excuse me, but aren't you Hope Creswell?"

"Why, yes," she answered in surprise.

The man waved his hand, and in a blink, a photographer stood at his side snapping pictures of her. She put up her hand; the flash was blinding.

"Isn't it true you are involved with Chase Hatton? How did you two meet? Is it true you dated in high school?"

He fired off questions so rapidly she wasn't able to even formulate a response.

"Excuse me, gentlemen, but I believe you are interrupting the lady's meal," a voice said pointedly.

"Uh...we're sorry," the reporter said, his voice a little shaky. He and the photographer scampered off.

Her eyes adjusted and she found Antonio Vasculli standing by her table. He wore an expensive, dark business suit with a snazzy gray and red tie. His jet black hair was slicked back neatly, and his dark, clear complexion set off his brilliant, white teeth, reminding her oddly of a shark. His face was handsome, with strong features and deep chocolate eyes, and he appeared to be in his mid-thirties. She was surprised to find he was better looking than his pictures made him out to be. He gave the impression of a man who knew how to work hard to get what he wanted, and would never accept anything less. "Are you okay, Miss?" he asked politely.

"Umm...yes, I think so."

He started to leave, but she put a hand on his arm. "Thank you so much."

His hand covered hers. "Not a problem. I hate to see a lady in trouble. Is your boyfriend going to be joining you?" He motioned to the chair across from her.

"No. No, actually. I've just been waiting for a girlfriend, but I think she must have forgotten about our date." She looked around for her "girlfriend" for show.

"What a shame. Maybe you would consent to join me, then?"

She smiled up at him. "I think I'd like that."

Antonio pulled out her chair for her, and placed a hand on her back. His hand fell on her bare skin, below where the straps of her white sundress crisscrossed over her shoulder blades. She shivered slightly. He pulled a chair out for her, and then sat down across the table.

"You're not waiting for someone?" she queried.

"No. Actually, I eat here frequently by myself, so your company is welcome. I'm not much of a cook."

She nodded. "Well, I guess I should introduce myself." She held out her hand. "I'm Hope Creswell."

He took her hand, covering it with his other hand. "Antonio Vasculli. So, you are Hope, Chase Hatton's girlfriend. I recognize you from the pieces of the video they have been showing on the news. I can't wait to see the whole thing."

"Oh no," she said quickly. "Chase and I are not seeing each other."

"No? But I assumed from his acceptance speech—"

"Oh, that was just a sort of...inside joke." She thought quickly. She had heard it said the best lies contain some portion of the truth. "Chase and I did date in high school. But I caught him cheating on me the night of senior prom." She took a sip of water. "I was recently assigned to do a story on him, up until a few days ago I worked for *The Chicago Globe News,* and got talked into shooting a video with him. Things got a little...hot, on the set, but I would never have anything to do with him again after what he did to me."

Vasculli listened attentively. "And he mentioned you in his speech, because...?"

She feigned embarrassment. "I don't know why, exactly. Because he knew the press would hound me, I guess, I'm not sure. In high school—you have to remember I was only seventeen or eighteen—I asked him to write me a love song. His saying he wrote all of his love songs for me was a way to, I don't know, take a jab at me, to embarrass me or something."

The waiter appeared at her side. Antonio gave his order, handed the waiter his menu, and looked at her. She gave her order, but after the waiter left, she said, "Breakfast is on me"—he raised a hand in protest—"to thank you for sending that reporter away. He caught me off guard, I guess."

"It was my pleasure. My mother would be ashamed of me if she found out I didn't come to the aid of a woman in need. And I insist on buying breakfast. Not feeding a beautiful lady, such as yourself, would also be ungallant of me."

She blushed, taking another sip of her water. "You are anything but ungallant."

"Thank you." He took a drink of his water, too. "You said you worked for *The Globe?*"

"Yes. Just a small-time reporter/photographer, doing family-centered pieces. Apparently too small-time, as the boss let me go last week. That, and I was...involved, with someone on the staff, and I had just broken up with him."

"Do you think that had something to do with it?"

"Possibly. I know it's not smart to get involved in workplace romances. Sometimes I just...get carried away, I guess." She gazed at him meaningfully and she saw a spark in his eyes. Maybe playing up the nympho role would be beneficial.

"What are you going to do now?"

"I haven't quite decided. Maybe something with my photography. But enough about me, Mr. Vasculli, what—"

"Tony, please."

"Tony. What do you do for a living?"

"Oh, a little bit of this, a little bit of that," he answered vaguely. "I mostly own things. Shipping lines, construction companies, real estate... pretty boring stuff."

"Oh, I don't think so," she commented as their food arrived. "That must be a lot to manage."

"It can be," he admitted. "That's why I allow for plenty of time to entertain myself," he added suggestively.

A shrill noise issued from his side of the table. Apologizing, he leaned over and lifted a leather briefcase onto the table. He opened it, fished out the whistling, vibrating cell phone, and answered it.

"Antonio Vasculli. Yes, Robert, would you hold one minute?" He covered the phone with his hand. "I'm sorry, it's business. I'll be right back." He stepped out into the lobby.

She stared at the briefcase. She could hear Antonio's loud voice in the distance, though she could not make out what he was saying. A folder stuck out of the briefcase. She glanced over her shoulder. Antonio stood by a tall planter with his back to her. She leaned across the table to get a peek at the writing exposed on the folder. She made out the letters R.M. on the tab. Could it stand for Robert Mulrooney? The briefcase had a combination lock, but hadn't he just opened it without turning the numbers? Maybe it was still unlocked. She reached a hand tentatively toward the release.

"I hope you didn't miss me too much," came a deep voice from behind her. She froze, her heart skipping a beat. As he moved around her shoulder, he noticed her hand on his briefcase.

"I was just noticing this lovely briefcase. I have to admit, I was tempted to smell it. I have a thing for the smell of leather."

"Do you, now?" Her host seemed to take this as a sign of some appealing perversity. "I'm sorry, Hope. But I have to go. Trouble on one of the sites."

"Oh!" she said, pretending to be disappointed. "Well, I guess a man like you doesn't get to relax much."

"On the contrary, I make it my point to relax. Would you consider relaxing with me at dinner on Friday night?"

She waited a beat, letting him think she was considering his proposal. "I'm not sure; I just got out of a relationship..."

"But you are tempted, no?"

She smiled. "Sorely."

"Be here Friday at seven. Oh, and wear a nice dress, if you can. They have dancing." And with that, he was gone. She congratulated herself on a job well done, and headed home.

HOPE COULD HEAR THE phone ringing as she tried to unlock the door. Thinking it might be Chase, she scrambled to get inside. Leaving the keys in the door, she dove for the receiver, flopping on the couch as she answered.

"Hey, babe!" His voice sounded fantastic.

"Hey, stranger. How's it going?" Her smile radiated from within.

"Good. Except I'm missing the lady in my life."

"Oh!" She groaned. "I miss you, too."

"So why don't you come out and see me?"

"What? Just hop on a plane and fly out to...where are you, now?"

"Toronto."

"Just fly to Toronto to see you?"

"What's wrong with that?"

"I don't know. It just seems kind of...extravagant."

"Hope, I've got the money, and dammit, I want to see you!"

"I want to see you too, honey, I do. I've been thinking of you constantly. And sleeping in our bed, or not sleeping, to be more accurate, is about killing me."

"*Our* bed?"

She played with a piece of fuzz on the couch, laying on her stomach and kicking her feet up behind her. "Did I say that?"

"You did."

"Hmmm. I guess I think of it that way now."

"Really? What are you wearing, by the way?" he asked suggestively.

A slow smile grew on her face. She kicked off her shoes as she answered, unbuttoning her sweater and shrugging it off. "A black teddy and thigh-high fishnet stockings."

"Oooh! I hope those beach towels are still up."

She glanced over to the windows where the light was streaming in. She had taken them down for Mr. Mewford, so he could still watch the pigeons strutting around on the ledge outside, taunting him, and bathe in the swath of rectangular sunlight on her warmed oak floors. *I need to put those back up,* she thought absently. "What are *you* wearing?"

"Not a stitch."

"Oooh! You're killing me!"

"So, come out here then."

"Honey, I wish I could, but I'm working on this story and I can't—"

"What story? I thought you were fired?"

She grimaced. "I just want to write one more story, as a free-lancer."

"What kind of story?"

"Uh..." She knew he would worry if she told him she was investigating someone who almost definitely had mob connections. "A story about a politician." Part truth, part lie, this was getting easier. "Anyway, I'm meeting with one of his associates on Friday. Hopefully, I'll get all of my information then and I'll be able to come out there."

"So, what are you doing until Friday?"

"Research, mainly."

"Research, which could be done in, say...Toronto?"

She smiled. "You're relentless."

"Uh-huh."

"I'll think about it."

"I could have the jet fueled and ready to go in an hour."

"I'll think about it."

He sighed.

Mewford jumped up on the couch with a loud meow.

"How's Mr. Mewford?"

"You heard that?" Hope was petting her friend while he kneaded on her chest. "He's great! How's Hal?"

"Hal is thrilled that we worked things out, absolutely thrilled. In fact, I don't think I've ever seen him so excited...except when we hit platinum." He paused. "He misses you terribly, though."

She could tell he was angling, again, for her to come, and the worst part was, she wanted to. She wanted to badly. She wanted to give it all up and run into his arms. But she knew this was something she had to see through to the end. She giggled. "In that case, I'll be on the next plane."

He laughed. "I'm sorry, hon. It's just, I sit here with Hal wanting to read me all the minute details on documents and all I'm thinking about is how soft your hair is and how good it smells, and about how you tease me and keep me in line and make me laugh. I think about your sweet voice and all the times we've had together and all the things I want to do with you, and to you— Ah, great! I think Hal's at the door. He probably wants to read me the fine print on my cable bill."

"He's just trying to watch out for you."

"I know, but that's why I hired him, so I wouldn't have to read the fine print. All right, babe, I've got to go. I'll call you later."

"I love you, Chase, more than you know."

"I love you, too. I'm sorry I'm so grumpy."

"You're entitled. I'll see you soon, I promise."

"Bye, babe."

"Bye." She hung up the phone, and sat petting Mewford, who had curled up on her chest morosely. "Well, I guess it's just you and me, buddy." Scooping him up, she returned him carefully to the pre-warmed couch. She ran through articles on Robert Mulrooney on her computer. He didn't appear to be the type who would get involved with anything shady. Balding with glasses, he looked like your a-typical father of four or more. He probably sang in his church's choir and washed the car wearing shorts and dark socks.

She sat with elbows on the bar, chin in her palm, staring at the screen. Only she wasn't seeing Robert Mulrooney anymore, she was seeing Chase. Chase rising out of the waves, pushing back his wet hair, his pecs glistening in the sun like some male version of a water nymph. Chase's love-charged eyes as he held her up, then lowered her. She remembered feeling his hands on her hips, and then her sides as he let her drop, still held tightly. She remembered her heart beating with a wildness equal to the thundering waves around them. She flashed to another scene, when she froze when doing the dishes as he slid his arms around her, his full lips so close to her ear.

She shook herself and stood up, rubbing her arms. The memories of him were so vivid, it was as if she could still feel his hands on her, still smell his clean, masculine fragrance. She wondered how it was that God had given each person their own special, recognizable scent. She moved over to the window, trying to walk away from his imagined presence, which was a definite turn on, without the promise of satisfying her hunger.

She gazed out the windows at the traffic below, hearing the vague honking noises as they drifted up to her. Now, she saw his sweet face as he agreed to help her find Phillip at the People's Choice Awards, as he held her the night she had come to him in the rain, without asking anything in return, and now she felt the ache that was much deeper than the yearning her body had for him. She needed to feel the way she felt when she was with him. Whether naked or fully clothed, in bed or in a limo, she needed to feel the love that radiated from him and filled her so completely.

She picked up the phone and dialed Hal.

CHAPTER TWENTY-FOUR

Hope sat in the hallway outside Chase's hotel room. She had flown through the night, the pilot having to delay their take-off because of a sudden storm raging in Chicago. She took a taxi from the airport and arrived at six o'clock in the morning at his doorstep. As she had raised her hand to knock, it occurred to her he had been up late last night and given a concert to a stadium full of screaming fans. She had turned around and leaned with her back against the door, sliding slowly down to sit and wait to hear movement inside. She was almost falling asleep when, an hour later, the door down the hall opened and Hal stepped out.

At first he frowned, probably thinking she was a fan who had somehow gotten through their security measures, but when she smiled at him, he ran down to see her.

"Hope! It's so good to see you." He hugged her and held her hands as they spoke. "What are you doing out here in the hall?"

"Well, I knew Chase was sleeping and I didn't want to wake him."

"Our rooms are adjoining. Why don't you sneak in through my side?"

She squeezed him. "Oh, Hal! You're the bomb!"

She crept into his bedroom and dropped her bag quietly at the foot of his bed. He lay on his back with the sheet at a diagonal across his midriff, one knee bent to the side, one bare thigh exposed. He gave the impression of some Greek god caught napping, she decided. She wordlessly stripped off her clothing, still gazing on his sleeping form, and then slid underneath the covers. She felt the welcome heat of his body and inched closer until their skin was touching. His rhythmic breathing ended abruptly as he took in a deep breath.

"Hope!" His arms came around her immediately, and he buried his face in her hair. "What are you doing here?"

"Shhhh! Go back to sleep."

He pulled her in, squeezing her, wrapping his arms around her chest, and adjusting the sheet so nothing separated them. She squirmed even closer, making sure every point on the back side of her body was touching him.

"I love you," he murmured with a contented sigh. His fingers strummed chords on her arm reflexively, a movement so familiar and so singularly Chase it made her smile.

"I love you, too." Within minutes they had drifted off to sleep.

CHASE WOKE TO THE SOUND of birds outside and the woman he loved in his arms. Life couldn't get much better than that. She felt so deliciously warm and soft. He didn't want to wake her, but the call of her bare flesh was too much for him. He sat up on his elbow and gently pushed back her silky brown hair to expose her neck. Pulling the sheet down over her shoulder, he touched her porcelain skin. He brought his warm lips to her shoulder, then worked his way up her lovely neck. She woke up and turned over in his arms, smiling up at him.

"Hello."

Chase grabbed her up into his arms. "I thought you weren't coming," she heard him whisper in her ear.

When he pulled away, she held his face in her hands. "I guess I found you irresistible."

"I was beginning to wonder..."

"Wonder no more," she said, running her hand up the inside of his thigh. She pushed him down on the pillows and began to kiss up his chest, her lips and tongue rolling over his flesh as she moved on top of him.

She brought her lips to his while her body continued to move over him, warm, pulsing, robbing him of all reason. As the blood rushed from his head to other parts of his body, giving him a slightly euphoric feeling, he wondered if this could really be true. Was she really here with him after all this time? After all the waiting and wanting and hurt? Could she really still love him, or was it all some dream?

She pushed away from him, sitting up. His eyes followed her every move and she drank in the power she had to move him. Questions kept floating through her mind. Could a love as powerful as this last, or was it as fleeting as the perfect light for an outdoor photograph? As she rode the wave of their passion, she realized she didn't care. She just didn't care. If this was fleeting, so be it. She would love him the best she could for as long as she could, and treasure every moment of it.

When at last they lay together, their bodies liquid and relaxed, he broke the silence.

"I'm glad you flew out here." They both laughed at his statement, given as it was in the wake of their intimate moments. "Are you hungry?"

"Starved! Are you?"

He nodded. "Should I take you out somewhere nice for brunch and then show you the sights?"

She thought about this. "To be honest, I could care less if we go anywhere, just as long as we're together."

"In that case, why don't we order room service and soak in my big tub for awhile?"

"Now that," she said, sitting up to check out the sunk-in tub that sat in the corner of the room, "sounds divine!"

He ordered sandwiches and fruit. They ate, then turned on the water and soon sat across from each other in the deep tub, their legs intertwined in the middle. After several minutes of soaking, she lifted the shampoo she'd set beside them.

"Let me do it."

She peered at him, eyebrows raised. "You want to shampoo my hair?"

"Yeah. Come over here."

She slowly moved to sit between his legs, watching him with suspicion as she did so. She handed him the bottle of her cheap shampoo. "I suppose someday I should get some grown-up shampoo," she commented.

When he took the cap off, he exclaimed, "So this is the stuff! This is the stuff that has been my downfall."

She laughed, but then it turned to a moan as his strong hands began to work her hair into a lather. "Mmm. What are you talking about?"

"Man!" He inhaled deeper. "Whenever you pass by me and I catch a whiff of this stuff, it makes my insides do the rumba."

"You're kidding. I've been using this stuff since I was, like, six years old."

"I know. And it's always driven me crazy."

"You never mentioned it."

"It's kind of a strange thing to tell a woman, don't you think? 'The way you smell sends me into orbit!'"

She laughed, flattered.

"Lean back now and I'll rinse you."

She tipped her head back, letting his hands support her and lead her gently into the water. Her hair spread out over the surface.

She studied his upside down image as she floated. She sat up suddenly and turned to him. "Chase, I know this is strange, and some weird quirk I have, but I just keep waiting for the other shoe to drop.

Like we can't possibly be this completely happy, and lucky, to be back together again. Do you know what I mean?"

"Yeah. I feel the same way, too."

She flipped back again and rested the back of her head on his shoulder while he wrapped her tightly in his arms.

He kissed the top of her head. "And I even feel a little guilty sometimes. Not many people are fortunate enough to be able to say they have found the love of their life, but I have."

She squeezed his hand, touched by his sweet words.

"Chase?" They both jumped at Hal's voice in the next room.

There was a great deal of splashing.

"Uh...yeah, Hal?" He sounded flustered.

"I just wanted to let you know we'll need to leave for the stadium in half an hour."

"Oh, okay. I'll be out in a little bit."

They scrambled to get ready. "I have to be there early for a promotion and to sign autographs. You don't have to come until concert time if you want. You may get pretty bored."

Her lips lifted as she shimmied into a pair of black jeans. "I want to be where you are," she said simply. He smiled and pulled a t-shirt on over his head, messing his hair up.

She sauntered over to him, wearing just her jeans and a bra and reached up to fix his hair. He grabbed her hips and kissed her, and then they finished getting ready.

HOPE COULD NOT BELIEVE how incredibly sexy Chase was on stage. There was just something about a man with an electric guitar slung in front of his pelvis that gave a girl the hots. His ass and hips looked *oh-so-good* as he moved to the rhythm. She had heard all of the music before on the radio, but to see him sing it, live, on stage, just a few short feet away, set her a-tingle. The drum echoed the beating of her heart, and the high-pitched *zing* of the electric guitar mirrored her insides, strung so tightly with lust she thought he could make them zing, too. The husky tenor of his voice as he belted out lyrics seemed to reach inside, filling her with an expectant heat.

When he came off stage to change clothes, he grabbed her with one hand and pulled her to him to kiss her. He was obviously way revved up, too, as he smashed her against the wall, his tongue diving into her mouth, sending pulses throughout her body, in front of a dozen stagehands. He plunged into her, changing the angles, his mouth open and hard on hers, their bodies moving up and down on the waves of their passion. He moved her hands from his sides and slowly brought them over her head, pinning the wrists against the wall with one hand, while using the other hand to unbutton his shirt. He pulled away and watched her, both breathless, as he fumbled with the rest of the buttons, a slow, satisfied smile stealing across his face.

She peered at him, lust still clouding her eyes a little, her smile mirroring his. She felt the vibrations of the audience's applause pounding through the wall and through her, escalating her heart rate even more. His body glistened with sweat in a virile sort of way, and she imagined riding on the sweat over his body, the moisture making it easy to slide and creating wonderful sensations for them both.

"I am so turned on right now!" she managed to get out, her voice raw from passion as much as from screaming out his lyrics.

For his part he leaned in closer, his forehead against hers, still having to yell over the crowd. "I can't wait to get you back to the hotel room so I can do the things to you I'm dreaming of doing to you right now!" He ended with a growl.

He pulled away and stood a foot from her, but never took his eyes from hers. Peeling his shirt off and accepting a towel from a stagehand, he wiped his chest and the back of his neck, then handed it back and held his hands out so someone could help him into a new shirt, all the while looking at her as they both let their breathing come back to normal.

He jerked his head at his dresser with a flash of a smile. "Thanks." Someone handed him a bottle of water, which he downed instantly, and then he was gone.

After his second encore he came off stage and threw his arm around her, blowing out some air tiredly and yelling with a smile, "Let's get out of here."

They strode back to his dressing room. The door clicked closed and there was relative quiet for the first time in hours. He unbuttoned his damp shirt, pulled it off, and started collecting things off his dressing room table—his brush and some toiletries—and throwing them into a bag. She came up from behind him and grabbed him around the waist, brushing her lips against the skin of his back.

"I don't know if I can wait 'til we get back to the hotel," she murmured, catching his eye in the mirror.

He swept everything from the table onto the floor and turned around to grab her by the hips. She laughed as he lifted her onto the table. She brought her legs to wrap around his waist as she rubbed her hands across his chest.

When Hal walked in, their lips were locked together and she was running her hands through his hair.

"Uh." He cleared his throat. "I just wanted to say, good show. I'm leaving now." He closed the door.

They both laughed, breathing out the sexual tension. "I guess we better wait 'til we're back at the hotel, huh?"

"Probably for the best," she agreed.

CHAPTER TWENTY-FIVE

Later, when Chase slipped into bed next to her, he had on only a pair of sexy black cotton boxers, she, just her camisole and black panties. He put his hands on her shoulders as they lay facing each other, their foreheads together.

He sighed. "So, what did you think of the performance?"

"I...thought...the performance...was *totally*...hot!" she said, punctuating the statement with kisses.

"You did?" he said, feigning surprise. "And I thought your performance—in the dressing room—was totally hot!" He kissed her in return. "And I was hoping for an encore."

She nibbled on his earlobe. "Mmm, how very rock-star-ish of you." He chuckled. She flipped, her back toward him, and he pulled her into an embrace, slipping his hands underneath the cami to caress her breasts. "My God!" she said, reflecting. "I never expected to be so turned on by seeing you play. You and that guitar. And the kiss you gave me backstage nearly sent me to my knees."

His hands stilled on her breasts. She held her breath, waiting to see what he would do. "Chase?" She heard quiet breathing. "Chase?" she said again, turning over, but he was asleep. She smiled, brushing the hair gently away from his face. "Rock stars!" she muttered, and turned over to reach for the lamp. She snuggled closer to his already warm body, and fell asleep.

When she woke up, she saw she had overslept and needed to hustle to meet the pilot for the return trip. Carefully, she shimmied out of bed, letting Chase's arm fall over her side. As she dressed, she watched him sleep. Not exactly pretty, she determined. His mouth was slightly open, his hair ruffled, but he was her Chase, and she loved him. She bent over the bed, pushing a few strands of hair away from his eyes with her fingertips, and brushing her lips across his. With a pang in her heart, she hoisted her duffle bag over her shoulder, and slipped out of the room.

WHEN SHE GOT HOME, there was a message on the machine.

"Hey, honey! I just called to tell you about a weird experience I had. I woke up yesterday morning with a beautiful woman in my arms I didn't go to bed with, and this morning, I woke up minus the beautiful woman I did go to bed with. What a strange hotel! I hope you didn't just leave me 'cause I didn't put out, 'cause, believe me, I can make it up to you." There was a long pause, and she thought he had hung up and was just about to reach down to play the message again when she heard him say quietly, "I miss you, babe. Come back soon."

A pain shot through her so intense she brought one hand to her heart, one to her stomach. Resolutely, she went to take a shower and get dressed for her date with another man.

HOPE FIDDLED WITH THE clasp of her black clutch. She had worn a dress as he had requested, and carefully woven a black ribbon through her hair. A rhinestone studded comb helped to hold the mass of curls in place, and long, diamond, drop earrings hung from her ears. She had inherited them from her mother, who had inherited them from her mother, along with the matching necklace, which Ved gracefully across her collarbone. She gazed out over the dance floor, searching for her date.

Suddenly, hands were on her bare shoulders and cool lips brushed the back of her neck, making her shiver. "You look beautiful tonight, my dear."

She smiled coyly. "We need to get you a bell so you can't keep sneaking up on me like that."

Antonio Vasculli spun her around. "You're not nervous, are you?"

"Maybe a little."

"No need to be," he said, bringing her hand to his lips. "We're going to have a nice dinner, do a little dancing"—he pulled her close and whispered smoothly in her ear—"and then I'm going to take you home and make love to you."

Her breath came in sharp, and she struggled to compose her face before he pulled away. She dropped her head. How do you respond to a statement like that?

Antonio cupped her chin in his hand, and raised her face. "You are exquisite when you blush." Her lips were parted in surprise, and he pressed his mouth to hers lightly, but with authority. After he had finished kissing her, he led her, his hand on the small of her back, to a table near the dance floor, nodding to the maitre de, who had obviously saved it for them. The musicians were tuning their instruments, and the dance floor shined to a high gleam.

They had barely sat and opened the champagne Vasculli had ordered for them, when her cell phone rang. She dug it out of her purse only to see Phillip's cell number emblazoned on the screen. She shoved the phone back into her purse. Why was he calling her?

Vasculli leaned back in his chair, watching her speculatively. "Feel free to answer," he said coolly.

"Oh, it's nothing important." She strived to keep the uneasiness out of her voice.

Antonio turned the stem of his champagne flute as it sat on the table, studying her, perhaps trying to judge whether or not it was important to push her. After a moment, it became clear he had decided to let it go. He leaned forward with a smile. "So, what have you been doing with yourself, seeing as you're no longer employed?"

"Umm...I've just been fooling around with my camera a little," she lied, "trying to improve my technique. If I get some good shots, maybe I can interest an art gallery in them." She shrugged. Her phone rang again. She snuck a look. Phillip. What could he want?

"Go ahead, answer it."

"No, I don't want to interrupt our evening—"

"Nonsense. Besides, it will make me feel better if I have to take a call later."

"O-okay." She picked up the phone and turned sideways in her chair as she pushed the button to receive the call. "What do you *want*?" she hissed through gritted teeth, without preliminaries.

Vasculli leaned back in his chair, sipping champagne and eyeing her steadily.

"What the hell do you think you're doing?"

Her face colored. "Excuse me?"

"What the hell do you think you're doing, sitting there sipping champagne with Antonio Vasculli?"

"What business is it of yours?" she snapped angrily, her eyes dancing around the room, searching every male in the vicinity.

"Hope," Phillip said with irritating calm, "you can either step out to the patio and discuss this with me, or I can come in there and create a scene. Your choice." His voice sounded so snide, she wanted to reach through the phone and strangle him. She looked over her date's shoulder and saw Phillip standing on the patio outside, which was closed for the evening, in a tux, waving at her animatedly with a huge smile on his face.

She seethed. "You'd just do that too, wouldn't you?"

"I just would," he returned lightly.

She snapped the phone shut. "Tony, I am so sorry, but my ex is out on the patio and he promises to make a scene if I don't come over there and talk to him about whatever it is he feels the need to talk to me about."

Antonio turned around to stare at Phillip, who waved at him pleasantly. "Are you sure you want to do that? I could just—"

She didn't want to hear what he could just do. Just off him? Just feed him to the fishes? Just make him a pair of cement waders? "No. This is my problem, and I'll take care of it. And besides, that would be giving him just what he wants, a scene. I'll give him five minutes and then get rid of him for good." She slammed her napkin down on the table and strode purposefully across the room.

"What the hell do you think you are doing calling me when I'm out on a date?"

"Out on a date with Antonio Vasculli? Huh! Did you get tired of your little rock star already? What, not as good as I was in the sack?"

She narrowed her eyes. "Don't overestimate yourself, Phillip. Chase is..." *Fantastic! Phenomenal! Everything I have ever hoped for and more!* She wanted to scream her answers at him, but instead she said simply, "THIS IS NONE OF YOUR BUSINESS! I thought I had made that clear!"

He grabbed her arm roughly. "Dammit, Hope! You are my business. You may not be my girl anymore, but I damn well still care about you. I just can't turn my emotions on and off like a faucet like you apparently can, hopping from bed to bed like some sex-craved whore who can't get enough of—" She made a move to slap him but he caught her arm, squeezing it painfully. He stared at her, his eyes taking on a mean and calculating tint, ignoring the angry tears that had sprung to hers. "So, where is Hatton anyway? Did you kick him to the curb when he couldn't satisfy your needs? Or maybe he just couldn't get it up for you."

She came at him like a wild cat, and he had to raise his other arm to block her blows. "DON'T...YOU...DARE...TALK...ABOUT...CHASE...THAT...WAY!" She delivered a furious hit with each word, her eyes sparking in the streetlight.

He grabbed her other arm and shook her once, viciously. "Listen, Hope! We don't have much time." He gestured with his head toward the restaurant.

She glanced over her shoulder. Vasculli had risen from the table with a look of grim determination.

"Look, I'm sorry I shook you. But I needed to get your attention. Now you can stop trying to pretend Chase Hatton means nothing to you and you're really here on a date. You're investigating Vasculli, and let me just tell you, Hope, you're way out of your league here."

She was a little stunned from the brutal shaking she had received, but she managed to counter with, "You have no idea what league I'm in, Phillip. No one does. No one ever gave me a shot at *The Globe*—"

"Is that what this is? An attempt to prove yourself? Hope, you have nothing to prove. You're a fantastic writer and an even better photographer, anyone can see that."

She was confused by his change of tactics.

They peeked back and saw Vasculli was nearing the door. "Sweet-heart," he said earnestly, "this man can hurt you. If he even so much as suspects—"

"Phillip," she interrupted, "I'm a big girl now, and it's no longer your job to fight my fights for me."

The door opened and Vasculli stepped out onto the big stone pavers of the patio. "I think you better let go of the lady."

Phillip peered at her, but she was unmoving in her resolve. He set his jaw and backed away, throwing up his hands. Antonio made a move toward him, but Hope tried to steer her date toward the door.

"Tony, let's just go finish our meal—"

Before she could say anything further, the Italian man reached out and sucker punched Phillip in the jaw. He stumbled backward and righted himself on the low brick wall surrounding the patio.

"Tony, please...let's just go and finish our dinner!" she cried desperately, her worried eyes on Phillip.

Phillip had his fists clenched. She had to stop this! He took a step forward but then his eyes flitted over her face. She took the opportunity to mouth, *"Please!"* as hot tears rolled down her cheeks. For s second Phillip just stood there, his jaw flexing. Then he exchanged one final dark look with Vasculli, turned and left the patio.

For several moments she and Antonio stared after the retreating figure, listening to the sharp sound his heels made as they struck the sidewalk. Finally, Antonio turned to her as she leaned heavily on his arm. "Are you okay?"

"Yes. No, I don't feel very good." She put a hand to her stomach, and the reputed mobster helped her into one of the wrought iron chairs gracing the patio. It was true, her head was still ringing from the violent way Phillip had treated her and nerves were making her feel queasy.

"What do you say we skip the dinner and the dancing, and we'll just go back to my place, where it's quiet?" He looked at her meaningfully.

She felt a wave of revulsion. How could he be thinking about that after what she had just been through? She wanted to say screw it all and just hop the first flight to Chase, but if she went back to Antonio Vasculli's place, she might get an opportunity to snoop around and find information that could incriminate him. Making her decision, she breathed, "That sounds good."

As they reentered the restaurant to grab her purse, however, the band began to play "Unforgettable."

"Wait," Antonio said. "Can we have just one dance before we leave?"

"Certainly." She smiled. As he led her to the dance floor, she commented, "I have to admit, I haven't danced in quite some time."

"What about in the video?" Antonio asked in surprise.

"We were only on the dance floor for about fifteen minutes, and before that, it had been years."

"But you looked like a real pro."

"Thank you," she responded, thinking, *that's only because I was dancing with Chase.*

When they reached the middle of the dance floor, he pulled her to him firmly, gazing into her eyes a beat before he began to sway to the music. Her gaze did not flinch. She found being with him was like watching a small animal skitter across a busy highway. Even though you know you might be about to witness a horrible scene, you somehow can't seem to look away. He was easy to dance with, and she was soon able to follow without even concentrating very hard.

"You're a beautiful dancer," she commented.

"Thank you."

"I love this song. Have you ever seen the video?"

"With the footage of Nat King Cole singing in black and white, and his grown daughter, Natalie, singing along?"

"Yes. That's one reason I love this song. I mean, what a tribute to her father to be able to sing with him some twenty-five years after his death. Plus, there's the fact that the music is so beautiful, as are the lyrics."

Antonio ran the back of his hand down the side of her face. "You are absolutely stunning when you are excited about something."

She felt her face get hot. He curled a hand under her chin and lifted her face to kiss her. Her insides churned. Although Antonio Vasculli was attractive, it felt wrong to let him kiss her, cheap. *Just think about Chase. Pretend you're kissing Chase.*

The song ended and he made a big display out of dipping her as Chase had done at the end of the video. He was too egotistical to notice this dip wasn't filled with the same kind of heat and passion. He drew Hope up, saying in a commanding way, "Let's go."

CHAPTER TWENTY-SIX

Chase was putting his guitar in its case when Hal stuck his head into the living room, which connected Hal's bedroom to Chase's in their suite.

"Umm...I've got a call for you from Phillip Rutledge."

He straightened. "Phillip Rutledge?" he repeated, his jaw starting to tighten. "What does *he* want?"

"I would have gotten rid of him, but this sounded urgent. It's something about Hope." Chase noticed the concern in Hal's eyes. He reached for the receiver.

"Yes."

"Chase!" Phillip sounded relieved. "Listen, I know the last person you want to talk to right now is me, but please don't hang up."

"What do you want?"

"I think Hope is in trouble."

His expression became serious. "You've got my attention."

"I saw her this evening dining with Antonio Vasculli. She must have overheard Jack talking about him the other day when she was in the office and decided to investigate him on her own—"

"Hold on. Hold on. You're talking too fast. Who's Antonio Vasculli?"

"He's a local crime boss. Okay, 'reputed' local crime boss. They've never been able to stick anything on him. But I'm telling you, Chase, he's one scary dude. He's into money laundering, extortion. You name it, he's been accused of it. And people have been known to disappear in cases he's involved in—"

"Where's Hope now?" Chase interrupted.

"Well, I followed them when they left the restaurant, and he took her to his place on the Upper West Side. I tried to talk to her, tell her this guy is trouble, but she wouldn't listen to me. Maybe she'll listen to you."

"She damn well better," he said grimly. After a pause, he added sincerely, "Thanks for calling."

"You're welcome. I still love Hope, you know, but I get that she's in love with you. I just don't want her to get hurt, is all."

"Neither do I. I'll fly out there as soon as possible and talk to her."

"Good. If you need any information, you can reach me at *The Globe* or my number is listed. Good night."

Chase hung up the phone.

"What's up?"

"Hope may be in trouble. I'm going to have to fly out there."

"No problem. We've got two days off anyway. You want me to call Jeff?"

"I know it's late. Offer to pay him double. I want to get there as soon as I can."

"You've got it."

WHEN THE LIMO PULLED up to Antonio Vasculli's "place" on Riverside Drive, all Hope could do was gape. On the drive over, Antonio had casually mentioned he had recently purchased his residence for thirty million dollars.

On the outside it resembled a city library, constructed of white marble in the French Renaissance jewel box design with bronze grills on the balconies. She was only half-listening to Vasculli's recount of the history of the house as he led her in, but heard enough to know Samuel Jensen had built the house in 1909, the same architect who'd designed Moulton Hall.

The interior was no less grand than the exterior, and while she was fascinated, she felt the building had more of the feel of a museum than a home, and she couldn't imagine living there. All in all, she preferred Chase's understated home and she began to miss him all the more. Antonio gave a quick tour, which still took an hour as they had to cover over 12,000 square feet. They ended up back in the library, where Antonio poured her a snifter of brandy. She kicked off her shoes, her feet aching from all the walking, and curled her feet under her on the couch as they drank.

"I wish I had brought my camera with me. I could probably spend a week in here taking pictures."

"Well, we'll just have to see about your coming back to do that." She could hardly miss the suggestive nature of his comment.

"I could do a coffee table book on Chicago architecture. Get an expert to handle the text, and I'd do the photos. I think I could sell that. It could go into all the tourist spots around town..."

Antonio laughed at her enthusiasm. Without saying a word, he reached over and took the snifter from her hand and set it on the gorgeous black walnut table in front of them, next to his own. She froze as he scooted closer, then put his hand on the back of her neck and drew her in for a kiss. He pulled away, keeping one hand on her neck, and running one hand intimately along her leg and hip. She fought back her fear and revulsion and the urge to cover her breasts as his eyes lingered there before looking deeply into hers.

He said with quiet menace, his grip tightening slightly on the back of her neck, "You know, Hope, I do not share my women."

A chill ran up her spine. He released her and took another long swallow of brandy. He stood, reaching down to grab her hand and bring her to her feet. "You shivered a moment ago. You must be cold." He rubbed her arm, and then brought his mouth to her shoulder, biting her in a painfully sensual way that made it clear he was a dangerous man, and he would be fully in charge of wherever this was to go. "How about we take this upstairs and get under the covers, and I'll warm you up?"

She fought back the wave of panic. "Do you think I could use the restroom first?"

"Certainly."

He made a move to show her the way, but she kissed him quickly on the lips to placate him and to reassure him of her intentions of furthering their intimacy. "You just stay here and finish your brandy; I remember where it is." She smiled seductively. "I'll be right back."

As soon as she was out of sight of the doorway, she scurried down the hall. She had noted earlier his study was conveniently located across from the bathroom. She opened the French doors that led to the study and hurriedly crossed to his desk. She spotted a top drawer on the right with a lock on it. She withdrew a screwdriver from her purse, which she had placed there for just such a contingency, and began to try to pry it open. She was leaving marks in the mahogany desk, but she couldn't worry about that now.

The wood creaked as she put her weight into the handle of the screwdriver, and then the drawer sprang open. In delighted surprise, she began to rifle through the contents of the drawer, glancing up every now and again to make sure she wouldn't be discovered. It only took a moment for her to come across exactly what she was looking for, a contract for a new housing project, already signed by Councilman Mulrooney, when she knew for a fact the deadline for bids wasn't until the middle of next week. Mulrooney was illegally awarding contracts to Vasculli, no doubt for a hefty fee.

She took a small camera out of her purse, and took pictures of the pertinent information. Just as she finished, she heard Antonio's footsteps on the marble down the hall. She rushed to replace the folder and her tools. She spit-rubbed the scratches until they were hardly visible.

When Antonio walked in, she was sitting in his chair leaning back with her high-heeled shoes crossed on top of his desk. She scrambled to her feet.

"All right, you caught me," she said sheepishly. She strolled around to the opposite side, trailing her fingers along the edge of the elegant desk as she did so. "I get off a little bit on the feel of power." She leaned on the desk in front of him, continuing to rub her hands along the edges of the desk. "And *this* is power!"

"Well, there's only one thing to do then. Make love to you right here."

With surprising speed, he began to clear the desk, sweeping off fountain pens, papers, and even knocking a lamp to the carpeted floor. She barely had time to react before he pushed her back onto the desk, kissing her wildly and then backing off to undo his tie. He drew the widened loop over his head and tore his collar open. His hands were on her breasts and his tongue ran along her neck.

"Oh!" she cried out, frantically pressing on him. "I'm going to be sick!" She managed to push him off and sat up. "Do you have a trash can or something?"

He stood there panting and staring at her for a second, his eyes still glazed over with lust. Then, as if finally understanding what she was saying, he sprang around the desk and retrieved a heavy, gold wastebasket. She leaned over pretending to be ill, and moaning.

"Oh, Tony...I'm so, so sorry! I've ruined everything! Oh...I think it was the champagne...and Phillip shaking me. Mmm, and then when we were, you know...oh, I am just mortified. I was trying to just get past it, but I don't think I can." She continued to breathe over the trash can with a hand on her stomach.

"Are you feeling better?" he asked after a few moments.

"Well, I don't think I'm going to be sick, but I have this raging headache. Tony, I'm sorry, but I think I need to go home."

He sighed, clearly disappointed. "Well, that's okay. You can't help it if you feel sick, I guess." He made one last desperate suggestion. "Maybe if you just lie down for a while..."

She shook her head mournfully. "I don't think so, Tony."

"All right then," he grumbled, no longer trying to hide his dissatisfaction. "I'll have Milo take you home." He escorted her down the long hall to the foyer.

"Can I get a rain check, maybe next week?" She smiled at him weakly as he helped her out the door.

"Sure. Sure. Here's my business card. Call me." He shoved his card into her hand as she bent down to get into the limo.

Antonio closed the door behind her. "Make sure you remember where you drop her off. I want to know where she lives," he told Milo quietly.

"Yes, sir."

She sank into the leather seats. She should feel exhilarated. She'd done it. She had evidence Antonio Vasculli and Robert Mulrooney were in cahoots. But instead, she felt dirty and cheap and frightened. She couldn't wait to get this story done and get to Chase and just melt into his arms. She curled her knees up and hugged them to herself. Phillip was right, she wasn't cut out for this work; she never had been. She began shaking uncontrollably. She put her head down on her knees and began to weep. She didn't know exactly why she was crying, only that she was overwhelmed.

"Are you okay, Miss?"

She sought for some control. "I-I'm fine," she rasped out. "Just tired...and I don't feel well."

"Let's get you home, then." She wiped her face and looked up into the mirror. She saw kindness in the driver's eyes. He pulled away from the curb. "Where to?"

"If you could just take me back to the restaurant, I need to get my car." She glanced around outside her window, becoming calmer.

"Mr. Vasculli told me to take you home, Miss. I don't think he wants you to be driving in your condition."

Her eyes quickly returned to the rearview mirror. The dark gray eyes that met hers in the mirror from beneath the driver's hat now had an edge to them.

"I'm perfectly capable of driving my own car," she returned with an air of haughtiness, trying to conceal her alarm.

The driver seemed to consider this for a minute. "As you wish," he said finally.

She sighed in relief. Maybe she was just letting her imagination get the best of her. All those movies she had watch about mobsters had her nervous. She would return home, write her story, and before long she'd be winging it to wherever Chase was currently situated.

CHAPTER TWENTY-SEVEN

H ope was up all night working on her story. She ran out of coffee and trotted down to the corner shop to get a fresh cup and some beans. On her return, as she strode down the hall of her building, she slowed her steps. The door to her apartment was ajar. She was certain she had closed it. Cautiously, she crept forward. As she neared it she could see the wooden doorjamb had been cracked. Someone had been in her apartment! With her hot coffee in one hand, and the small bag of groceries in the other, she warily pushed the door open with her foot. A groan escaped as she surveyed her apartment.

Couch cushions had been slashed, their white fluffy batting strewn everywhere, books had been jerked from decorative wine crates, their torn pages mating with the pillow fluff, her lamp lay smashed on the floor and stools were knocked over. In dismay, she stepped into the room, afraid to look into the kitchen area and see further damage. As she approached Mewford hopped up on the bar, mewing plaintively.

"Oh, Mr. Mewford! Thank goodness you're okay."

She gingerly set her grocery bag down on the bar, her eyes scanning the cabinets, which lay open, empty except for pots and pans, all of the dishware lying smashed on the floor. *My God, didn't anyone hear the ruckus?* But then she remembered most of her neighbors had already left for work, and the retired people who remained in the building were, perhaps, too hard of hearing to have noticed. She let out several small soft "ohs!" before her eyes landed on her laptop.

Strangely it was not smashed, the screen flipped open as she had left it, her inbox visible.

Her inbox visible. It had not gone into standby, which meant she had either just missed the vandals, or...they were still in the apartment. She dug in her purse. She heard a floorboard squeak and looked up, catching a figure reflected in the door of the microwave approaching from behind. She made a dash for the front door but was intercepted by another burly man who grabbed her around the waist, picking her up off the floor and dragging her toward the kitchen.

"Let me go!" she screamed, but his tight grip around her midsection strangled the cry. He swung her around, throwing her against the post that ran from the bar to the ceiling. He clapped a rough hand over her mouth. He was about average-height, with dark, close-cropped hair, almost as short as the stubble on his face. He wore a one-piece jumpsuit with the name of a laundry service embroidered on the left-hand side of his chest.

"Okay, darlin', that's enough!" He leered at her as she stood gasping for air, smashed by the weight of the lower half of his body, pressed against hers. "God! She's a pretty little thing, isn't she?" he commented to his friend with a low chuckle. "Now, listen, sweetheart, there's no need for this whole thing to get out of hand. We just want to ask you a few questions, then we'll leave, okay?" She gave a slight nod as he stared into her eyes. "I'm going to let my hand down, and I don't want to hear a peep from you. Not a peep!" His hand lowered to just below her throat. He let his eyes wander there. "Built, too," he commented.

The second man stepped closer to get a look. He was shorter and not as heavy, but his muscular frame was evident even through the jumpsuit he wore. She let her gaze shift back to the man in front of her. His hand had drifted further down her shirt, and he began to undo buttons, pulling the blouse loose from the top of her jeans. He grunted his pleasure and slid his hand around her breast and began to fondle her.

"Hey," the second intruder said in an irritated way, "we're not here for that!"

Despite his words, she could see his eyes were riveted to her body as well. He took a step closer, his resolve weakening. Meanwhile, the first man shifted his position, bringing one arm up to lean it across her upper chest, putting pressure on her windpipe. She could feel he was excited as he forced his hard body against hers. He started to dip his head toward her chest, but he never got there as she brought her forehead down, hard, into his face.

He screamed and staggered backward, hands to his face. She made another break for the door, but a third man she hadn't noticed before blocked her path. She turned back in time to see her molester bring his hands down, covered in blood. A steady stream began to drip off his chin.

"Geez! Stupid bitch broke my nose!" The other men chuckled without sympathy. She stared in fear as his eyes narrowed forebodingly. "You're gonna pay for that!" He clutched a handful of her shirt and pulled his elbow back. His fist connected solidly with her face, and her head hit the wall with a sickening thud. He released her shirt and she slid down the wall, crumpling to the floor and blacking out.

CHASE STAMPED DOWN the hall, wondering why Hope would be stupid enough to try to investigate a mobster. Had they finally gotten back together, only to have her fling her life around like a ball attached by elastic to a wooden paddle? And why hadn't she told him about it? Why hadn't she trusted him? *Because,* he answered himself, *I would have told her she was being a little fool!* He'd had plenty of time on the flight over to work up a full head of steam. *And for that matter,* he added, *in this age of space travel, why did it still take so*

long to fly from the coast to the Midwest? He fed the anger, because the anger kept the fear at bay.

Until he saw the door. He ran the last several feet and pushed it open. The first thing he saw was the pool of blood on the floor.

"HOPE?" he shouted in a panic. He looked behind the counter, but saw only ruined dishes. He ran into the bedroom, into the bathroom.

He kept calling, although he knew the small apartment didn't have any other places to hide her. "Hope? Oh, God, Hope!"

"Chase?"

He ran back to the front room. The kid from the roof? "Kip?"

"I saw it, Chase! I saw the whole damn thing!"

"What did you—?"

"These guys came in and tore the place up, just tore it up. They were looking for something, I guess. They had one guy as lookout at the door. He must have seen your girlfriend coming, 'cause all of a sudden they all went into the bedroom, and a few seconds later she walked in and they jumped her."

"Was she hurt?" Chase stared with alarm at the blood on the floor.

"Oh no, man. That's not her blood. She was so cool! They were...uh...messing with her, and she head-butted this one dude in the face and he was bleeding everywhere!"

"And then what happened?"

"Well...he got really pissed. He knocked her out and then they put her in one of those rolly laundry cart things and just carried her out of here. Rolled her right through the lobby, man!"

"Did you see what they did next?"

"Of course," he said proudly, "they put her in this laundry van and drove away." When Chase's face fell, he quickly added, "But I think I know where they took her."

"You do?"

"I've seen that van before, when I walk to school. It's always parked in this section of warehouses nobody seems to use much, which I've always thought is strange, seeing as it's a laundry truck and all."

"Do you have a car?"

"Yeah, dude, I have a car."

He grabbed the teen's jacket and pulled him with him out the door.

"But I can't drive it. I'm grounded."

"Well, I'm sure the hell not grounded. I'll drive!" He dragged him down the hall.

"I don't know, man..."

Chase stopped suddenly. "Kip, they could be killing Hope right now."

"Yeah, maybe. But if I let you drive my car, my mom will *definitely* kill me. She told me not to ever—"

He gave the teen a look of exasperation, and then had a flash of inspiration. "What if I gave you concert tickets?"

"Come on! It's parked in front. But hey, I called the police ten minutes ago. They're supposed to meet me here."

Chase pushed him into the elevator. "We'll call them on the way."

WHEN HOPE CAME TO, she was lying on her side along the cold metal floor of a stripped-down van. She had duct tape covering her mouth, hands tied behind her back, as well as her feet.

"Hey, look who's up." The heavier-set man knelt beside her and started stroking her face, his eyes lit up as he again slid them over her body.

The slighter man kicked him. "Knock it off! Tony wouldn't like that."

The van came to a jarring halt, and the big man made a move to pick her up. "I said get your stinking hands off her!" The smaller man stepped in front of him and scooped her up easily, trudging, stooped over, to the back of the van. The driver threw the doors open, and she was handed down into his arms. The man carrying her never said a word, never made eye contact, as if she were just another pile of laundry.

Mr. Handsy, as she now named the bigger man in her head, rolled open a large door on the side of an unmarked warehouse surrounded by broken-down equipment, forklifts, and bobcats, which looked like they hadn't moved in years. The day was bright and she was surprised they would just carry a woman, trussed up like some cannibal's dinner, out in the open. But, from what she could see, the place was deserted. The warehouse they brought her into was also relatively bright, with lots of narrow windows high along the ceiling on all sides. The majority of the space was nearly empty, maybe a couple of dozen crates, with a bunch of empty palates scattered about. The last quarter of the room was floor to ceiling crates, unmarked except for some shipping numbers burned into the wood. The air smelled mustily of oil and dirt, and the more welcome scent of the wooden crates. There was a broken-down table and a half dozen chairs in the middle of the room. They pulled one of these aside to stick her into.

The three men almost immediately got started on some animated conversation about the Sox game from the previous night. She had a sort of surreal feeling. *They're going to kill me and move on to conversation about who should win the Kentucky Derby while they're cleaning up the blood!* But they simply ignored her. She heard a faint noise outside and prayed somehow help had arrived. But when the door rolled back, her heart skipped a beat. In strolled Anthony Vasculli, trailed by two thugs, and he did not look happy.

CHAPTER TWENTY-EIGHT

They pulled up to a rundown warehouse in Kip's burnt orange '76 Malibu. Chase turned off the ignition when he was about fifteen yards away from the laundry van. He handed Kip his cell phone.

"Tell the police exactly where we are, and if you see anyone, duck down."

Kip nodded silently, his usual gusto gone. Chase heard him start to dial as he carefully shut the car door behind him. He crept forward until he could see into the door, which had bounced open a crack when the thugs had tried to slam it shut. He saw a bunch of men standing around, one in a suit, and he saw Hope in a chair. He allowed himself a sigh of relief, at least she was okay. But as he watched, the man in the suit cracked her viciously across the face, knocking her to the floor. He started in surprise, feeling the fury leap inside him like a fire someone had just thrown gasoline on.

"HOPE," ANTONIO SAID jovially, as if she weren't sitting there in front of him bound and gagged, "so good to see you." She stared at him stonily. He looked at the men behind her, who had come to a sort of awkward attention. "Why is there blood on her shirt? I thought I gave you explicit instructions she was not to be harmed."

"Uh...that's 'cause Joey, here, got a little fresh with her and she head-butted him in the snoot." He chuckled, but then cleared his throat as he could see the mobster wasn't amused. "That's Joey's blood, boss. We didn't do nothin' to her."

"Is that so?" He eyed Joey coldly. "When I give instructions, Joey, they are to be followed to the letter. Do you understand?"

Before the man could answer, one of the two muscular men who had come in with Antonio dealt him three quick blows to the body and a crushing right hook to the chin. Hope's eyes grew wide as he fell near her feet, unconscious.

"Get him out of here," Antonio instructed. The guy who had dropped him dragged his body off to one side. She watched with concern, even if part of her thought justice had been served.

"Now, Hope." Antonio strutted back over to her. "I am sorry for my cohorts' ungentlemanly behavior." He slowly began to button her shirt up, his eyes lingering on her body as he did. Halfway up, he stopped and rubbed the back of one of his knuckles between her breasts. "You know," he said only loud enough for her to hear, leaning in, his eyes set on hers, "I had planned on undressing you myself." He opened his hand, so the back of it just touched the curve of her breast as it moved up and down. He sighed. "And then you had to go and ruin everything."

His eyes became hard, and he finished buttoning her shirt quickly. He grabbed hold of a corner of the duct tape covering her mouth and, with a savage yank, ripped it off. She gasped in pain. Antonio turned his back to her and walked a few feet away, turning again to face her with arms crossed over his chest.

"Where is the film you took in my office?" Perhaps seeing the spark of surprise in her eyes, he added, "What? Did you think you were the only one with a camera?" He took a step forward. "Where is it, Hope?"

She set her jaw without commenting, staring at him in defiance. Even if her hands had been untied, she still wouldn't have had time to block the blow that sent her sprawling to the floor. She moaned as she lay there, and then felt hands on her upper arms, jerking her up to the chair. Her shoulders ached from the strain of her body weight, and she breathed in the pain jaggedly.

She had no more been put in her seat, when the door opened and a man brought in Chase's limp form, supporting him under the arms. *Chase? But that was impossible. Chase was in Canada somewhere, safe, with Hal...safe...*

"Looky what I found snoopin' around outside. Chase Hatton! When he wakes up, do you think he'll give me his autograph?" They chuckled coarsely. With a heave, he plopped his burden down and Chase rolled face-up in front of her. She looked on in horror.

"Isn't this nice?" Antonio said grimly. "The happy couple reunited." He stared down into Chase's still face. "Well, you wouldn't listen when we hit you, maybe you'll listen when—" Antonio made a move to kick Chase.

"NO!" she screamed, falling to her knees at his side. "*Please!*" She sobbed. "Antonio, I'm begging you! I'll tell you where it is." Her shell-shocked eyes fell on Chase. "Please! Just untie me so I can help him, and then I'll tell you right where to find it." She peered up, her eyes wild with desperation.

Antonio shrugged; tied or untied, she was no threat to five men. "Untie her."

As soon as she was free, she bent over Chase's prone form, her shaking hands pushing the hair from his face.

"Hope?" Antonio said impatiently.

Without looking up, she said dully, "It's in the paper towel holder."

"What?"

"Back at my place!" she snapped. "I saw your men coming and I shoved it into the paper towel holder to hide it."

Antonio snapped his fingers and two of his men took off.

Chase stirred.

"Oh, God, honey! I'm so sorry."

"Nice of you to join us, Hatton," Antonio commented snidely. "A murder/suicide is so tidy. Doesn't leave any open ends." He pulled a gun from his pocket and aimed it at the pair as Chase rose unsteadily to his feet with Hope's help. "Just think of the headlines: 'Rock Star And His Hope Found Dead.'"

His sardonic laughter died on his lips when a loud, amplified voice cut through the stifling air. "Chicago PD. COME OUT WITH YOUR HANDS UP!"

The only one aware of their impending arrival, Chase reacted faster than anyone else. When Antonio turned toward the door, he grabbed Hope's hand and took their chance to run. Before anyone even knew they were missing, they were able to make it almost all the way to the edge of the stacks of crates. When Antonio realized they had scampered off, he took a shot at their fleeing figures. The bullet ricocheted off the corner of a box, splintering it and sending shards flying, but the pair had already turned the corner.

As they raced among the rows of crates, they could hear gunfire and shouting from the front of the warehouse. They could also make out the pounding feet of a pursuer. Hoping to find an exit somewhere along the far wall, they were disappointed to discover only more pillars of crates leaning against it.

Chase could hear someone getting closer. He glanced around feverishly and spotted the small windows near the top. "Up, Hope," he said breathlessly.

Without hesitation, she began to scramble up the boxes, and for a minute he was reminded of her lithe figure scaling the side of Mt. Lowe. She glanced back. "Chase?"

"Keep going," he ordered. She was an open target, and he wasn't about to turn his back on anyone who might be gunning for her.

She reached the top and peered down. "Chase! What the hell are you doing?"

Putting off answering her, he responded, "See if you can get through the window and if you think I can."

As she obediently slithered through the window, he turned his ear again to the warehouse. Whoever had followed them was just feet away on the other side of the boxes. He could either expose himself by climbing up to Hope, or take his chances in a confrontation. He set his face grimly as he saw a shadow carrying a pistol on the side of a box.

The man in the suit rounded the corner. "Where's Hope?"

"She's gone," Chase announced with a hint of triumph in his voice.

"No matter," he commented, waving his gun as if swatting at an annoying gnat. "We'll get her. She's a lovely girl, Mr. Hatton. You were very lucky to have her, but I'm afraid that relationship, and all others for that matter, is over for you."

"Listen," Chase tried to buy some time, "there's no way you're getting out of here. You can leave now with just an attempted kidnapping charge. Why up the stakes to murder?"

Before the man in the suit could respond, a box tumbled from atop of the stacks. In the split second it took to fall, the man looked up, hearing the wood creaking. Chase, too, sized up the situation and dived to the side. The heavy crate hit the man squarely and his gun went off.

Hope half-climbed, half-slid down the tall pile of boxes. Hitting bottom, she came to Chase, as he slumped in a corner between the boxes and the wall.

"Chase!" She bent and they both looked at his bloody sleeve. A small, strangled cry of alarm escaped from her mouth.

"It's okay. I only cut it on the edge of a box. I'm fine."

He scrambled to his feet. The gun lay about two feet away from the mobster's outstretched hand. The crate was broken open, resting on Antonio's shoulder where he lay moaning, spilling its contents all over his back and the floor. They appeared to be bundles of some powdery substance, but Chase wasn't sticking around to find out what it was. He hurriedly picked up the gun as he heard more feet approaching. Pushing Hope behind him, he backed them against the wall, the gun raised.

"Drop it! Police!"

Chase had never been so happy to comply with an order before.

"Chase Hatton! What the hell are you doing here?" the officer asked, as his partner peeked around from the opposite corner.

"It's a long story, Officer." Chase turned to Hope, grabbing her by the shoulders and leaning down to look her squarely in the eyes. "You're okay?"

She nodded dumbly and he pulled her into an embrace. They held each other for several moments without speaking, hearts still pounding in their chests.

CHAPTER TWENTY-NINE

Chase was up to something. Every time Hope turned around he was either whispering with Hal, or was on some mysterious phone conversation he would label "business." *Funny business,* she thought, but she didn't pry. She did, however, observe.

Things had wrapped up in Chicago quickly; Vasculli and his cronies had been sent to jail, and the story was splashed all over the front page of *The Globe*. But as far as she was concerned, she had left that life behind. She had been on the road with Chase for the past two weeks, enjoying every minute of it. She sat across from him now, at a Cleveland hamburger stand, sharing a plate of fries.

"Have dinner with me tomorrow night at my parents'?" he asked abruptly.

She paused, a French fry poised halfway to her mouth. "In Lincoln?" she asked, incredulous.

"It *is* where they live. So, yes, that would be most convenient."

"What are you up to?" she asked him, waving her fry in circles in front of his face.

He snapped at the fry with his teeth and ended up with half of it in his mouth. He leaned back in his chair, his arms behind his head. "Nothing," he returned, the picture of innocence.

She smiled at him, but then turned thoughtful. Her face became serious and she dropped her eyes for a moment, picking at the fries absentmindedly.

"What's wrong?"

"Hmmm...oh...nothing, really..."

He pushed the hair back from her face, laying a hand easily on her shoulder. "It doesn't sound like nothing to me," he prodded gently. "Come on..."

"It's just..." She took a deep breath and tried to articulate her thoughts. "The last time I saw your parents, it was prom night. They were so happy. We all were so happy." She faltered. As she struggled to put her thoughts into words he was reminded of the night he had found her on the swing set, torn up on the inside, and so vulnerable he wanted to just sweep her up in his arms. He rubbed her hand where it sat on the table and waited patiently.

She looked up, staring off into the distance, squinting in the bright sunlight. "I don't think I ever told you this, but I really love and respect your parents, as much for making you the man you are, as for their own special traits. Your dad was always so funny and kind and generous and sort of...wise...in an offbeat way. And your mom, she was just dynamite. Nurturing, but strong...easy to be with, both of them." Her face, which had gone soft in remembering, clouded.

"And?" He tried to softly nudge the words out of her.

"I'm afraid, Chase," she said in a rush. "Afraid of seeing the disappointment in their eyes."

"I don't understand."

She smashed the end of a French fry down like she was putting out a cigarette. "My God, Chase, I hurt you. Your mom must hate me. I'd hate me if I were her. She should hate me." She became increasingly agitated. "It was awful what I did."

"Hope! Honey, I explained it all to her."

"And she understood?"

He could see on her face that she was letting herself believe it for a second. "Yeah," he replied, trying to sound convincing, but his voice waivered. The fact was his mother had been quiet on the phone when he had talked to her about it.

She flew out of her chair, standing behind it and gripping the top. "See, I knew it! She hates me and I can't bear that, Chase. I really can't." She glanced around, realizing her voice had risen. But, as it was much later than the regular lunch hour, they were practically alone.

"Hope," he said, shifting to rub the back of her thigh and pulling her between his legs, "I love you. And whatever hang-ups my mom may or may not have, she'll just have to get used to it, because I'm not letting you go this time."

Slowly, a smile edged its way across her face. "How did I get this lucky?" She caressed his face and kissed him sweetly. "I love you, too, Chase. And I'm not going anywhere."

He smiled brightly. "You'll come to dinner, then?"

She hesitated. "What's on the menu?"

"I asked Mom to make fried chicken and mashed potatoes, and she said she was going to make an apple pie—"

"You had me at fried chicken."

"Good." He stood to give her a squeeze.

THEY PULLED INTO THE Hattons' driveway. The shadow of the house fell across them as they got out of the car, the lawn dappled by the huge elm tree that still stood sentinel. Hope looked at the house with a sigh. It hadn't changed. God, how she had missed this place! She saw herself playing catch with Chase on the front lawn, running to glide along the Slip and Slide, tossing the Frisbee, and she could almost hear the laughter coupled with the *tick ping* of the table tennis ball as it bounced from side to side.

"Hope?"

"Huh? Oh." he stood with his hand stretched out to her. She took it briefly, and then slid an arm around his waist, laying her head for a second on his shoulder.

"Wait. Before we go in." She jerked her head in the direction of a knotted hickory down the lane. "For old time's sake?"

He grinned and they both broke into a run. He admired the fluid way she still ran, hair streaming behind her, elbows keeping rhythm with her feet. They reached the tree at the same time, both running a hand along its rough bark as they passed and then bending over with their hands on their knees, gulping in air and laughing brokenly.

"Ha! Not quite as easy as it used to be."

She shook her head with a smile, still winded, and he threw his arm over her shoulder. "Come on," Chase said tenderly, "let's go inside."

"HEY, MOM!" CHASE GAVE her an enthusiastic hug and a kiss on the cheek, and then stepped back next to Hope who hadn't moved much past the door.

"Look at you," she said, ruffling his hair playfully and fighting back the tears of joy. "Hope, welcome home." Her words were kind, but Hope noticed she couldn't keep the coolness out of her voice.

"Thank you for having me, Mrs. Hatton. It's good to see you again."

Before the awkward moment could extend any further, Chase's dad came bounding down the stairs. "Well-l-l, look what the cat dragged in! Hey, Chase." Greg Hatton clapped his son on the back and shook his hand warmly. "Hope." He swallowed her in an embrace. "So good to see you!" His sincerity brought a genuine smile to her face. "You look fantastic! Not quite the girl who used to race you across the field," he added, elbowing Chase in the ribs with a grin.

"No," he agreed. "But she did just give me a run for my money a second ago."

Greg stepped forward and took both of Hope's hands in his and kissed her cheek.

"Well," his mom said with forced gaiety, "who wants some fried chicken?"

"I do!" they all answered at once.

She laughed. "All right, then. Let's eat."

The meal passed pleasantly enough with Mr. Hatton asking numerous questions about Hope's adventures in Chicago and her photography.

"I'm trying to put a portfolio together to present to galleries in hopes maybe one day someone will allow me to have a showing."

"As soon as someone sees her work, they're going to snap her right up. She's unbelievably talented," Chase commented.

"You may be a bit biased."

"I'd love to see your work," Chase's father interjected.

"I have some photos out in the car I could bring in after dinner."

"I have plans for after dinner," Chase said mysteriously.

"You do?" Hope studied him with a smile, but his face didn't reveal anything. "You know," she mentioned between bites, "Chase is pretty talented along the photography line, too. Have you seen the pictures he's taken at the beach?"

"No," Mr. Hatton replied, raising an eyebrow in his son's direction.

"He's got an excellent eye."

"Yes, he does." Hope caught the wink Chase's dad gave him.

Chase laughed, and then looked over at his mom accusingly. She had not entered into the conversation all evening.

She shrugged and silently mouthed, "What?"

After they had cleared the table, she finally spoke up. "Hope, could you please help me hang the laundry on the line?"

"Mom, I'll help you with that." Chase made a move to take the laundry basket from her.

"No, Chase." She put a hand on his. "This will give Hope and me a chance to catch up."

He paled. "I don't see why I can't help you two—"

"That's all right. I'll help your mom." Hope spoke with quiet resolve, like a person walking into an audit, resigned to her fate.

When the two women went outside, Chase and his father moved to the window over the sink to watch them.

"I didn't know Mom used the laundry line," Chase said thoughtfully.

"She doesn't."

Chase looked at him in alarm and made a move toward the door. His father put a hand on his arm. "Trust your mom, Son."

They continued to stand, leaning on the counter and peeking out the window. After a few minutes, his dad noted, "She has nice smelling hair." When Chase turned to look at him quizzically, he elaborated, "Hope. Hope has nice smelling hair."

Chase smiled slowly. "That's an odd comment."

His dad shrugged, returning his gaze to the window. "I'm an odd fellow."

"I'll say."

Greg Hatton punched his son's arm, and they continued to watch in silence.

Hope followed Mrs. Hatton grimly. A warm, gentle breeze blew through the trees, lifting the fresh scent of laundry detergent into the air, belying the tension between the two completely. She knew the older woman was still angry with her, and she couldn't blame her. She would take any criticism headed her way; she deserved it. They stood on opposite sides of the clothesline, the basket in the soft, green grass near their feet.

"Hope...I've been trying to figure out what to say to you all during dinner." She paused and Hope waited nervously for her to continue. Mrs. Hatton removed clothespins from a baggie she had brought with her, clipping them on the line near the end, as she spoke. "I am glad to see Chase so happy with you. But there was another time he was happy with you, and things didn't turn out so well." She paused, her hands hovering near a clothespin, her eyes on Hope's.

"Yes. You are right. And I made a mistake then. I won't make that mistake again. I love Chase, Mrs. Hatton. I always have. He makes me feel happy and warm and secure. You raised a good man, and I am grateful to you for that."

"Thank you," Mrs. Hatton replied, taking another clip and moving down the line.

"I should have believed in him more. I shouldn't have let my mom convince me to move away with her that night. But when I saw Susie McNamara kiss him..." Hope became upset and this time it was Mrs. Hatton's turn to wait while Hope regained control. She stretched a sheet over the line as Hope talked, taking them from the basket one by one. "I know now I misread the situation, but taken out of context, the kiss, the conversation about her pregnancy, it was very convincing evidence he had cheated on me, and was in fact, still cheating on me. I was devastated. I was eighteen. And I had always felt unworthy of Chase. He was so good, and I was...uncertain of whom I was. I'm not any longer. I know it must have been difficult for you to watch him suffer, and I can understand if you never want to forgive me." She teared up again. "All I can say is I'm sorry. So sorry! I was young and foolish. I should have given him a chance to explain himself. Instead, I ran away. But I love him and I'd do anything to have a chance to prove that to him, and to you."

The basket lay empty, the sheets strung in a neat line across the yard. Hope picked the empty basket up and rested it on her hip. Mrs. Hatton watched her thoughtfully as Hope turned to head back inside.

In the kitchen, the men hastily began scraping dishes into the sink, pretending they had not been watching the entire time.

When she came through the door, Mr. Hatton called out, "Hope, why don't you show me those pictures now?" He threw an arm over her shoulder and started to walk with her out to the car.

"What about the dishes?"

"Don't worry about that. We'll get them later. I'm really anxious to see your work. I've always been interested in photography myself."

Chase heard their voices fade as the door swung to behind them. He turned back to the window. His mom was wandering toward the swing set. She sat down in a swing and gently swayed back and forth. Chase dried his hands on a towel, struck by how the scene mirrored the night he had found Hope sitting there, and went outside.

"Mom?"

She looked up at him. "She's quite a girl."

He sighed. "I know. I really love her, Momma. She makes me happy."

"I can see that."

"We won't make the same mistakes this time around."

His mom stood and embraced him. "My little boy, turned man!" She pulled back and looked at him. "I only want what's best for you, you know."

He squeezed her, his eyes shut tightly. "I know, Momma. I know," he whispered. "Hope's what's best for me."

When the two strolled in hand in hand, they found Hope and Chase's father engrossed in studying photos. They were spread out in a rainbow fashion across the glossy, dark wooden dining table where Chase's father sat, obviously enjoying himself. Hope stood behind his father, who now showed a little gray at the temples, bending over to point something out to him. His dad looked up over the frames of his glasses at his wife as she entered. She smiled.

Seeming to take this as a sign, his dad cleared his throat. "Chase. Don't you and this young lady have some plans for tonight?"

"We sure do." Chase came around the table and grabbed Hope up in a bear hug. Winking at his mother, he guided Hope toward the door.

"Where are we going?" she asked, her curiosity getting the better of her.

"Never you mind," he responded firmly.

CHAPTER THIRTY

"Miniature golf." She smiled and leaned over in the car seat to kiss him. "You're so sweet!"

"I am, ain't I?"

"You're in for some serious necking later, buddy!"

"Mmm..."

After eighteen holes of grim combat, they got back behind the wheel of his yellow Camaro, which his dad kept stored for him to use when he was home.

"Don't worry, Hope. With some practice, someday maybe you'll be as good as me."

She socked him in the arm. "One stroke. One lousy stroke. And I'm pretty sure I saw you using your foot wedge."

"I did not!" He snorted indignantly.

"We made a lot of good memories in this car," she said, changing the subject and leaning her head back against the leather, smiling slyly.

"I'll say." He leaned his head back against the seat, too, and reached over, cupping his fingers behind her head and rubbing her cheek with his thumb.

She looked into his wonderful green eyes and felt a sudden wave of sadness. "There should have been more," she said quietly. It felt good to be home, for the most part, but it also reminded her of what they had lost.

"Yeah." They sat silently for a while. "Did you ever think, though, maybe this was the way things were suppose to be? Maybe we wouldn't have appreciated what we had if we'd been together all along."

"Hatton," she said with a smile, "how did you get to be such a damn optimist?"

He laughed and started the engine. "We have one more stop."

WHEN CHASE PULLED INTO the school parking lot, she beamed. "Man, it seems like eons, not years! It hasn't changed much though. New sign."

He parked and turned off the engine. "Want to take a walk around?"

"Sure."

They ambled around the campus arm in arm as the twilight fell, reminiscing about teachers and games and fellow students. "I wonder if it's changed much inside," he mused. "Let's try a door."

"Oh, I'm sure it's locked."

But the door opened for him. "Come on," he said with a grin.

She hesitated. "Do you think there's something going on tonight? There weren't any cars in the parking lot."

"I don't know; let's see." He held the door open for her, and she ducked under his arm.

"Oooh!" she said in hushed tones. "This is kind of creepy. Are you sure we aren't gonna get caught by Old Man Meyers and arrested for trespassing?"

Lights turned on at the end of the hall, and she was shocked to see her former principal standing there with his customary megaphone in his hand. "Old Man Meyers, huh?"

"Uh...Mr. Meyers..." Even though he didn't seem nearly as big and scary as he had when they were in high school, she was nervous. Her palms began to sweat. "We were just..." She looked at Chase for help.

Chase stepped forward and offered his hand. "Good to see you, Mr. Meyers."

The principal shook his hand. "Chase."

"Still use the megaphone?"

"Oh yeah!" He held it to his mouth to demonstrate. "Hatton! Creswell! Shouldn't you be in fourth hour?"

They all laughed, and Chase looped his hand easily around her shoulder.

"Success seems to agree with you, Chase. You guys look like you haven't changed since the last time I caught you making out in the hall. I wish I could say the same for me." He rubbed his bald pate. "But, you know, you guys were always respectful. Not like kids these days." He sighed, then laughed at himself. "Now I really do sound like Old Man Meyers. Well, I've got some paperwork to catch up on. You guys go ahead and look around. I'll be in my office if you need anything."

"Thanks," they chimed in unison.

"Boy," she said under her breath as they watched him trod away, "he's not nearly as scary as he used to be. Has he shrunk?"

"I think you're just not as intimidated by him as you once were."

"I'm not so sure about that. Didn't you hear my knees knocking?" She released a relieved laugh. She stepped over to some charcoal drawings on display along the wall. "Wow! These are good! I wonder if Mrs. Boyd is still here."

"I doubt it. She seemed like she was about a hundred years old when I had her."

She chuckled. She dragged Chase down the hall. "Look! They've got a soda machine now."

"Not fair!" he whined. "Speaking of sodas, the ones I had earlier are going to make a pit stop necessary. Why don't you go, too, and I'll meet you out here."

She gave him a kiss. "Okay." She released him, but then pulled him back for a deeper kiss. "Something about being back here is making me all hot and bothered."

"Mmm...maybe I'll get lucky tonight."

"You play your cards right, Mister"—she nibbled him on the chin playfully—"you can never tell."

He watched her as she turned to enter the restroom.

When she rounded the corner by the sinks, the first thing she saw was a long floral dress hanging on the last stall door. She sucked in her breath in wonder, and took a few steps forward, mouth hanging open.

"Look familiar?"

She jumped as Chase's mom stepped out of the stall.

Her hand over her heart, Hope's eyes returned to the dress. "It-t looks like—"

"Your prom dress. Chase couldn't find one exactly like it, but he came darn close," Julia said, examining the fabric.

"Ch-chase found this?"

"Uh-huh."

"But, I don't understand."

Julia lifted the hanger off the top of the door and handed it to her. "You're supposed to put this on." Her smile was radiant.

She took the gown from Chase's mom and stood staring at it, transfixed. Mrs. Hatton gave her a gentle shove toward the large handicap stall. "Go on."

When she stepped in, Julia shut the door behind her and held it closed. Slowly, she slid the lock closed, and Mrs. Hatton removed her hand from the top of the door.

"Anything you need should be in your overnight bag in there. Chase had me bring it from your hotel. Did you enjoy your miniature golf?"

"Ummm..." She was still stunned and it took a minute for her brain to decipher the question. "Yeah...yes," she said, slipping her top off and unsnapping her shorts. "You knew we were going golfing?"

"Yes, it was all part of the master plan."

"The master plan for what?" she asked a second later, stepping out of the stall in the dress.

"Spin around and I'll zip you up."

She did as she was told, lifting her hair so the zipper was accessible. She looked into the bathroom mirror. It was surreal. The dress was so similar to the one she had worn that night. It had large, bright flowers akin to the one she had worn all those years ago, and the design was almost identical. Instead of being crinkly, however, the fabric was smoother, silkier. It was flattering.

Mrs. Hatton gazed at her in the mirror. "You look utterly beautiful," she said, her eyes sparkling. "Can I help you with your hair?" Hope relinquished control, and Chase's mom began to brush her long hair. "I'm sure your mom did this for you on the night of prom. I was sorry to hear of her passing. She was a really good friend. I missed her a lot when you two moved away."

Hope glanced up quickly into the mirror to see if Mrs. Hatton was again angry with her, but she was still smiling. She twisted her hair up and secured it.

"I'm not as good at this as your mom was. Jeff and Chase didn't need much help with their hair."

Hope turned to the Julia and squeezed her hands. "Thank you, Mrs. Hatton."

"Hope...I was too hard on you earlier. I was wrong to be. If I had been in your position—seen Greg kissing some girl, discussing plans for her pregnancy—I would have ripped his eyes out. Scratch that. I would have ripped her eyes out and then ripped his out. I had no right to judge you." She looked down at their hands. "I know you would have never hurt Chase on purpose, and he wasn't the only one hurt that night." She looked up. "Will you forgive me, Hope?"

Hope was too overwhelmed to say anything. She simply hugged Julia tightly for several minutes. When they pulled away, both women were sniffling. "Oh, dear! Now we've got the waterworks on and we'll ruin your makeup. Come here, come here!" She rushed her into the stall and wiped her eyes with toilet paper she ripped off the roll. "I'll leave you to finish getting ready, but if you need me, I'll be right outside." With a final squeeze, she was gone.

Hope sat down on the toilet. He had gotten her a dress. Her eyes fell on a small white box near her bag. She reached over and picked it up. She opened the lid. A wrist corsage, just like the one he had given her on prom night. She got up slowly and slid the beautiful orchid and baby's breath over her wrist as she glided again to the mirror. She assessed herself. A few wrinkles had begun to appear around her eyes and mouth, but Mrs. Hatton had done a good job with her hair. She hadn't changed all that much. One thing definitely hadn't changed, she loved Chase Hatton, and Chase Hatton loved her. When she stepped out into the hall, he was waiting for her. He was leaning against the opposite wall, talking with his dad, wearing the same tux he had worn to prom, and looking devilishly handsome. When his dad stopped midsentence, Chase turned. He straightened, his eyes wide and bright. He stepped over to her side, not taking his eyes from hers for an instant.

"You look even more beautiful tonight than you did eight years ago."

"Y-you...this..." She ran a hand over her dress, speechless.

He laughed lightly. "Come on." He led her into the gymnasium, which was dark except for a single spotlight on the middle of the floor. As they hit the circle of light, he took her hand and raised it to his lips. "We never got to have our last dance." Chase took her into his arms, and from somewhere nearby in the darkness, music started to play. A voice began to sing The Temptations, "My Girl."

She spun around the dance floor with him, wrapped in awe and bliss. He began to sing to her quietly, that golden-toned voice he was famous for singing with, just for her.

His voice choked and he stopped singing. He drew their hands in and laid them on his chest, his swaying stopping as he bent slowly to kiss her. Her tears spilled onto her cheeks.

"Hey, hey, hey. No crying." He brushed away the tears.

"I'm just so happy. I can't believe you did this for me! I don't deserve this."

"Nonsense. Hope, ever since you came back into my life, I've had this constant smile plastered all over my face. Besides, this is as much for me as it is for you. I wanted another chance to hold you tight, just like this." He bent to kiss her again, and they continued to dance, she with her head on his chest, Chase laying his cheek on her hair.

After about twenty minutes, he said, "Hope, we've got the band for as long as we want them, and I could stay here forever dancing with you...except I think they have a basketball game in here tomorrow night, so it may get a whole lot less private...or, we could go back to my parents' place and take a walk by the pond. What do you want to do?"

"A walk sounds nice."

"Okay. Just wait here for a minute, I'll be right back." He took a few steps into the darkness, but then came back. "You're not going anywhere, right?"

She laughed. "I'm not going *anywhere!*"

"Good!" He left to pay the musicians, and then came back to her side. "Let's blow this popsicle stand." He grabbed a hand and escorted her to the door. Outside, Chase's dad was having a discussion about the school's football team with their former principal, while Mrs. Hatton stood gazing out of a window.

"Were you in on this Mr. Meyers?" Hope asked accusingly.

He nodded. "Chase called me a couple of weeks ago." He bent and kissed her on the cheek. "I've got a little soft spot for romance, too," he said quietly, with a wink.

"Thank you, so much! Both of you!" She kissed each man in turn, and then turned to Chase's mom. "Thank you for making this night so special for me!"

"You're welcome, honey."

"Come on, milady," Chase said with a courtly bow. "Your chariot awaits."

She stuck her hand through his crooked elbow and soon they were eating asphalt in the infamous Camaro. All the way home, she gushed about how beautiful everything was and asked him to divulge all of the steps he had taken to pull off her wonderful surprise. He was happy to oblige, having kept the secret for weeks. "It was kind of something I fantasized about for, oh...eight years or so."

Their animated discussion continued all the way down to the banks of the little pond they had gone skinny-dipping in once upon a moon.

They had strolled out to the end of the dock, and she breathed a contented sigh. "Oh, Chase! It's as lovely as I remember. Truly it is." Suddenly, her eyes fell upon a little white box on top of the support post at the end of the dock, seeming to glow in the moonlight. She turned to find him kneeling on one knee beside her. "Oh my goodness!" she said, her voice trembling. "What are you doing?" she breathed, her voice barely a whisper.

"Hope Alexis Creswell." He looked steadily into her eyes. "I've loved you since the day I met you, actually since the minute I laid eyes on you. And with each day I've spent with you, I've grown to love you more." He reached up and took the box from the post, opening it to reveal the ring nestled inside. Her hand flew to her heart. "I want to love you forever, to be forever lost in your eyes.

You've stolen my heart. Hope, won't you marry me? Give me your heart, and make me whole again."

Her heart swelled so full she thought it would burst; it actually pained her a little. "Yes, Chase, yes. Oh yes, I want to marry you—" The rest of her answer was smothered in kisses as he rose, picking her up and swinging her around, the sound of their laughter ringing around the edges of the pond, and then bouncing back to them in delight.

EPILOGUE

H ope trudged out of the doctor's office still stunned.

It was exactly four months since she and Chase had been married on the beach backing up to his house. It had been a small ceremony, just Hal, Chase's parents, his brother, Jeff, and Jeff's wife...some of the band members...and a few girlfriends from Chicago. She had spent the intervening months collecting shots for her portfolio and touching base with several contacts in the art industry. She and Chase had fallen in love with and purchased a small cabin at the foot of Mt. Lowe, where Chase had secluded himself to work on a new album, while she combed the nearby woods and lakes looking for "the perfect shot."

And now, she found herself pregnant.

She didn't know how it had happened. They had been careful. They both wanted children, lots of children—as she had been an only child, and he just one of two—but they had jointly decided to wait while she tried to get her art off the ground and he promoted his new album. How was she to tell him now all of their plans had flown out the window when the stick had turned purple?

A baby. In the abstract, it had seemed so desirable; in reality, the prospect was terrifying. She had no doubt Chase would be a fantastic father. He had grown up with an ideal family, quirky, but loving, always by his side, always supportive. But all she had known was an abusive father, and a mother who worked hard to support her, but was often absent. There had been no nieces or nephews to cuddle. She didn't even know if she had ever held a baby before.

Touched a little bootied foot, sure. Taken a picture of one, of course. But changed a diaper? Hope Creswell—now Hope Hatton—mother? How had this happened? In the abstract, it had seemed ideal. In reality, it seemed ridiculous.

And what about Chase's career? He already had tour dates lined up. Traveling together as a couple had been so easy, but with a baby in tow?

Her head was spinning even hours later, in the footlights of the auditorium at Chase's concert. She wasn't singing along like she usually did. She wasn't dancing. She wasn't even tapping her foot to the music. What was more, He seemed to have noticed, too. He kept glancing offstage as he sang.

"Hope!" Hal shouted above the noise. "Do you think I could talk to you for a second?"

She peered at him blankly for a minute, and then nodded. Hal led the way to a backstage waiting room, which had a few comfy couches and a small kitchenette. He sat down on a couch opposite her.

"Why don't you tell me what's on your mind?"

She glanced at him hesitantly. She hadn't told Chase, knowing he had to perform, and not sure how he was going to feel about the news. But Hal...he had to know; it affected him, too.

"I'm pregnant."

"What?" Hal sprung off the couch. "You're kidding? Congratulations! This is fantastic!" At her lack of exuberance, he paused, his brow furrowing. He crossed to sit on the coffee table in front of her, his hands on her arms. "You're okay, aren't you? The baby's okay?"

"Yes. Yes. Everything is fine."

"Well, good. You had me worried there for a minute. Chase must be thrilled. I'm surprised he is even able to perform."

"I haven't told him."

"You haven't...why?"

"Hal, we've only been married a couple of months. Chase and I decided to wait for a while. He's got this album coming out—"

"Listen, Hope, when I went into business with Chase, I knew his music was important to him, but I also knew it wasn't the most important thing in his life. I didn't know at the time *you* were, but now, seeing you guys together...this is what it is all about for Chase. And, for the two of you to have a baby, to create life...if you don't think he is going to be absolutely overjoyed to find out you're pregnant, then you've got him all wrong."

She let out a huge breath she didn't even know she had been holding. Her smile broke over her face in an instant. "Thanks, Hal!"

"You bet. Now we better get back or Chase is going to go nuts."

Chase seemed relieved to see them in the footlights. He immediately came over to her at the first break. "Hey, what's going on?" He squeezed her arms gently, and bent down a little to peer into her face.

Seeing his look of concern, she just couldn't keep it in any longer. "Honey...we're going to have a baby."

His face registered his shock, and for a minute her heart sank. "What did you say? Did you just tell me you're...?"

She nodded.

"No kiddin'?" A slow smile spread over his face. "I'm going to be a daddy?" He paced in a little circle with his hands on his hips. She watched him carefully. "No kidding? WOW! WOW!" He put his arms around her and lifted her off her feet with a whoop. "This is fantastic!" He beamed. "Oh, oh, oh!" He put her down, his face showing concern. "You're okay, aren't you?"

She laughed. "Yes, Chase, I'm fine."

"Wow, a baby!" He turned to the nearest stagehand, who held out a towel for him to mop his brow with. "Did you hear that? We're going to have a baby!"

"Yes, sir."

"Hal!"

Hal laughed. "Yes, I know, Chase. Congratulations!"

"Wow! This is SO cool!"

"Chase, you have five seconds!" the stage manager called.

"Okay."

"FOUR." People whipped around him, tugging his shirt off, depositing a fresh one over his head. "THREE." Someone handed him the towel and he wiped his face. "TWO." Someone straightened his hair. "ONE." He started to head on stage, but turned back to slip his arm around her and kiss her, hard, on the mouth. Without another word he entered the stage lights, leaving her breathless and radiant. She could hear his voice as he waved off the musicians.

"I'm sorry, everyone, I missed my cue. But I think you'll understand when I tell you...I just found out I'm going to be a father!" The crowd erupted and the band members set down instruments and came over to congratulate him. "Oh my gosh! I just told twenty thousand people before I told my mom! She's going to kill me! Hold on a minute...do you guys mind if I make a quick phone call?" The suggestion was greeted with wild applause. "Okay, shhh...shhh...Mom? Hey, it's Chase... Good. Good... I am. In fact, I'm on stage right now. But I had to call to tell you something. What would you say if I told you that you were going to be a grandmother?" He held the phone away from his ear as she shouted. "She's pretty happy," he told the crowd. "What? Yeah, Hope's fine. She's right here. Hope, she wants to talk to you." He held the phone out and Hope shook her head. He waved her on stage. "Come on."

Petrified, she took a few steps forward. *Don't look at the audience! Don't look at the audience!* she told herself. She crossed the stage to his side.

"Ladies and gentlemen, this is my wife, Hope!" The clapping and whistles were deafening. He grabbed her and kissed her passionately for several seconds before releasing her. Hope, a little red in the face, took the phone and headed backstage. "How about I play you a little rock and roll now?" The music started and Hope had to go deep into the building before she could hear the congratulations shouted into the phone.

"MOMMY!" OLIVIA RAN through the gallery, heedless of decorum, her little canvas slip-ons beating a happy cadence on the polished wooden floor.

"Hey, Toots!" Hope bent down to scoop the bright, five-year-old up into her arms. "How are you?"

Livvy's white sundress was spotless, and her sunny blond curls were swept up on her head in what she and her mommy liked to refer to as her "princess 'do." The two made a pretty picture. Hope wore a similar white sundress with large black polka-dots, and over it, a sheer, short-sleeved, black jacket that stopped above her waist and buttoned at the top with one large button.

"Mommy! Mommy!" Josh ran up to them, interrupting in typical three-year-old fashion.

"Joshie!" his older sister scolded. "*I* was talking to Mommy."

"I've got a present for you," Josh stated brightly, ignoring the baleful look his sibling shot him. Chase rolled in behind the pair, pushing a double stroller containing their still-sleeping twins, grinning at her over Josh's head.

Hope pretended not to see the enormous bouquet of flowers tucked conspicuously behind Josh's back. "For me?" she said in surprise, squatting down to look into his big blue eyes. Josh shook the long blond hair he wore in a style similar to his rock star father's out of his face, and pulled the flowers out from their hiding place with a flourish. "Oh my!" Hope looked up into Chase's sparkling eyes. "They're beautiful!" The huge bouquet was made up of daisies and a number of flowers she didn't recognize in pinks and purples and yellows, wild and flowing.

Chase took in every inch of her legs, accentuated by her sleek black heels, as she straightened up slowly.

She leaned over the stroller to give him a kiss, smiling at the twinkle in his eyes she recognized, knowing it meant he was turned on.

"Mommmy...?" Olivia began, stringing the word out and looking at her with her I'm-so-cute-don't-I-deserve-a-treat eyes.

Hope sighed, feigning exasperation. "I think I have ice cream treats in the mini-fridge in my office."

Needing no more invitation, the pair took off running toward the back, jostling for position just as she and Chase used to, screaming ecstatically.

"In the top part...and watch those flowers, Josh!" she called after them resignedly, realizing their little ears were already well out of range. Both Hope and Chase instinctively checked the stroller to see if the commotion had rousted the twins, but Sam and Jules lay with their heads turned toward the middle, resting them on top of each other, their cheeks flushed and mouths hanging open, oblivious.

With a sigh of relief, Chase observed. "I can see why they like coming to the gallery."

She chuckled. She stayed apart from him, her arms clasped behind her back, swinging a leg through a streak of sun from the windows that made the wood shimmer where it touched the floor. "And why do *you* like coming to the gallery?"

She smiled coyly as she looked up at him, sending a shiver down his spine. He walked purposefully toward her, seizing her by the hips and scooting her back against one of the dividers her artwork was hung on. She groaned as he nuzzled her ear. "I'm in love with the artist." He pulled back to look at her meaningfully.

"You are, huh?" She giggled and blushed slightly.

"I love that I can still bring out the school girl in you. It makes me want to get you alone all the more."

She tried to ignore the sensations Chase had created when his lips had brushed over her ear. "Well, I'm afraid *I've* got a thing for this rock star," she teased, nibbling on his bottom lip, tempting him needlessly.

He took possession of her lips, kissing her so wonderfully deep it seemed to resonate within her, pulling on a deep-seated chord, playing her like his favorite guitar. A melting began in her middle and spread, consuming her senses. She felt herself almost going under.

They heard the jingle of the door somewhere behind them as a customer entered the gallery, and he removed his lips from hers, but remained close, opening his eyes slowly and letting them roam over her face. Hearing footsteps now, he released her, standing back and clearing his throat, a slow smile replacing the need that was on his face seconds before.

She stood with her arms behind her, clasping the walls of the divider, still looking at him, but now her smile mirrored his, reflecting the shared secret of their stolen intimacy. At last, when she felt her lust-weakened knees could again support her body, she pushed away from the wall, taking a deep breath, almost unwilling to let the glow he had brought on vanish.

"How was your morning?" she said finally with forced casualness, his ears only meant to catch the continued intimacy woven in her voice.

"Terrific!" He smiled, frozen as she was.

The customer came around the corner of a divider and he dropped his eyes. He shifted his weight from foot to foot, looking at his toes for a minute before lifting his head to continue. "We went to the library"—he let a sigh escape, briefly mourning the loss of their closeness—"and then read books for about...thirty hours...and chased bubbles up and down the beach. How was yours?"

"We made a big sale overseas..."

Something in the way she said it alerted Chase. He watched her face curiously.

"A million dollars big," she announced with barely concealed excitement.

"You sold a picture for a million dollars?" he said in shock.

"No, silly!" she replied, swatting his arm playfully. "The dealer bought five."

"Still...that's two hundred thousand a piece," he whistled, genuinely impressed. "A million dollars will sure buy a lot of beakers," he added, referring to the Cancer Research Fund, which received all the profits from her sales.

"Yeah!" She grinned, no longer able to hide her delight at the prospect. She started to saunter back toward her office in the rear of the Hope Hatton Gallery, but he grabbed her hips again and pulled her back, sliding his hands down her arms.

"I say we go out to celebrate," he growled, burying his face in the hair she had left down and curly today, and breathing in her scent.

"I don't know. The kids were up late last night..."

"Not with the kids; just the two of us."

She spun around, peering at him in surprise.

"Grandma needed some 'cheek-pinching time.' Her plane lands at five."

This time her squeal did wake the twins.

"Oh, honey!" she cried as Jules started to fuss. "Mommy's sorry." She unbuckled and picked up her still-warm daughter, snuggling her to her chest. "Did you have fun at the library?"

The apple-cheeked, honey-brown-haired cutie nodded her head with a smile, fingers curled to her lips as her pigtails danced up and down.

"We chased bwubbles."

"I heard! We better go check on Sissy and Bubba. They're having ice cream. Would you like some?" Her head nodded up and down vigorously and was coupled with a loud, happy cry from Sam, who Chase had just released from confinement. The two toddled off in the direction Livvy and Josh had taken, holding hands peaceably.

As they watched the pair go, she sighed with contentment. "They're so sweet, aren't they?" She felt his hands on her shoulders.

"Just like their momma," he replied, kissing her hair. He turned her to face him. "Now you've got them all sugared up, when are you going to be home?"

"I just need to see to a few details with the shipping of that order, and then I was thinking of knocking off early and coming home to spend some time with you and the kids."

"I think," he said with a kiss, "that's a fabulous idea."

WHEN HOPE GOT HOME, she found a note on the table.

We're at the Beckmans'.
Love you—Chase

Their neighbors, the Beckmans, were on some jaunt in the Amazon or the Antarctic or something. *Antarctic,* she decided, after reflecting a moment. *They were on that quest to hit every continent. The Amazon was in the spring.* The Beckmans' normal pool service couldn't cover a few of the days they were gone, so Hope and Chase had offered to fill in. She quickly went to the bedroom and shimmied out of her dress, pulling on a pair of blue jean shorts and a navy t-shirt with a red Chevy symbol emblazoned on the front.

When she entered the gate to her neighbors' elaborately landscaped backyard, Chase was already dragging the pool with a net attached to a long pole. Josh and Livvy sat on the edge at the shallow end, their feet swirling in tiny circles as they watched the sunlight dance off the water. Sam and Julie were back in their stroller, parked in the shade, chattering away animatedly, as if they had been selected as a council of two to solve the world's problems.

"Hey, Babe, you look good!"

She looked down at her tennis shoes and shorts; she had donned a baseball cap to ward off the sun, pulling her long hair through the hole in the back. "I think you've been out in the sun too long."

"Not hardly," he said with a wicked grin. "I'm almost done here."

"Okay." She toyed with the idea of pulling her socks and shoes off and dipping her feet in the pool with Josh and Livvy, but she thought she should look around first and see if there was anything she could do to help. "Hey, guys!" she called to the pair.

"Hi, Mummy!" Josh answered. Livvy popped up and started running toward Hope for a hug. Not to be outdone, Josh chased after her, only to be outmaneuvered by his older sister in the last several feet. "You always get the first hug!" he complained.

Cutting off any response from Livvy, Hope reached over to tickle Josh's rib cage. "But *you* always get the first tickle, don't you, Mister?" Hope tickled him until he curled up into a little ball, leaking peels of laughter. Livvy took off toward the tennis courts. "Uh-uh-uh, Young Lady! Not without your shoes, you don't."

Livvy laughed and ran back to get her little canvas shoes and frilly, white socks.

"I wanna play tennis, too," Josh called, pulling on his shoes as well.

"What do you say to a set of doubles, girls against the boys?"

"I say," Chase responded, "you're on!" He wheeled the twins' stroller over, Hope helping him down the patio steps.

While Sam and Jules chased ants around in one corner, Chase and Hope watched the comic attempts their older children made to hit the ball, swinging at it a good seven or eight times before the ball ever reached them, then hopping back to take another few whacks at it. At one point, Livvy actually connected and sent it past a surprised Chase.

"Way to go, Liv!" he called happily.

"Good job, girlfriend!" Hope slapped her a high-five.

"You're gonna be one great little tennis player," her proud daddy called.

"Nah. Her sport's volleyball, right Liv-Girl?" The pigtails nodded enthusiastically.

"What about basketball?" Chase countered.

"Right!" Hope rolled her eyes.

"Can we go play with the ants, too?" Josh asked, nonplussed.

"Sure." Chase ruffled his hair. "I'll just give your mom a little tennis lesson."

"Sure, you will," she rejoined, rocking from foot to foot, ready to parry anything he sent over the net.

Within a short amount of time, Chase found himself huffing and puffing, his shirt stuck to him with sweat. Hope had incredible skill and reach, getting to balls he thought for sure he'd put past her. He flashed back to their first table tennis match, where he had been defeated by her, surprised he hadn't learned his lesson by now. She zinged another ball past him and he bent over, resting his hands on his knees and panting, "Had...enough...schoolin'...yet?"

She laughed lightly and came to the net. When he met her, she kissed him sweetly. "Oh! You taste like salt."

"Yeah, I'm all sweaty. You're killin' me here!"

She laughed again and meandered over to the bench with him. They sat and he tried to find a dry corner of his shirt to mop his face with. He looked at his pretty wife out of the corner of his eye, then put his arm around her and leaned back, letting the sun warm his cheeks and eyelids.

Hope looked to the corner of the court where Sam was allowing an ant to crawl up his arm, and the others were screaming and running away, only to return and take off again with another squeal. It suddenly struck her what a perfect day it had been. She had sold a million dollars worth of art, plus, and spent the afternoon laughing and playing with her children and husband. Despite being only a little over four pounds when she was born, Livvy, and all her other children, were healthy and, presumably, happy. She couldn't have been more in love with her husband, and if life were a rat race, she'd say she'd gotten the cheese.

She pulled Chase to her by his t-shirt, kissing him and tasting the salty flavor of his sweat. "Let's go home, Salty-Dog, and you can take a shower."

He smiled, quirking an eyebrow as a silent invitation to join him. She slapped him on the chest, and then rose to collect their children.

ABOUT THE AUTHOR

M.J. Schiller is living large in the Midwest trying to balance all of life's chores and pleasures while writing about it. Her home is known to be messy, her thoughts random, her blessings many. When not writing she gets paid to hang out with her friends, her fellow lunch ladies. When not writing or scooping food for hungry fourth graders, she likes to karaoke and pretend she's one of the rock stars she writes about. One of her constant writing companions is her cat, Serena, who likes to curl up between her legs where she can feel the heat from the overheated laptop. Talk about living large!

ALSO FROM M.J. SCHILLER

ROMANTIC REALMS COLLECTION:

TAKEN BY STORM
AN UNCOMMON LOVE
LEAP INTO THE KNIGHT[1]
LADY OF THE KNIGHT[2]
A KNIGHT TO REMEMBER[3]

ROCKING ROMANCE COLLECTION:

TRAPPED UNDER ICE[4]
ABANDON ALL HOPE[5]
BETWEEN ROCK AND A HARD PLACE
ROCK ME, GENTLY[6]
MIDNIGHT MELODY

REAL ROMANCE COLLECTION:

UPON A MIDNIGHT CLEAR[7]

1. http://myBook.to/LeapIntoTheKnight

2. http://myBook.to/LadyOfTheKnight

3. http://myBook.to/AKnightToRemember

4. http://mybook.to/TrappedUnderIce

5. http://mybook.to/AbandonAllHope

6. http://mybook.to/RockMeGently

7. http://mybook.to/UponAMidnightClear

THE HEART TEACHES BEST[8]
DAMAGE DONE[9]
HOMETOWN HEARTACHE[10]
TAKE A CHANCE ON ME[11]
BLACKOUT[12]

DEVILISH DIVAS SERIES:

TO HELL IN A COACH BAG[13]
DAMNED IF I DO
THE DEVIL YOU KNOW
SATAN, LINE ONE
PITCHFORK IN THE ROAD[14]

---

8. http://mybook.to/TheHeartTeachesBest

9. http://mybook.to/DamageDone

10. http://mybook.to/HometownHeartache

11. http://getbook.at/TakeAChanceOnMe

12. http://mybook.to/BlackoutMJSchiller

13. http://mybook.to/ToHellInACoachBag

14. http://mybook.to/PITCHFORKINTHEROAD